Past Praise for t

For *The Second Chance Supper Club*

"This heartwarming story of two headstrong women who relearn how to listen to one another will delight fans of Mary Simses and Nina George." —BOOKLIST

"Nicole Meier's *The Second Chance Supper Club* is full of family, forgiveness, and fresh starts." —POPSUGAR

"*The Second Chance Supper Club* is a glorious celebration of new beginnings, sisterhood, and the healing power of food. A wonderful story!" —KAIRA ROUDA, *USA Today* bestselling author

"This is a devour-in-one-sitting read that is as atmospheric as it is emotionally resonant."
—MICHELLE GABLE, *New York Times* bestselling author

For *The Girl Made of Clay*

"With luminous prose and an artfully crafted storyline, Nicole Meier's new novel is not to be missed. *The Girl Made of Clay* is a moving examination of the limits of familial obligations—and the unexpected rewards of opening up your heart to someone who may not deserve it."
—CAMILLE PAGÁN, #1 Amazon Charts Bestselling Author

"Rich and vibrant, *The Girl Made of Clay* is a heartfelt story about family, forgiveness, and second chances. Meier's emotionally charged writing, vivid settings, and crisp dialogue weave a powerful tale that brings her characters to life and draws in the reader. I thoroughly enjoyed it!"
—KERRY LONSDALE, Amazon Charts and
Wall Street Journal bestselling author

Other Books by Nicole Meier

The Second Chance Supper Club

The Girl Made of Clay

The House of Bradbury

CITY

OF

BOOKS

CITY
OF
BOOKS

A Novel

NICOLE MEIER

Published by SparkPress, a BookSparks imprint,
A division of SparkPoint Studio, LLC
Phoenix, Arizona, USA, 85007
www.gosparkpress.com

Published 2024
Printed in the United States of America
Print ISBN: 978-1-68463-246-6
E-ISBN: 978-1-68463-247-3
Library of Congress Control Number: 2023915525

Interior design by Stacey Aaronson

To anyone who's ever loved a bookstore.

One

Jo Waterstone picked her way through the streets of downtown Portland. A promising sliver of sunshine peeked through the clouds, chasing away the previous night's rain shower.

Monday was her favorite day of the week. So many good things awaited her. A tidy checklist of such things was tucked into her I'm All Booked Up tote bag. Her hand patted the canvas exterior for reassurance as she walked. Glancing at the time on her phone, she lengthened her stride.

If nothing else, Jo liked to keep a routine. She counted on it.

And yet when she'd woken up that morning, she couldn't help but notice a strange nagging that something just wasn't right. It tugged at the edges of her brain when her feet hovered over the side of the bed, and then again when she poured her first cup of tea. She couldn't quite place her finger on it, but something felt amiss. It was like leaving the house and carrying the sense of dread over whether the oven was properly turned off. This feeling almost took her off track, causing a wrinkle in her morning routine. She'd already lost fifteen minutes cradling her mug and staring into the middle distance, trying to place the thought. In the end, she'd brushed the concern aside. Turning fifty (was she really fifty?) a few months earlier had suddenly set

her normally even emotions on an irritating pattern of unpre-
dictability.

It's nothing, she told herself as she wove her way downtown.
There was far too much to do at the bookstore to bother about
some inconvenient twinge in her belly.

As she rounded the corner, the smell of sugary warm
muffins floated in the breeze. Jo's mouth watered. Hopefully, one
of her staff remembered to pick up the breakfast order for the
morning meeting.

Her sight fixed on the three-story brick building that was
now up ahead. As always, a familiar flutter filled Jo's chest as the
large, cheerful marquee beckoned her closer. To Jo, this was the
best sight in the city. Glancing up, she noted the sign's pleasing
black lettering in extra-large font: BRUEBAKER'S BOOKS. NEW AND
USED. COME INSIDE AND DISCOVER YOUR NEW FAVORITE READ.

It was a reassuring sight, instantly comforting her.

There was no place else Jo would rather be on a damp Monday
morning. This place had been her North Star for two decades.
More than that, it was her life.

Fishing out her keys, she turned the lock and then slipped
through the set of glass doors. Once inside, the soothing hush of
a hundred stacks welcomed her. There were books as far as the
eye could see. Jo paused to inhale, and her shoulders dropped.
There was nothing more satisfying than the sight of so many
rows of books—their spines turned out, a rainbow of colors
arranged in an endless array, just waiting for the right reader to
come and pluck a new armchair adventure.

Jo should know. She was the gatekeeper to this bookish corner
of the world.

"Good morning!" Her shift manager, Anna Singer, rushed
over and briskly locked the double doors behind her.

"Morning." Jo eyed the glowing iPad in her hand.

"Busy day." Anna's smile was tight and all business.

This was typical Anna. She was very much a Hermione Granger, clever and helpful in the best of ways. Somehow, Anna balanced both school and work with smooth precision. Jo admired this about her coworker.

But she knew better than to label Anna by her book personality out loud. While most customers seemed to enjoy this quirk in Jo's personality, Anna did not.

Jo was known for identifying people with their matching book character. Whether she was trying or not, she habitually cataloged people by protagonist or book type. Maybe other book enthusiasts were the same. Jo wasn't ever quite sure.

"There's no one like you, Jo," people often commented.

Jo would force a smile and try to laugh along. She wasn't sure if this was a compliment or not.

Over the years, as patrons streamed in and out of the store, Jo honed her ability to suggest titles. Each person came in searching for something, only they weren't always sure what. Oftentimes Jo suspected what they wanted even before they had a chance to open their mouth. She just had a hunch, like how one knows after witnessing a shift in the clouds what the weather might be.

It was in the way customers carried themselves, the way their expectant faces searched the aisles in a slow-building pursuit. By the time they encountered Jo—who was available from opening to closing five days a week, every week without fail—she'd already determined where to guide them for their next choice read. She took pleasure in the beam of happiness that illuminated their faces as they paid the cashier and strode toward the exit, confidently carting a reusable bag brimming with paperbacks.

"Thank you," they'd all say to her as they passed.

"Happy reading," she'd answer back.

Some people told Jo this practice of hers was a skill, a talent. Others even teased it was a superpower. She always shrugged it off. She didn't consider it so special.

She watched now as Anna rechecked the door lock.

"Feeling worrisome?" There was something tense hanging in the air. The way Anna's brows dipped between her eyes troubled Jo.

Anna shrugged. "Can't be too careful."

Anna was right, Jo supposed. Just a week prior, an inebriated man pushed his way into the store minutes before opening. Filling the lower level with a sour smell, he proceeded to urinate behind the souvenir section. It took three determined employees to corral the disoriented man and deliver him back onto the street with a stern warning. But the damage had been done. Portland could be tricky that way. The streets held every walk of life, from the artistic to the odd, the destitute to the well-off. That's just how it went. It all added to the flavor of what "kept Portland weird."

Jo took a moment to peel off her jacket. It would be the only still part of her day, before the OPEN sign glowed red, before the throng of bibliophiles, tourists, and regulars packed the rooms.

As she took in the front room, the scent of leather, dust, paper, and something uniquely woody filled her nostrils. It was what customers often referred to as being "smellbound." People entered the store and were transfixed, as if held under a spell by the alluring aroma of new and gently used literature. Jo understood just what these dreamy readers meant. The store, with nine different rooms named after various iconic authors (Shakespeare, Twain, Hemingway, Austen, Shelley, Morrison, Kesey, and so forth), was every booklover's fantasy. Shelves and shelves of reading material were neatly organized in wooden cases, touting every subject and storyline imaginable. There were staff picks, new releases, used treasures, and rare editions housed under one roof.

It was pure heaven.

Jo followed Anna to the back of the store and wondered if she might be irritated by something else. The way she scurried along appeared more urgent than usual.

"Hello, everyone," Jo called as she made her way into the break room. Before her was a large rectangular table displaying various bottles of pressed green juice, a basket of fruit, and a full platter of muffins. Despite the well-organized preparation for the meeting, only half of her normal employees were present. A flicker of concern passed through her. Something was definitely off.

"Hey, Jo."

"Morning, Jo."

"Not everyone's here yet, boss."

"I see that." She frowned. "Where's everyone else? They haven't called in sick, I hope. We still have boxes of Easter books to unpack in the Beatrix Potter room, and the nature writer from Bend is due to arrive this afternoon to do his signing."

A few employees exchanged dubious glances.

"That guy canceled an hour ago."

"What?" Jo placed her hands on her hips. It was poor form to cancel a book signing at the last minute, especially at Bruebaker's. Those events were coveted spots. Now they were going to have to return inventory that wouldn't be signed. "Why? Because of the storm? The weather center already announced the worst has passed. This is the Pacific Northwest, for goodness' sake. Everyone knows it rains."

"That was last night's news," Adam responded. Jo noticed his eyes shift to the others.

"So?"

"So, there was a gnarly accident that closed the bridge, and this next storm's supposed to be intense. They're calling it an atmospheric river. I think it's already delayed flights." Adam rubbed at his jaw. His shoulder-length hair was still slick from showering. Jo had the urge to tell him he should have combed it before shoving it into a ponytail, but she bit her tongue.

Adam was a reader of revolutionists and adventurers. He was a fan of titles like Che Guevara's *The Motorcycle Diaries* and Cheryl Strayed's *Wild*. Anything about a young person striking out on his or her own, traveling the land, or seeking out social injustice interested him. He was a young man with a blooming passion.

Adam was twenty-seven, and Jo was fifty. In his eyes, she was likely ancient. Sometimes she got the sense he needed to overexplain current events to her. This morning was no exception.

Jo shook her head and looked past Adam. The store would be opening soon, and they were wasting time. "Can someone try contacting the rest of our staff, please?"

Jade, from the morning inventory team, spoke up. Not one to normally talk in a group setting, her round face flushed. "Also, Regina Anderson has been trying to reach you. She's called the store more than once this morning."

Something hard and pebble-like lodged itself in Jo's throat. She wasn't exactly sure what this meant, but the implication was enough to fill her with anxiety. The company's unfriendly CEO normally only liked to communicate via email. "Regina's been calling for me? Did she say why?"

Jade shook her head, her long bangs falling into her eyes. "She said something's happened with Mr. Bruebaker."

"What?" The pebble in her throat calcified.

"She didn't say anything else. She said she tried your cell, but you weren't answering."

Jo cursed herself for not turning on her ringer earlier. She knew better. With jumpy fingers, she searched her pockets. Everyone stood around the break room in silence, waiting for her to react. Her hand seized the cold device just as it buzzed.

"Hello?"

"Jo!" A strained voice came over the line. "Oh, thank goodness you're there."

I'm always here, Jo thought. Except she hadn't been that morning. She turned her back to the roomful of faces and pressed her phone closer to her ear. Regina sounded like she was someplace public; a cacophony of voices droned on loudly in the background. Jo's mind raced, trying to determine where she might be calling from.

"Is everything all right?" Jo asked.

"Just a minute, I need to step into the hallway." There was a muffled sound while Regina pulled the phone from her ear.

What's happened with Mr. B? Jo's feet paced in a small circle while she waited. Usually she knew everything that had to do with her boss and his store.

You're my right hand, he'd told her more than once. *I tell you more than I tell my own children.* She squeezed her eyes shut and pictured the last time he told her this. It had been over steaming cups of Earl Grey in the cramped break room after an author event. The remark was punctuated by his signature wink as he blew into his tea. Jo never tired of that wink and the sense of confidence that came with it.

She'd been faithfully reporting to work for twenty-two years. Well before Regina came onto the scene, Jo was there getting things done. She was the longest-standing store manager employed in the bookstore's history.

And Jo's personal relationship with the store's founder, Arnold Bruebaker, had also grown over the years. What began as a mentor-mentee rapport slowly turned into something more familial. Jo liked to think of Mr. Bruebaker as a kind of father figure, seeing as she didn't have a living parent of her own. Secretly, she knew Mr. B had similar feelings. He was a good and generous man. Her true boss had retired—or so he claimed—a few years back, leaving the business of things mainly to Regina.

Regina, Jo thought as she rolled her eyes. The store's CEO might be hardworking, but she was mostly absent. She didn't know the store like Jo did—not even close.

"Listen, Jo," Regina breathed heavily into the phone. Jo could almost smell the familiar French roast on her breath. "We've got a real problem."

"Okay?"

"I don't want to scare you, but Arnold has suffered a stroke."

A stroke?

"What? When?" Jo's knees weakened. She reached for the back of a nearby chair.

"Yesterday."

"Oh no." Her intuition had been right. Something had gone wrong. Only she hadn't known it at the time. She was woozy just thinking about her beloved boss in a fragile state or worse.

"I'm at the hospital now," Regina continued. "I'm waiting for Arnold's daughters to arrive. Their flights have been delayed. I've been talking to his doctors and relaying the information in their absence. It's not good, Jo. He's in bad shape."

"He is?" She tried swallowing, but the calcified pebble expanded in her throat. A million questions ran through her head, and yet her lips were numb. How could this be happening? She'd just chatted with Mr. B not more than a week ago. He'd been fine. In fact, for an eighty-six-year-old man he was in surprisingly good shape. Jo knew he didn't eat very well, the food in his refrigerator always balancing on the edge of what she'd considered hazardous expiration dates, but he also liked to come downtown to "stretch his legs" for exercise on a regular basis. Considering his age, he was still quite active.

"I'm sorry you have to find out this way. It all happened so fast. Anyway, he's in the ICU at the moment. The doctors are monitoring him."

"Oh my gosh." Jo felt her eyes brimming over. "Can I come see him?"

"No. I'm sorry, but they don't want visitors. It's family only. I'm just a stand-in until Suzanne and Jane arrive."

"Oh." Jo was trying very hard not to cry over the phone. She wasn't even allowed to visit. "What can I do, then?"

There was an uncomfortable pause. "Close up the store."

Jo blinked. She couldn't have heard correctly. Clearly she was in shock. "I'm sorry, what did you say?"

"Jo." Regina's voice suddenly had an edge. This was more like the Regina that Jo knew, the woman who could be found skimming Lean In, by Sheryl Sandberg, in the business aisle while she waited for Jo to update her on numbers. "It shouldn't be any surprise that Arnold's daughters have wanted their father to sell the store for years now. It's just not profitable, and he's supposed to be retired. It's been a drain on them in many aspects. The lease is up for renewal, and the price will be increased to a crushing amount. You know that as well as I do."

"I do?" Jo *did* know this on some level. The city owned the historic building, and she'd heard prices downtown were skyrocketing. Still, Bruebaker's Books was a fixture. It was also Mr. Bruebaker's dream. He wouldn't think of shutting it down. The bookstore was woven into the very fabric of Portland life. Everyone knew that, even Regina.

Bruebaker's was the most popular establishment in all of Oregon, maybe even in all of the Pacific Northwest. Not too far back, it had been heralded as the Eiffel Tower of the Pacific Northwest. It wasn't any wonder that Mr. B felt the need to check in every once in a while, even after he had "retired." His baby had grown into a massive institution, and it was vital to the community, and beyond that, it ran like a well-oiled machine.

This doesn't make any sense. Jo felt her limbs giving way and wondered if this was what it was like to have an out-of-body experience.

"Come on, Jo. Don't play dumb," Regina said. "This isn't the first time you've heard this. Besides, his daughters can get power of attorney if they really want to. Right now, Suzanne and Jane need to focus on their father's health, not his struggling business. They've asked me to close up the store. Effective immediately. They want to be done with the space and move on before the estate hemorrhages any more money. They'll be facing mounting costs with their father's care. It's all too much. I've agreed to follow through with their wishes."

And just what are you getting out of this deal? Jo envisioned a hefty severance as she squeezed the phone in her hand. An acrid mixture of anger and fear churned inside of her. This wasn't at all what Mr. B would want. He loved the bookstore more than life itself. He always had.

How dare Regina? How dare Suzanne and Jane? Were they really that laser focused on the money? That wasn't even the point of the store. It was never about the money. It was about the literary community—and so much more. *But the minute Mr. Brue-baker is rushed to the hospital, all they can think about is closing up his business? Without his consent?* It was absurd. Jo knew there was more than enough money tied up in his big house to make matters comfortable.

What were Regina and Mr. Bruebaker's daughters really after?

"Even if I were to agree and do as you say," Jo asked through a clenched jaw, "what do you propose I do about all of our customers? About the staff? About the slate of upcoming author events?" Jo glanced over her shoulder, feeling the weight of a dozen sets of eyes bearing down on her. Surely Regina would come to her senses and realize closing up the store was far more complicated than she'd anticipated. Wouldn't she?

"I'll deal with the logistics." Regina's tone turned prickly. She clearly did not like to be challenged. "We'll get a statement drafted as soon as possible. For now, why don't you post a brief something on social media about the store closing for a family emergency? Don't give specifics yet. Employee compensation and your, er, severance will be discussed at a later date. For now, my obligation is to follow the wishes of Mr. Bruebaker's daughters. Your obligation is to close the store. You have two hours. We'll chat later. I have to go."

The line went dead.

Two

"Two hours?" Jo asked aloud. Her stomach hollowed as if she'd been punched with a firm fist. She collapsed into a metal folding chair, her head spinning. What Regina was suggesting was impossible, unimaginable. A kind of tunnel vision set in. Was she dreaming? It was like she'd shown up to work that morning and instead tumbled into some kind of alternate universe.

Several bodies were suddenly at her side, bent over and peering into her perspiring face. It was only then that she was aware of the questions coming at her.

"What's going on?"

"What did she say?"

"Is everything all right?"

Still dazed, Jo looked up at the cluster of nervous faces and felt her color drain away. She was going to have to tell them the truth. They deserved that much. "No," she said. "Things aren't okay. Mr. Bruebaker is in the hospital, and it appears we have to shut down the store. Immediately."

The room filled with white noise as she sat in her chair and reverberated from the shock. Bruebaker's was closing its doors.

"Close the store?" Adam peered closer. "What does that even mean? And what about the author events and customers and, you know, us?"

"I . . . I don't know." Jo swallowed. He was right.

She wrung her hands and fretted over where to even begin. With a long to-do list, she didn't have the luxury to speculate what may or may not result from the store's closing. The empty feeling of walking through the Beatrix Potter room on the second floor and not finding the rug covered with tiny bodies gathered for the usual Shel Silverstein reading must be ignored. The awful disappointment over canceling so many expectant authors and their book signings must be accepted. And any grieving for the hundreds of would-be faces entering the bookstore for the first time would have to wait—maybe forever.

On top of the overwhelming sense of loss, closing for even one day was going to be a blow to the community. Surely Mr. Bruebaker's daughters were overreacting to his stroke. They hadn't even considered what the news of the store closing might do to him once he recovered. Had they? With any luck, Jo told herself, the whole event would blow over and they'd come to their senses. Surely this wasn't a forever decision.

It couldn't be.

For now, she and her team needed to focus on turning away customers, postponing author events, trying to pause shipments of new inventory, and a whole slew of other logistics she couldn't yet wrap her mind around. She tugged at her woolly crewneck sweater, its collar suddenly giving her a choking sensation. How on earth would they be able to get the word out on social media, to their distribution channels, and to the long list of employees, who were now apparently out of a job?

Oh God. Her employees. This was a disaster.

"What are we gonna do for work?" Grayson, a wiry stock boy in a Pabst Blue Ribbon T-shirt, wondered aloud. His eyes skittered around the room, searching for answers. "My roommate just

moved out, and my rent is due, like, tomorrow. I'm screwed
enough as it is. I can't afford to lose my job."

"That's rough." Adam shook his head.

Grayson sagged. "Tell me about it."

"I'm sure Mr. Bruebaker's family will figure something out."
Jo reached over to pat his bony shoulder. Physical interaction
with the staff wasn't something she normally practiced, but this
poor kid looked as if he needed it. He was so thin she wondered
if he was too strapped for cash to buy proper groceries. It was
then that she realized her fingers were trembling. Swiftly, she
dropped her hand and walked away before anyone noticed. The
truth was, she had no idea what anyone would do. This whole
crisis came on without any warning. Other than pay employees
for work that day, she wasn't sure what else the store would
cover.

"Does this mean I'm going to lose my benefits?" another
voice asked.

A low murmur rippled through the group.

Jo placed her hands on the end of the table and hushed them.
"Calm down, you guys. Sick or not, Mr. Bruebaker is expecting us
to take care of the store. Let's just focus on our job and get this
place closed down like we've been asked. One step at a time for
now. Okay?"

The group grew silent.

Adam scratched his head, looking unconvinced. "But we've
never closed. This place is open 365 days a year. It's a staple.
Even on holidays. People count on us."

Jo watched, the buzz of injustice growing infectious. Her own
nerves zinged in reaction.

"Yeah!" Grayson said.

"Yeah, he's right. This place is iconic."

"Totally."

"What're you gonna do, Jo?"

Jo winced. The onslaught of responses came at her like hot arrows, each one with surprising swiftness that left a sharp sting. The staff had a point.

"I don't know," she muttered, getting up to wander from the break room. She made her way to the nearby row of registers at the front of the store. "I need to think."

There simply wasn't time to be upset, not yet anyway. Jo would follow through with Regina's orders for now. With any hope, she could find a way to convince the three women they were making a big mistake, and they would reopen the store in a day or two. In the meantime, she shuddered to think of the potential loss of sales for even just one afternoon.

Stretched before her, on the main level of the store, stood neat display tables containing a rainbow of journals, postcards, pen sets, and other gifts. Along each of the four walls were floor-to-ceiling bookcases, all labeled and organized by genre. In the center, long linear partitions created snaking checkout lines, waiting to be filled with happy customers cradling their treasured merchandise. Jo's heart grew heavy as she looked around. Today there wouldn't be any customers, nor the following day or possibly even the next. Her beautiful store currently had no future.

And without a store, Jo didn't have much of a future either. Just the thought of it made her seize up. Before she could control it, a guttural sound escaped from somewhere deep within. To keep herself from crumbling entirely, she clung to a rack of bookmarks and held tight. She tried to catch her breath before the others saw.

This can't be happening.

The sudden banging of a side door caught her attention. Jo

whirled around just in time to see the building's maintenance man enter wearing a somber smile.

"Hey there, Jo." Truman tipped his head in her direction. His khaki-colored pants rode low on his waist as he strode over to where she stood. As always, he carried with him a tool belt and the faint whiff of sawdust. He was always in the building, repairing a bookshelf or gluing a display case back together. As busy as Bruebaker's was, it wasn't necessarily prosperous. Jo once overheard Regina refer to the bookstore maintenance budget as nothing more than string and duct tape. The store took on a lot of wear and tear.

The woman wasn't too far off with her observation.

"Hey, Truman. Why are you here so early? Did Regina call you?"

"She did." He sagged.

What was on his agenda? By the way flecks of day-old salt-and-pepper stubble dotted his jawline, he'd obviously skipped shaving and instead rushed over as soon as he got the call. It was still very early in the morning, after all. And Truman didn't usually show up until late afternoon.

Truman had been around Bruebaker's for nearly as long as Jo. He'd become a kind of friend over the years, often stopping by the break room to shoot the breeze over a cup of black coffee or to deliver bags of apples picked from his tree at home. Jo saw how the employees were collectively fond of him, with his relaxed, even nature. She liked the way he listened to the stories of the younger employees, always patient and thoughtful with a response. Perhaps it was why much of the twentysomething staff viewed Truman—who, like her, was in his early fifties—as a kind of surrogate uncle.

"It's a shame about Mr. B," Truman said, his voice soft.

Jo drooped. Hearing Truman use Mr. Bruebaker's nickname made it feel more real. "I know."

"The boss wants me to help you shut the place down," Truman said. He glanced around anxiously, his hands jingling the loose change in his pockets. "She said something about nailing boards over the front doors and posting up some kind of permanent sign."

Jo shuddered. Nailing boards? A sign? It all sounded so over-the-top and ominous. "Good grief. It's like we're condemned or something."

Truman shrugged. "Kinda sounds like it. Doesn't it?"

"Do you agree with such drastic measures? Do you think we really need to shutter the place just because Bruebaker's daughters want it gone?"

Truman rocked on his heels. His jaw moved back and forth, as if he was mulling over the facts. "I don't really know. Mr. B sounds pretty sick. Seems like his daughters don't think they have much of a choice. Regina said it's a financial thing. She made it sound like things are dire. Know what I mean?"

Jo nodded. She did know. The store had not been profitable for some time. Still, the growing queasiness in her stomach made her feel as if what they were about to do was wrong. Family wishes or not, giving up on the store just didn't feel right.

Plus, her loyalty was to Mr. B, not Regina or his daughters. Truman didn't have the same relationship with him as she did. This was her mentor, her friend they were talking about. Jo's eyes pricked at the memory of sitting at Mr. B's kitchen table just a month earlier, eating saltines and tomato soup while they discussed the state of the publishing industry. Those regular lunches with Mr. Bruebaker were one of her most cherished pastimes. It was as close to having a family meal as she could get. The thought of him now lying in a hospital bed, with no one but Regina to look after him, made her fist clench.

"Regina says no visitors are allowed, but maybe I should just go over there anyway. Maybe I can talk some sense into her and let Mr. B know what's going on." Her voice trailed off as she pictured her plan.

Truman shook his head. "Have you ever been in the ICU?" he asked.

"Not really."

"Well, I have, and it doesn't work like that. You have to be family to get inside. Even then, most patients are out of it or unconscious in there. It's not a place to have a business meeting."

Jo nodded and sniffed. Of course, on some level she *did* know this. She supposed she was in denial. It was all she could do to hold back the tears.

In an effort to keep busy, she wandered over to the cash registers and opened each one to check the contents inside. Truman leaned up against the counter and waited. Her hands dove into each drawer, making sure there wasn't anything left over from the night before. She glanced up once. Truman looked on quietly. Self-consciously, she moved faster. She hoped he didn't notice her trembling.

In all her years, she'd never been asked to shut down the store. Sure, there were contingency plans in place for natural disasters, active shooters, and even a robbery. But those were all hypotheticals. None of them actually ever happened. As far as she was concerned, Bruebaker's would last a lifetime. And now she was fully unprepared for handling such a bewildering turn of events, especially since it threatened to end everything she'd ever known.

Slamming the drawer of the final register, she felt her eyes water.

"Truman," she whispered, "I don't know how to do this."

Deep lines hugged his temples. His face rearranged into an empathetic smile. "I know what you mean. We've been coming into this place almost every day for nearly two decades. It's like a second home to me. Hell, it's like a second home to a lot of us. To tell you the truth, I was kinda hoping that when I showed up to board the entrance, you'd talk me out of it."

Jo dabbed at her eyes, confused. "You were?"

He nodded.

Her chest squeezed. The way Truman talked, he made it seem as if she had a choice in the matter. She didn't. Regina had made her position clear. And, apparently, so had Mr. Bruebaker's daughters. Just what did Truman expect her to do? Wave a magic wand and make the whole thing better? Open the doors and let the customers inside despite it all?

A dozen scenarios ran around in her head. None of them stopped the trembling. There didn't seem to be any way around closing the store.

"Truman, I can't—" She was interrupted before she could continue.

Adam peered into the room, his eyes shining with enthusiasm. He had an almost electric quality to the way he now carried himself, and it felt a bit suspicious. Adam was known for stirring the pot.

Most of her staff members were right on his heels, their faces expectant.

"Hey, Jo. I need to talk to you."

"Okay." Jo frowned. She didn't know what Adam was up to, but the last time Adam looked this way, she'd discovered he'd taken it upon himself to assemble displays at each of the endcaps in the Ken Kesey room. He had erected chalkboard signs posing rather controversial and intrusive questions to patrons. He claimed he'd been inspired by stories penned by the Oregon author and wanted customers to feel equally stimulated. The plan backfired. It took no time at all for the complaints to reach Jo, who'd been working with a new sales employee on another floor. Adam was swiftly reprimanded and asked to disassemble his project.

Jo studied him and wondered if he was planning to resurrect his old signs for the store's closing. Maybe he had a new way to alert customers of this unhappy development.

"What is it?" Jo stopped what she was doing and crossed her arms.

"So I know Mr. Bruebaker's family wants us to lock up and go home and all. And that Regina supposedly thinks everything in here"—he waved his arms around—"should be sold off or destroyed or whatever. But I don't want to see that happen. This place is an institution. And what they're saying is all very *Fahrenheit 451*, if you know what I mean."

Jo sighed. He was being rather dramatic. "Adam, calm down. No one is talking about burning any books."

"You say that, but you can't be sure. Can you? Don't you remember when the mayor closed down The Arcadery on the east side after those two girls OD'd? That place was iconic, and people begged to have it reopen. But rather than work with the owner to turn things around, he just erased it off the map. Who's to say that won't happen here?"

She ran a hand over her face. Her gut gave a sickening twist. He wasn't wrong. Still, she needed to get control of this situation. Adam's rebellious nature sometimes had a tendency to become infectious.

"Okay, so what exactly are you proposing? That we protest?" Jo measured her words, unsure if she wanted to hear his answer.

Adam brightened. "Yes. Why not? I think we should refuse to go."

"What?" Jo felt her eyes grow wide. He couldn't be serious. Maybe her ears weren't working properly under the stress, but she could've sworn Adam just suggested she disobey Regina's orders to leave.

Jo dropped her head into her hands. What was the best way to honor her beloved boss? Surely he'd want the store to go on, with or without him. Jo knew this in her core. Yet the idea of sheltering inside the building for any amount of time seemed crazy. It was a bookstore, for goodness' sake, not a hotel.

But still . . . a small part of her also knew that Adam's idea of defying Regina's orders might be their best chance to force the daughters' hands. If the public got wind of what was going on, they might rally behind the bookstore employees. Something good might come of it. She honestly had no way of really knowing. But what she did know was that if the store had a fighting chance of reopening, then Jo and her staff would once again have jobs.

And the life that I love could resume, she thought.

Truman, who'd been listening, let out a low grunt. Jo shot him a questioning look. By the way he had his elbows propped behind him and wore a sideways grin on his face, she couldn't tell if he was amused or impressed with Adam's outburst.

Jo cleared her throat. It was important Truman didn't egg on Adam's impetuousness.

"I don't think it's okay to write this place off. It's the easy way out," Adam said.

Jo pushed air through her nose. He was looking at this through the lens of a willful child, refusing to pick up his toys and go home. "Adam, this is serious. Regina made it crystal clear. The family is worried about Mr. Bruebaker's health and the financial instability of the business. We don't have permission to do as we please. We don't own the place. And I'm pretty sure we don't even officially work here after today. Do you understand?"

"Yes." Adam stood taller, the fabric of his faded denim shirt pushing out. The edges of his determined face hardened. She looked beyond him to the half dozen staff members who stood behind him with similar expressions.

Her heart sank.

"So, knowing all of that, you still don't want me to shut the store down?" Jo asked.

Anna stepped forward. She reached out and placed a hand on Adam's arm, signaling she'd take it from there. "We understand the store needs to be closed to the public for now. We obviously don't want to put the business at risk. But it's important to show how strongly we feel about keeping Bruebaker's alive, despite what Mr. B's daughters think is right. What Adam means is that some of us hope to stay and see if the store can be saved somehow. Personally speaking, I can't imagine letting the first editions in the rare-books room go. We all know Regina doesn't care about stuff like that. I mean, I wouldn't be able to live with myself if I didn't at least *try*."

A long, uncomfortable stillness filled the space between them.

Jo's mouth went dry. Anna had a point. It was one thing for such an outlandish proclamation to come from Adam. But now Anna, perhaps her most levelheaded employee, was on board with this idea as well. This gave her pause.

"I will consider staying and seeing if I can convince Mr. B's daughters to let the store reopen. But I'm going to have to do it alone. I don't have any intention of getting you—the staff—into trouble. It's not your burden to bear. Do you understand?" Jo scanned the room, trying to gauge their reaction.

"No." Adam didn't skip a beat. "We don't understand. Some of us really want to stay as well. We're just as passionate about the place as you are."

Jo's stomach dropped.

Truman lifted himself from his position at the counter. "Sounds to me"—he tipped his head in Jo's direction—"like you've got a bit of a revolution on your hands."

Adam shot a balled fist high into the air above his head. "Hell yeah we do!"

"Occupy Bruebaker's!" another voice shouted.

"We're not taking no for an answer!"

Someone in the back let out a whoop.

Anna met Jo's stunned gaze with a jutted chin. They were dead serious.

A rush of heat swept over Jo's rigid body. It appeared they were taking over the store. The question was, to what end?

Three

*T*wo hours had come and gone, and Jo was still nowhere close to forming a solid plan. At the urging of the others, she'd phoned Regina and asked for more time. There was too much to do, she claimed. She was given until noon.

It appeared time was the primary concern for others too. A surprising text from Suzanne Bruebaker popped onto Jo's screen.

> Suzanne: Hello Joanna. Any problems closing up the store?
>
> Jo: No, just needed more time to tie up some loose ends. Working on it with my staff right now.
>
> Suzanne: Good. Please expedite.

Jo couldn't help but snort. Suzanne was an Olive Kitteridge all the way: a woman without apology. Jo wanted to inquire after Mr. Bruebaker's well-being, but the three dots on her screen disappeared, letting her know Suzanne was done with the conversation.

Three other workers quickly ran off when Adam began marching around the sales floor chanting, "Power to the people!" Jo knew he was joking, but she didn't find it funny. A sales associate named Jimmy and his counterpart from one level above both rolled their eyes and muttered that they didn't exactly share Adam's unbridled social activism tendencies. After swapping a few whispered concerns, the two collected their things and said goodbye. Right behind them was a quiet librarian type named Fiona.

"Um, Jo?" she asked.

"Yes?"

"While I love the store and hate to see it close, I have my mother to think of. She's sick and—"

"Say no more," Jo responded. This poor girl had no obligation to stay. After all, their plan wasn't really a plan at all—more like a wild hair.

Other than Anna and herself, the rest of the group included Adam, Grayson, Jade, and two others from Jade's morning inventory team who seemed to be quietly arguing among themselves. Then there was Wendy, a woman from the café who remained silent as she twisted the loops of her crocheted scarf around her fingers with nervous expectation. Wendy was one of the many female employees who had a predilection for all things Jane Austen. Jo just wondered if Wendy had it in her to follow through with their radical plan.

The last were Jack and Leo, two rather unknown staff members from the upstairs Hemingway room. If these two read anything at all, Jo believed they were likely fans of stories in which characters sought utopian settings where conventional rules did not apply. *The Beach* by Alex Garland came instantly to mind. Both Jack and Leo had the look of what she called "fun seekers," young men eager to engage in something exciting and possibly dangerous. It was obvious in their goofy grins.

Jo chewed on the end of her reading glasses and studied each of their faces, determining who else would go. *They should all go and leave me to try this on my own*, she thought. But she also understood there was no deterring some of them.

"Um." One of the women from the inventory team met Jo's quizzical stare. "So, we've been talking and . . . well, I think we're gonna go."

"What? No, really?" Adam groaned. "Why?"

The woman's face colored as she shrank back in her chair. "Well, it's just that this all kind of is happening so fast, and we're not sure it's, um, wise. And, you know, we've got our families and partners and people who will be pretty concerned about us. You know?"

Adam opened his mouth, but Jo cut him off. "Yes, we do understand. This is a very big thing that we're suggesting. It's perfectly understandable; in fact, it's very smart of you to bow out now before it gets more complicated. Your job at Bruebaker's does not include any of this." Jo opened her arms and gestured around the room. "Thank you for your honesty. Feel free to head on out through the side door. Truman hasn't locked that up yet."

They uttered thank-yous and scurried out of the room. Adam audibly deflated at their departure. His band of rebels was shrinking.

Wendy's phone buzzed, and she turned away from the group to answer. Everyone exchanged quick glances. It didn't appear any of them knew her very well. Was she an asset in their predicament?

A series of low murmurs and head nods later, Wendy snatched up her bag and wished them well. The group watched her scarf trail behind her as she swiftly exited the building.

Jo and her team—or what was left of it—sat around the table in the break room and blinked. Of the twelve staff members who clocked in to work earlier that morning, only seven remained. Truman, bless his patient soul, was also hanging back to finish boarding up the entrance. Jo also suspected he wanted to lend a bit of moral support. He didn't say as much, but Jo got the sense he didn't want to leave the building until she did.

A pang of gratitude shot through her.

"Everyone moving forward with the revolution?" He poked his head around the corner, a hammer and nails in one hand.

Jo sighed and shrugged in his direction.

Adam, of course, beamed. Somehow Truman's willingness to treat the cause seriously gave him the credibility he was seeking. "Hey, man, thanks for the support."

Truman held out the palm of his free hand. "I'm remaining neutral on this one. Just want to make sure everyone is doing okay, that's all."

"We're trying," Jo said. She intended to ask Truman just how neutral he really was once he was finished with his tasks. He was the only other middle-aged person in the room; she needed perspective from someone with her level of maturity. She secretly wished Truman would pull her aside, tell her how crazy and dangerous it was to even entertain Adam's ideas, anything to talk her out of being there one minute longer. But he didn't. Truman held a poker face.

Truman cocked his head.

Jo met his gaze. "At the moment, we're doing our best to land on some sort of compromise."

Adam folded his arms across his chest and leaned back in his chair. The way his lips pressed tightly together, Jo could tell he had no intention of compromising anything. This was his stance, and he was sticking to it.

"Ahh." Truman wandered off again to finish his job.

Seeing that her number one protester wasn't budging at his end of the table, Jo decided to see if she might convince the others to go home. She turned in her chair to face Grayson, who was busy eating his way through the fruit bowl. This kid really needed a proper meal.

"Grayson, what about you?" Jo asked. She studied him. Were Grayson's reasons for sheltering in the store more about his inability to pay rent and buy groceries, rather than standing up for the salvation of the business?

Caught off guard, he shifted a lump of banana to the side of his cheek with a raised brow. "Me?"

"Yes, you," Jo said. "What are your motives for staying? Are you really prepared to take on the bookstore's owners and possibly get into trouble? You may risk losing some kind of severance pay if you agree with Adam's little campaign. Plus," she said, addressing the room, "who's to say Regina or Mr. Bruebaker's daughters will even take this thing seriously right now? They're preoccupied at the hospital. We might wind up spending the night in here, for all I know."

Just acknowledging this out loud made her stomach queasy. The building was massive, and it was no place to sleep over as a form of makeshift protest. Jo found herself equal parts devastated and daunted over the very notion.

Grayson worked the large bite around in his mouth, his Adam's apple protruding as the food went down.

"Uh, yeah, that sounds like a risk for sure. But, like, it's the only job I have right now, and I really can't afford to lose it. Plus"—he sent Jo a sheepish grin—"I'm pretty sure I'm about to be evicted. So there's that."

"Uh-huh." Just as Jo suspected—this kid was in it for the free shelter.

"Grayson," Adam interjected, "I get it. May as well stick around here where you're needed."

"Or not." Jo scowled. She planned to pull Grayson aside later and ask whether or not he had any family who might take him in. She really didn't feel like being responsible for more people than necessary. To her, each one of the faces huddled around the table was a potential liability. What if they got into real trouble?

Her goal was to try and quietly convince Regina and Mr. B's daughters to let her reopen. She'd try to focus on packaging up their existing online orders and maybe organizing some inventory. The idea was to remain low profile and professional—if that was even realistic—in her approach. Having more people remain in the building didn't exactly fit with this plan.

If she agreed to allow them to stay on—which still felt extremely risky and far-fetched—she needed to limit her responsibilities. At present, she wasn't sure Grayson was capable of being responsible for himself, let alone an all-out coup.

Shelving her worries over the staff, Jo angled her head toward Anna in the corner of the room, furiously typing away at the laptop. Jo had tasked her with researching all there was to know about strokes. It was important to know what kinds of obstacles Mr. Bruebaker might be facing when—*if*—he recovered.

"How's it going over there? Find anything helpful yet?"

"Working on it, boss."

Her loose hair had been secured into a high ponytail, and at her side was a pencil and notebook filled with scribbles.

"You're a premed student," Jo said. "I'm counting on your know-how to get me some real information. I can't go into this blind. I need to know what we're potentially getting ourselves into."

"Just need another minute," Anna said.

Everyone took the awkward silence that followed as a chance

to scan their cell phones to see if any kind of statement about the store had been made online. So far, Regina hadn't announced anything.

"Well, I'm sure Regina will be speaking to the press at some point. She made her intentions clear. Closing the store is essential," Jo remarked.

"But *we're* essential," Adam griped. "People count on us. She would know that if she ever spent much time here. That lady never liked hanging around the store. When she did, she always made comments about how we should be embracing digital sales more. I mean, none of us have ever even seen her holding a book. She doesn't even care." He tossed his phone onto the table.

All around, heads pumped in agreement.

Adam's dedication to the store was endearing. But Jo worried he might not grasp how serious things could become. Essential or not, there could be a real risk in staying there. Who was to say Regina wouldn't resort to calling some kind of security if they refused to go?

"I understand your passion. Believe me, I do. Books are important, but in this case they're secondary to the Bruebaker family wishes. I'm okay to stay here and try to change the family's mind. But they want everyone out by the lunch hour." She glanced at the clock on the wall. It was five minutes to noon. "And now, we've run out of time."

As the words left her mouth, Jo suddenly felt as if she were floating. Her head became light. How was this all truly happening? Their cherished, bustling store had gone from running at full tilt to a standstill within the span of a morning. She placed a hand over her churning stomach. It was all too new, too upending, too raw. And the big question still loomed: Was she doing the right thing?

"Anna," she asked, "what did you find out about stroke recovery? How long is Mr. Bruebaker going to be in the ICU?"

"Well," Anna began, "it all depends on the patient. But from what I'm reading, the most rapid recovery usually occurs during the first three to four months. But some people still continue to recover well into the first and second year—40 percent of stroke survivors experience moderate to severe impairments and go on to require special care."

"Ugh." This was heartbreaking.

"Sorry, but it sounds like it's going to be a long road ahead."

A low murmur returned among the group.

"So?" Adam stood. "Are we doing this? I'm ready to stay overnight with Jo if we have to. What about the rest of you?"

The room was silent. Adam pressed on.

"I've been texting with my two roommates. They're servers at a brewpub in the Pearl District. They said they could deliver food if we needed. If you guys are in, I think we should stock up on a few provisions from the market down the block. And the closet upstairs in the kids' section has all of those colorful mats for the old summer sleepover events. That's food and shelter in case this thing runs longer than a day. Now all we need is Truman to give us access to extra keys, and we're all set."

"What about clothes, man?" Jack asked. "I mean, don't we need, like, deodorant and underwear at least?"

"Yeah, dude. You might stink after a while." Leo jabbed him with an elbow, and the two chuckled.

Jo frowned. She didn't know them very well, and from what she could gather, they were a bit on the relaxed side—a bad fit for staffing the Hemingway room. She made a mental note to change this once—if—things returned to normal. They were tall and strong looking, however. And since they were to take on the task of moving things around to accommodate the group, perhaps the more able bodies the better.

"Hmm."

They all glanced around. At this point they were a small group—plus Truman, who was still wandering around the building and finishing his work. Jo didn't know where he stood in all of this, but she hoped to find out soon.

The bookstore was his life, just like it was hers. There wasn't a spouse or any children or a houseful of pets waiting at home for Truman's return. He'd made that clear by all of the apples he regularly delivered. He'd said he would have kept them to make pies, but that was too much food for one person. Plus, he worked a lot of overtime. This job had defined him. It was difficult to imagine him giving that up—certainly not forever.

Jo rubbed her head. Her mind whirred. She thought about all of the customers who'd vocalized their fantasies of being able to linger in the aisles for days. They wanted to move in, to vacation among the stacks. It was a romanticized notion, but the sentiment was real. People wanted to lose themselves in their love of books.

But to temporarily move into the store was something else entirely.

If Jo and the others were going to pull this off, it was important to go into this harebrained scheme with eyes wide open. True, it was impossible to know all the ways it could go wrong. Yet she couldn't imagine anything more wrong than losing Bruebaker's.

A low buzzing of adrenaline coursed through her limbs as she considered the commitment she was about to make. Not everyone would be happy. In fact, they might all lose severance pay, or even be arrested. But the alternative might be worse. Mr.

B might wake up and realize she did nothing to protect the store. And her number one allegiance was to Mr. B.

It was a risk, Jo finally decided, worth taking.

"Okay," she announced, her voice audibly shaky. "Let's do this."

Four

*U*nlike the others, Jo decided against running home for supplies. Despite the looming notion of remaining inside for an unknown period of time, she felt obligated to stay at the store. Someone needed to supervise the comings and goings of the staff. Plus, unlike everyone else, she didn't have any pets to check on or loved ones to update back at her small townhouse. It was just her.

Going home now would be a reminder of the nothingness awaiting her if their mission failed. Just thinking of it now caused Jo to slam her eyes shut, willing the image to disappear.

Instead, she escaped to the one place in the store that was hers alone. Being the manager, Jo was granted a humble yet sufficient office located on the building's basement level. Inside, an apartment-sized desk, a table lamp, and a roller chair made up the space. Attached were a bathroom and the world's smallest shower. She'd only rinsed off under the funny little brass faucet a handful of times, but now it might come in handy. And perhaps most importantly, there was also a change of clothes. This small convenience was added last month after a stressful episode of ripping her blouse on a splintered book pallet minutes before hosting a prominent author event. She'd realized the prudency in having an extra outfit or two on hand.

Jo was a planner. Calendars, printed charts, and plentiful

provisions were what made her feel most comfortable. Because of this, she'd stocked the drawers of her desk with face wipes, a toothbrush, and feminine products. There was even a drawer dedicated to first aid. Just the sight of it filled her with a tingling satisfaction. One never knew when disaster might strike.

Today, Jo decided, was definitely a disaster. Which kind, she wasn't sure yet.

Racing down one flight of stairs, Jo arrived in her office and shut the door.

Collapsing into the squeaky faux leather office chair, she shivered. It was cold and damp down in the basement, with its broken fluorescent lighting and cave-like cement walls. But the space also provided brief moments of sanctuary during her busiest days. There was a secure feeling to it. Jo was pretty sure the place could double for a bomb shelter if required. No one else on staff had an office on-site. This was a piece of the store that was meant just for her.

For that reason, she had always been grateful.

Jo switched on the little table lamp and pulled open a drawer to fish out her tube of lavender hand cream. Out of habit, she rubbed an ample amount into her parched skin and waited. The air around her filled with a dreamy floral scent. Lavender was supposed to be calming, and right then she'd do anything to quiet her jittery nerves.

What have you gotten yourself into? Jo tilted her head back and stared at the ceiling. She couldn't yet believe she'd agreed to go against Regina's wishes and barricade herself inside the store. Did she need a head check? Was this the stupidest thing she'd ever done? Her mind was filled with a mix of excitement and dread. And her mouth was very dry. She wondered if that was a bad sign. She couldn't fall apart, not if she was really going to do this thing. She was a leader. It was important to remain strong and sure.

If only she could transport some of these feelings to Mr. B. Surely she would be there to support him, if she was just allowed. Jo slowed her breath and tried to focus on sending him all the positive energy she could muster.

"I'm rooting for you, Mr. B," she whispered.

A soft knock came at her door. Truman's face poked inside.

Reflexively, Jo's hands went to her hair. No doubt her blonde, wavy bob had turned just as out of control as her thoughts. When she caught Truman's eye, she dropped her hands and flushed. She ushered him inside. "Hey. There you are."

He entered the small space and leaned up against the far wall, a hammer hanging casually from his belt loop. The ease with which he carried himself, even in a crisis, amazed her. "I was wondering the same about you. Seems like everyone decided to give up the ghost and go home, huh?"

"No. Actually, they ran out to grab clothes and plan to come right back. Believe it or not, about half a dozen or so employees want to try and wait this thing out. They're not giving up hope."

Truman whistled. "That's really something. You've gotta hand it to those kids. They're not the unmotivated generation everyone pegs them out to be after all."

She laughed. "Yeah, I guess you're right."

He nodded. He crossed his arms then, his expression turning sober. "And you? What did you decide?"

Jo felt her chin tremble a bit. "I've decided to stay."

"Really?" Truman's neck snapped back in surprise.

"Guess I drank Adam's Kool-Aid after all," Jo answered. This clearly wasn't what he'd expected to hear.

His eyes narrowed into a thin squint as he rubbed at his

stubble for what felt like an eternity. Jo fidgeted. She wasn't sure if he was going to tell her she was out of her mind, or if he was considering helping her in some way.

Finally, she could no longer stand the suspense. "Well? What do you think?"

His eyes opened up and landed squarely on hers. "I think you're a brave woman. That's what I think."

"Am I being an idiot?"

He grunted. "Who's to say you'd be any less of one if you abandoned the place? I mean, there's no real way to tell what the outcome is going to be. You're sticking around to try and find out, and I think that's admirable."

"You do?"

"I do."

"Huh." Jo's shoulders lowered. She wasn't sure what to say. She'd supposed—maybe even hoped—that Truman might talk her out of it.

And then another thought occurred to her. "Truman"—Jo leaned forward—"any chance you're feeling brave too? I could use someone with your skill set to stick around and help. And honestly"—she paused, swallowing—"I could use a friend."

Again, he reacted with the indecipherable squint and hard stare into the middle distance. Jo bit her tongue and waited for him to answer. Maybe asking this of him was too much. After all, they were coworkers. He didn't owe her anything. Actually, he owed Mr. Bruebaker—and by extension, the Bruebaker family—a lot more. And she was guessing that's where his allegiance was. That was probably where it should remain.

"Sure. I'll stay and see if we can make Mr. B's daughters reconsider," Truman said. "Why not? You all seem to have your hearts in the right place. And I'd really hate to see this business crumble to dust. It's too important to let that happen. Deep down, I bet old man Bruebaker would be happy to see us try and save it, even if it does mean defying the orders of his CEO. Plus, no offense, Jo, but you're gonna need backup if these employees of yours get too crazy."

Jo wanted to pinch herself. She could hardly believe his words. "No offense taken. Gosh, thanks, Truman."

"You bet." He offered a wry smile and a clap of his hands. "Now, where do we start? I've never participated in public disobedience before."

"Me neither." They traded a nervous laugh. Even though this was more of a private disobedience, she knew what he meant.

The sound of footsteps came as Adam bellowed from one floor above.

Jo rose from her chair. "I bet our troops have a pretty good idea of what to do. Let's go find out."

"After you." Truman waved her through the door.

Jo thanked him and tried to tamp down her rising anxiety. Straightening, she hoped Truman couldn't tell just how un-brave she really felt.

"Let's go."

Adam, Anna, Jade, and the rest of the gang clamored with excitement, sleeping bags under their arms, totes filled with food and supplies strewn across the table. They looked like a bunch of mischievous children about to have a camping night. For the first time that day, Jo couldn't help but feel drawn into that adventurous state of mind.

Five

"A case of beer and a pack of frozen waffles?" Jo stood over a cardboard box, dumbfounded. "This is what you bring back?"

Jack and Leo glared back with offended expressions. "It's all we had at our apartment," Leo said. "We figured there's a big fridge and toaster oven in the break room. So, I mean . . . why not?"

"Ugh. Morons." Anna tossed her hair. She crouched down and picked through the box, clearly searching for anything of value. "Typical guys, bringing a bunch of carbs with zero sustenance. We could be stuck here for days! Don't you think the taste of pale ale and processed breakfast food will get old pretty fast?"

"Jeez." Jack sneered. "At least it's something. Why, what'd you bring?"

Righting herself, Anna walked over to a cluster of neatly organized reusable shopping bags. Taking her time, she plucked out a sample of provisions from each, calling them out by name. "Protein waters, granola bars, gluten-free oatmeal, almond butter, dried spaghetti and tomato sauce . . . Shall I continue? That's the kind of stuff a normal person would've brought." She waved a package of seed bread in their faces with a huff.

"Excuse us, Anna. We can't all be premed and perfect like you."

"What's that got to do with anything? I have to be a doctor to pick out nutritious food?"

"Okay, you guys. That's enough." Jo peeled off her cardigan. The room was becoming hot with tension.

"Okay, you three. Jo's right. Simmer down." Thankfully, Truman interjected. "You each brought things that will be helpful. Anna, great variety. Well done. And, Leo, got any syrup for those waffles?"

Leo brightened. "As a matter of fact, I do."

"Wonderful. Why don't you all go put those things away in the kitchen while Jo and I check all the doors?"

The group—including Adam, in an oversized camper's backpack containing who knew what, and Jade, with an armful of pillows—made their way toward the break room.

"Morons," Anna could be heard muttering under her breath.

The guys traded a few jostles.

Jo sighed and shook her head. "Holy cow, Truman. It already feels like herding cats."

"And we haven't even made it to dinnertime yet."

Jo groaned as she followed him around the store, checking windows and doors at each entrance. She didn't know why, but securing the building would make them feel better. At least, that's what Truman kept saying.

As day turned to dusk and the sky outside morphed into a muted orange hue, Jo sat on a window seat and debated the best way to inform Regina. While the others broke out a bag of potato chips and tossed around ideas for the hours ahead, she'd slipped away to the third floor for a moment of peace.

Tucked in the naturalist section, surrounded by guidebooks on bird migrations and leafy pamphlets highlighting field biology, she found a floral cushioned seat to curl up on. She adored this section of the store and the inquisitive customers it attracted. It wasn't often that she had the chance to spend time up there, but when she did, Jo liked to observe scientific-looking readers pointing their noses at the pages with deep interest.

Pressing her cheek to the cool glass window, Jo hugged her legs and tried to imagine the reaction of Mr. Bruebaker's daughters once they discovered her plan. She already knew what Regina's reaction would be, judging from the umpteen unanswered texts filling her phone screen.

Text 1: Please message me with an update. You aren't answering your phone.

Text 2: What is the status of the closing? Signs posted?

Text 3: I'm very concerned. Not seeing anything on social media yet. Please call ASAP.

Jo's chest tightened. Regina was demanding at best, ferocious at worst. She'd gained a reputation over the years as an asset to the store's bottom line but also as someone to be feared by middle management. Jo was in the latter category. Regina wouldn't hesitate to pull substantial levers with Mr. Bruebaker's daughters, halting any plans not on her approved agenda. There'd be immediate concerns regarding liability, insurance, and "optics." This was one of Regina's favorite buzzwords.

Jo sighed. It was late afternoon and time to bite the bullet. She'd better call Regina and update her. Turning the phone over in her hand, she rehearsed a few lines in her head. But nothing sounded right.

Finally, she dialed.

"Jo!" Regina answered after half a ring. Panic laced her words. Jo swallowed back her trepidation and forced her voice into a light tone.

"Hi, Regina. I—"

"Where have you been? I've been calling you for hours. It's nearly 5:00 p.m. and we haven't heard a peep from you since before lunch. Suzanne and Jane want an update. And so do I."

Heat climbed up Jo's neck. How was she going to do this?

"Before I get to that," she said, "how's Mr. Bruebaker doing?"

"Oh yes. He's stabilized."

Jo exhaled. "That's good news, right?"

"Well, yes. Although he's still in the ICU. He woke up for a brief time, but he's fragile. The doctors want to run more tests and monitor the bleeding in his brain. But he's not getting worse. So there's that."

"Thank goodness." Jo let the relief wash over her. Maybe it meant he'd make a full recovery. Feeling boosted by the news, she decided to try her luck and make one final plea for the store. "So, given that he's doing better, shouldn't we wait and ask him what to do? I mean, he'd want to be involved in a decision as big as closing the store. This place is his pride and joy. Surely his daughters can see that. Right?"

Regina let out a long huff. "Jo, we've been over this. Suzanne and Jane are doing what's best for their father. And that includes making the hard decision to close the business. They don't even know if all his faculties will be intact if he does recover. He's in his mideighties, for goodness' sake. They don't have any intention of backing down. So I'm asking you, is it finally all locked up?"

Jo chewed the inside of her lip. The prickly heat climbed higher. Outside, the scurrying of what she likened to harried ants returning to their anthill filled the streets. People and bikes and cars traveled up and down the city streets with fresh urgency. Shoppers clutched their bags; professionals in business attire pressed phones to their ears, their legs carrying them in quick strides as nearby cars filed into the single lane leading over the bridge and out of downtown. The workday was over. People were going home—except for Jo and her staff.

"Jo?"

"Yes, sorry. I'm here."

"Are you at home now?"

Squeezing her eyes shut, she gathered up her nerve.

"No," she answered. "I'm actually still at the store."

"You are?"

"Yes. And I'm not alone. A few of us have been talking all day. We closed the doors and have posted signs out front, of course. We haven't been open to the public. But a group of us are . . . well, we're having a hard time leaving."

A pause.

"I understand. I probably would take my time saying good-bye to the old place myself. It's a sentimental thing for you. I can appreciate that."

Jo shook her head. Regina didn't comprehend as much as she thought.

"Yes and no. I mean, of course, you're right. It's very difficult to abandon ship over here. The store is so valuable to the community. It's so important to all of us. But, Regina, what I'm trying to say is that a group of us have . . . decided to stay."

Frosty silence filled the line.

"Are you still there?" Jo asked.

"What do you mean, exactly? You do recall I told you Suzanne and Jane ordered the place to shut? I was very clear."

Jo filled her lungs with courage. "I know. But we've decided to stick it out anyway. With all due respect, we don't agree with what you and Mr. Bruebaker's daughters are doing. I've known Mr. B for twenty years, Regina. That's a lot longer than you. And I just can't imagine he'd ever want this. So, for that reason, we are protesting. The store can't close. Not like this."

Even as the words left Jo's mouth, she couldn't believe what she was saying. "We don't want to imagine a Portland without Bruebaker's Books."

Again, silence.

Finally Regina seemed to snap out of her shock. "You can't possibly be serious, Jo." Her tone was acrid.

"I'm afraid we are." It was important Regina understand this was about more than her alone. This was a collective decision. The voice of the most dedicated had spoken.

And they weren't going anywhere.

"Unbelievable!" Regina's voice reached an alarming decibel. "You have no idea what you're doing. This is not how business matters are handled. You think holing up in the store, refusing to go home for the day, is going to win you any favors with Suzanne and Jane? Do you think it's going to bring Arnold back to his old fighting self just because his staff is feeling ornery? My God, Jo. You're taking this too far. I know the store is your life. Really, I do. But this is not the way to go about saving it. Believe me. It's just not."

A million responses rolled around in Jo's head. She wanted to tell Regina where to stick her condescending lecture. She wanted to reach through the phone and grab the woman by the shoulders to give her a good shake, to make her understand how senseless and coldhearted she was being in the wake of Mr. Bruebaker's illness. She wanted to scream at the top of her lungs that she knew exactly what she was doing, even though she really didn't. But Jo did none of these things. Instead, she took a breath and decided not to engage in whatever verbal fight Regina was picking.

"I'm sorry it's come to this, but I stand by my staff. We aren't going anywhere. Goodbye."

Jo hung up the call and let her head fall forward. The heat faded away, and her limbs went slack against the seat. One giant hurdle down, a million more to go.

Six

"So, where are we gonna sleep?" Grayson asked, tipping back in his chair and stifling a yawn. "I got up at the crack this morning, and I'm not gonna lie, I'm beat." Before him, empty beer bottles lay scattered on the kitchen table. Next to him, Leo and Jack patted their stomachs, looking pleased. It was well into the evening, and so far their seclusion had been nothing more than a work-related happy hour.

"There's that weird hammock in the Kesey room," Adam suggested.

"Or those benches on the first floor," Leo offered.

"Actually"—Jade, who'd been jotting ideas down on a large white paper, scooted out of her chair and stood—"I already set up all the mats and pillows upstairs in the children's section. They have the best carpeting up there. And there are blinds on the windows. I thought it could be kind of cozy."

"Wow." Grayson blinked back at her.

She blushed ever so slightly, her large eyes roaming around the room.

Jo studied their silent interaction. She doubted anyone had set up anything "cozy" for Grayson in a long while.

"That's very nice, Jade. Thank you." Jo smiled. "I like the idea of us all staying in one room. This building is too large for us to spread out right now. I think, given the situation, it's best we stick together."

"Yeah, thanks."

"Good idea."

Anna and Truman, who were huddled at the far end of the room, appeared to be discussing supplies and listing strategies for getting sold books out to customers should they continue to sell products online. They looked up.

"So are people really going to bed?" Anna asked. "It's only nine o'clock. There's a lot of work to be done."

Truman nodded stoically and folded his arms. He'd skipped the beers but had no problem taking down much of the delivery pizza they got an hour before. Jo wondered if he was an early bird like herself or if he was more of a night owl. It was funny how you could work side by side with someone for so long yet realize you didn't know too much about them.

She supposed she'd find out soon enough.

"Naw, we can't go to sleep right now." Adam rose and stretched. "Anna's right. We've got work to do. That's why I've typed up this statement." He held out his phone, the screen filled with type too small for Jo to read.

"What's that?"

"A kind of manifesto. I was hoping we could all sign it and send it off to the *Saturn* and see if they'll publish it." His eyes skipped around the room.

"A manifesto?" Anna wrinkled her nose. "As in the thing the *Unabomber* wrote?"

"Ha!" Truman slapped a hand over his mouth, but it was too late. A ripple of laughter moved around the table.

Appearing wounded, Adam continued. "No, not like the Unabomber. Jeez. Like a real statement. People need to know why we're locking ourselves inside the bookstore and helping to save this amazing institution."

Anna snorted. "Getting a little self-righteous, aren't you?"

"You know what I meant. Seriously, could you be any more judgmental?"

Jo waved them apart. "Okay, you two. Let's not fight about it. Adam, as your boss I'm asking you not to publish anything that the group hasn't collectively approved. I applaud your effort, but give us a chance to weigh in, okay?"

"Fine." Adam flopped back down into his seat.

"And, Anna, since you're our point person for gathering and writing down all information, that means we need to consider everyone's input without judgment. At least for now. Okay?"

"Okay."

"Good." This was all moving awfully fast. It was one thing to stage a quiet protest inside the closed store, proving to Regina and Mr. Bruebaker's daughters just how serious they were. But it was quite another thing to go public. Jo wasn't sure any of them were really ready for the attention they might get—positive or negative—if they broadcast their mission via the media. She needed time to absorb this idea of Adam's before they did anything too hasty.

Jo placed her hands in her lap. Without looking, she knew they were trembling again. The group needed to be strong, united, not tearing one another down. The bickering between Anna and Adam wasn't a good sign. There had to be some way to find common ground and stay on it.

"I like numbers two and three on this list." Truman ran an index finger down Jade's handwritten list.

They all came over to give it a read.

1. Organize the basics (food, beds, hygiene needs *not everyone using the same bathroom!).

2. Keep up online sales, prioritize local pickups.

3. Divide workers into shifts.

"What do you mean, shifts?" Jack asked. His eyes had a lazy droop about them. Jo frowned. While Jack was supposedly known for his ability to haul large boxes of inventory around the store, he didn't seem up to the job at present. A stack of abandoned UPS boxes waited in a corner. She suspected the beers had put him in a less-than-productive mood.

"I'm glad you asked." Anna held up her pen. "That one was my idea. There are seven of us, plus Jo. Who is technically still the boss, so she gets final say. But my suggestion is that we break up into pairs. Some clean or cook, some deal with social media, and some pull and pack up books based on our orders. Ever since I posted this afternoon on Instagram about temporarily shifting our focus to online sales versus in-store sales, we've received an upswing. If we all work together, we'll get more accomplished."

"Smart thinking." Jo had to hand it to her. Not only had Anna been frantically researching medical information online, but she'd also been brainstorming a strategy with Jade. They were all in new territory, yet she'd managed to stay focused. It really was quite impressive.

"Thanks."

"If this is the plan," Truman said, "I think I'd better give everyone a brief tour of the supply closet, in case you need any-thing."

Everyone nodded in agreement.

Walking out of the break room and past the row of front win-

dows at the front of the store, Jo startled. Every neck craned as a
flash of blue and red sped by, one police car after another. The sky
outside had turned a deep navy, and the bright lights cast distorted
shadows along the bookstore walls. A high pitch from the sirens
sliced through the stillness, giving off a foreboding air.

Then just as quickly as they'd come, the lights were gone.

Jo stopped holding her breath when the last patrol car disappeared into the distance. Neither Jo nor the others really knew the
depth of trouble they might get into, now that they'd chosen to stay.
It was in Mr. Bruebaker's daughters' hands at the moment. And
their father was in no position to speak. If only he'd wake up.

Jo prayed she could buy her team some time.

She understood, however, by the cascade of notifications
filling her phone screen, that Suzanne had indeed been informed.
Jo saw four missed calls within the past two hours from her. She
stared, a slight panic rising in her chest. On one hand, she should
call Suzanne and face the music. On the other hand, she might
buy more time to build up her courage if she put the daughters
off just a bit longer. Deciding it was best to preserve what little
calm was remaining, Jo opted to switch her phone to Do Not Disturb. Suzanne and her undoubtedly angry inquisition would just
have to wait.

"I wonder what's going on out there," Grayson whispered as
he scanned the darkened windows with wide eyes. "You think
anyone knows we're here?"

Jo looked from him to Adam.

"Don't worry." Adam clapped his shoulder. Then he turned
to Jo. "I know what you're thinking. The answer is no. I haven't
sent anything to the press."

"Okay, thank you."

"But that doesn't mean it won't happen at some point." He

trailed after her; the impatience coming off his breath was palpable. "I think you underestimate the many fans of Bruebaker's. This thing we're doing could be a monumental movement, if we allow it."

Jo stopped walking. Adam was right, of course. Anyone who searched the store's Instagram account would see an impressive three hundred thousand followers, which no doubt included the many regulars who wandered the aisles and attended author events week after week. The customers were quite engaged. Anna liked to remind her of how many comments and DMs the store's social media accounts accumulated just over the weekends alone. She understood there was a certain intimacy that resulted from this kind of engagement, one that hadn't existed when Jo first began working at the store. But their sit-in wasn't supposed to be public. That wasn't the original goal.

Jo studied Adam's pleading expression. Could he be right?

"Okay. I'll give your manifesto a read after we're done with Truman. But right now, we need to focus. If we want a real shot at saving this store, then we've got to get organized. Especially in regard to boosting online sales."

Adam did a fist pump. "Awesome!"

As she walked away, Jo tried to ignore the tug of uncertainty in her gut. What would Mr. B tell her to do? If only he'd get well enough to pick up his phone and let her know.

Seven

*A*s evening fell and everyone made their way to the Beatrix Potter room, the charming children's wing tucked away on the second floor, Jo announced she wasn't ready for bed.

In actuality, she was too afraid to lay her head down.

Anna had just alerted her to the already-growing public response to "the store's temporary closing due to a family emergency within the Bruebaker's Books family." The website and social media announcement Anna crafted was vague, yet customers began posting comments of support nonetheless.

@steverllreads: I support indie!

@literarylover: What? You're even open for Christmas. What's happened?

@bookstagrammer5: So sad. No Book Bingo this week?

@pnwpages: Hope everything's okay. Sending love!

@penandink22: ♥ ♥ ♥

Just as Anna said, there'd been a surprising climb in online orders. This was a nice development. Jo announced to the others she wanted to get a head start on these orders. She would be staying up late.

In honesty, it was better to stay busy. Otherwise, she might get quiet enough to hear the clanging voices of self-doubt in her head. To her surprise, Jade offered to stay up and help too. She admitted she was feeling restless and would be glad to put her energy into packing up a few books.

So off the two of them went, an iPad in one hand and a list of inventory in the other, and got to work.

The bookstore was different at night. Accustomed to a never-ending din of voices, the ebb and flow of bodies passing through the aisles like a current, Jo now found herself awed by the silence. Rooms weren't filled with eager tourists snatching up souvenirs, dreamy bookworms scanning titles, and first-time visitors snapping selfies among the stacks. Gone were the excited whispers and happy chatter of people moving through the hallways and stairwells. And absent was the familiar flutter of pages floating through the air like a welcome breeze.

Nothing but stillness now filled the once-bustling store.

Life as Jo knew it suddenly ceased to exist in this space. Instead was something else entirely. It was almost as if she and the others were merely ghosts roaming an abandoned building once occupied by the living. For all intents and purposes, 1:00 a.m. in the bookstore was an otherworldly experience.

Of course, as the manager, she'd found herself alone in the building more than once. She'd locked up the store many times over the years, tipping her head to a nighttime cleaning crew or listing last-minute instructions to the inventory team for the following morning.

"You're always here," a janitor once remarked, with a puzzled expression. "Don't you ever treat yourself to a day off to be at home and put your feet up, or maybe take a vacation?"

Why? To just be all alone? Jo had wanted to ask. She knew the man was trying to be nice, perhaps even pay her a compliment for working all hours. But Jo couldn't help bristling at the inquiry all the same. It was as if he were implying she should go out and get a life. But how? Other than her cherished book collection, there wasn't anyone or anything waiting for her outside of the store.

But never before had she felt this alone and secluded, standing among the store's darkened shelves.

"Wow," Jade said, coming up alongside her. "It feels like we've been accidentally locked inside a museum after everyone else has gone home."

Jo nodded. This made sense. Thick shadows shrouded the corners of the second-floor room and gave the feeling of something mildly spooky. Navigating through the fiction room, she passed a display of dystopian novels. Warily, she eyed the haunting book covers. A row of Margaret Atwood paperbacks had been arranged near the back wall, illustrations of tiny red cloaks popping out from the otherwise dark covers of *The Handmaid's Tale*. For some reason, seeing them like this put Jo on edge. They were like little warning flags, trying to get her attention.

"Let's get to the historical fiction section," she said, pushing the feeling away. "I need to find something over there that's from one of today's online orders."

Jade was right behind her.

Finally arriving at her destination, Jo forced herself to pause. Clearly the mounting stress was causing her imagination to run off with her. She was being silly. What did she expect—the books to come to life and release characters from the stories, right there into the vacant store? These were rooms she'd frequented thousands of times before. What was wrong with her? She really needed to pull herself together.

There was work still to be done.

There had been a lengthy discussion on whether or not to try and sell items from the rare-books room as well. Anna, showing considerate forethought, expressed concern that if these books weren't boxed up and protected correctly, then Suzanne and Jane might not preserve them the way they deserved.

Jo knew she might be right.

Bruebaker's housed precious first editions printed as far back as the nineteenth and twentieth centuries. This dedicated space, located in a secluded section of the top floor, was 850 square feet of dark wood shelving, ambient lighting, soft furniture, and a thoughtfully procured library of antiquarian books. The majority of the leather-bound books, which were meticulously polished and oiled every five to ten years in an act of preservation, weren't handled by hordes of shoppers the way the rest of the store's inventory had been. This private chamber was locked and maintained more stringently. For that reason, the group decided to leave the rare-books room undisturbed and hope for the best, should the store be turned over to someone other than themselves.

"Ah, here we are." Jo scanned the end of the alphabet, on the shelves marked Z, and her finger stopped at the Markus Zusak books. Plucking a paperback by the spine, she pulled out a copy of *The Book Thief*.

"Is that the last of our orders?" Jade asked.

Jo nodded. "Looks like it. Now we just need to get this down to the register with the others so someone can work on shipping them out in the morning."

The two made their way back toward the first floor.

Jo quietly studied Jade as they went. It was nice getting to know an employee whom she might otherwise not have. A big part of why Jo liked her job was the thrill over the sharing of information and stories. Everyone had a story, whether it was in a book or not.

What was Jade's story? Being part of the morning inventory crew, Jade did a lot of the behind-the-scenes work, making sure each item went to the right place in the store, shelving books, pulling items for Internet orders, creating merchandise displays, and keeping things organized and looking good. Jo imagined Jade had once been the type of sweet-natured little girl who might have pored over something wholesome like the Laura Ingalls Wilder books. Jo speculated that titles written by Sue Monk Kidd, perhaps *The Secret Life of Bees*, might be up Jade's alley now that she was an adult. Perhaps she'd seek out some titles for her in the morning.

"So," Jo said, "tell me why you're here. What is it that you like so much about this store that you're willing to save it?" Jo had wondered this all night. Why was this shy young woman, with her seemingly obedient attitude and nonconfrontational smile, teaming up with the likes of Adam and company? Yes, lots of people loved Bruebaker's. That was a given. But to drop your whole life for it—well, that was a different thing entirely.

Jade's fingers tugged at a delicate silver chain hanging around her neck. A small charm in the shape of a tree sat just below her collarbone. Jo wondered if it was a gift from someone special.

"I like my job," Jade began. A shy smile was revealed.

Jo dipped her chin, waiting for her to continue.

"My parents don't have the money to send me to college, so I'm doing classes online."

"Oh, that sounds smart. What are you studying?"

"I thought I wanted to be an English major, but lately I've been thinking I might want to be an elementary school teacher. I like little kids."

"That sounds like a good plan." Not having any children herself, Jo wasn't sure which qualities best made for an elementary school teacher. She could see, however, that Jade's sweet temperament could easily translate into a nurturing role involving young students.

"Thanks, I hope so," Jade said. "In the meantime, the rest of my time is spent here." And then, as if further explanation was required, she continued. "My parents work a lot. My friends from high school have mostly moved away. My days can be kind of lonely. Doing school at my computer, in my bedroom, sometimes feels like I'm living in a weird bubble. That's why working in a place like Bruebaker's, where the rooms are constantly filled with customers, it . . . I don't know. It makes me feel less alone. Does that make any sense?"

"Ah yes," Jo responded. "That makes perfect sense." She understood this kind of loneliness all too well. Until now, however, she hadn't been aware of the similarities she and Jade shared. The discovery made her heart ache. It was one thing for her to be alone at middle age, but another for Jade to feel this way when her adult life was just starting out. "I'm so glad we have the good fortune of having you on staff. Truly."

"Thanks."

A new thought occurred to Jo. "Do your parents know where you are right now? They must be worried."

Jade nodded. "Yeah, I texted them earlier. I don't think they're happy about my decision. They say it's too risky. It might jeopardize my chances at being hired as a teacher. They want me to call them in the morning. Probably to talk me out of staying any longer. We'll see. For now, I just want to help as much as I can."

"Please don't risk your relationship with your parents or your future job prospects over the store. Don't get me wrong—

I'm happy to have you here. But family is important. So is your professional happiness. Don't forget that."

Jo wanted to say if she had family nearby, she might not choose to stay locked up in a commercial building with no real plan. But she didn't have anyone worrying about her the way Jade's parents did. Her own parents died years earlier, well before Jo was ready to be on her own.

They'd had her late in life. Her mom was forty-two when Jo was born. "My little miracle," she always called Jo. She had been the center of their life, but then they died all too early. By the time Jo turned nineteen, her mother had succumbed to a fast-moving cancer, and her father suffered a number of setbacks related to a weak heart soon after. And that was it. She had no other family to speak of.

Just for a second, she allowed herself to feel a small pang of envy over Jade's concerned family. It must have been nice to have people care so much about you.

Shaking off the sentiment, she placed the book on the first-floor counter. "Okay, shall we head upstairs and try to get some sleep now?"

"Sure."

Jo clapped her hands together. It had been a productive night after all.

At least a modest heap of titles had been pulled for the next day's sales. *One task down, a hundred more to go*, Jo told herself.

No matter. Tomorrow would be another day.

Eight

"**J**o! Jo!" Somewhere in the distance, she could hear her name being called. She felt herself being jostled by the shoulders. "Wake up."

Bleary-eyed and thick with sleep, Jo stirred. The voice calling her was not coming from the end of a long tunnel but rather from the anxious person hovering over her. More alert now, Jo sat up and blinked. Truman's face stared back at her. For a moment, she had to remember where she was. Had it all been a dream?

"What's going on?" Her hands went to her face and then to her untamed hair. Had she overslept? When she and Jade finally tumbled into their makeshift beds, it had taken her a long time to quiet her spinning brain before drifting off. Now Truman was standing over her with a face full of urgency. She looked over his shoulder to see daylight creeping in through a row of windows.

"Regina Anderson is outside. She's been pounding on the front door and calling your name. I wasn't sure what to do, so I went down and talked to her through the window. She can't exactly come in because, as you know, I double bolted the side door in addition to placing the huge board over the front entrance. Regardless, she wants you to come out."

"Oh no." Jo tensed. A tiny tornado swirled in her chest. "Did she look mad?"

Truman hooked his thumbs into his belt loops and grunted.

"Uh, yeah. That's kind of an understatement. You'd better get down there before she does something rash."

"Crap." Jo felt around for her shoes. The muscles in her forearms burned. She hadn't even stood up yet, but clearly her body was paying the price of last night's inventory hunt with Jade. "What do you mean, something rash? What do you think she's going to do?"

Truman's head swiveled around, searching. "I don't know. It's not her building, but she could make it known that we're trespassing just to get us out of here. Maybe she'll call the cops. I don't think we ought to get these kids arrested. Do you?"

"No." Jo made sure no one was within earshot. Her gaze drifted.

Strewn around the carpeted room was a sea of empty floor mats. Rumpled pillows and various items of discarded clothing were the only evidence of a hard night's sleep. It struck her then how haphazard it had become in such a short period of time. Tiny tables and chairs had been pushed to the edges of the room, colorful displays of *Pete the Cat* and *Horton Hears a Who!* were jostled to the side. The space looked chaotic in the new morning light.

This didn't matter. She shook her head. Her primary concern was Regina.

"Okay, I'm ready." Jo stood and attempted to smooth the wrinkles from her cotton shirt. It was useless. There was no hiding the fact she'd slept in her clothes and that her teeth could use a good brushing. If only she had time to run a shower and sip some coffee, she might feel more human.

There was no time.

Truman shifted on his feet. He was jingling loose change in his pockets again. Jo sensed his rising unease. Clearly, he wasn't a fan of confrontation.

"I doubt Regina wants to call attention to our situation right now," Jo said. "It would be bad *optics*, to use her words. She doesn't like negative press. Especially if it means news that might jeopardize her career. Right now, she's a CEO who can't get her employees to listen to her. She's lost control. That's one thing she and I agree on. She probably just wants to yell at me."

"Not exactly what you wanted to wake up to first thing in the morning, is it?" he asked. He offered a crooked smile.

"No. Definitely not. But Regina disagreeing with our little mission was inevitable. I'll go see if I can make her understand." Jo returned the smile and walked away.

"Hang on," Truman called. He closed the gap between them and reached for her face. As his hand came to touch her cheek, she felt herself flush. It seemed like an awfully intimate act for someone who'd not so much as even hugged her goodbye at a company holiday party. But here he was, just inches from her face. His fingers were like soft feathers across her skin, sending a wave of fluttering in her stomach. Feeling his warm breath, she closed her eyes for the briefest of moments.

This is what it feels like to have Truman touch me, she thought.

"You've got blue fuzz on your face," he said, breaking her daze. He stepped back, producing a ball of lint.

"Oh, ha!" She laughed and willed the heat to leave her face. Part of her was relieved he wasn't pointing out something terrible, and yet a bigger part of her wished his intimate act hadn't just been about a piece of stray lint.

Maybe her morning breath turned him off. She backed away, averting her gaze. *Please don't let him be able to read my mind.*

"Hey, guys." Adam suddenly appeared in the doorway, breathless. He was surprisingly alert, considering the early hour. His hair was combed back into a neat bun, and he even appeared to have changed into fresh clothes.

"Hey, Adam," Truman said. Reflexively, Jo distanced herself even farther from him.

"I don't mean to interrupt you, but—"

"What is it?" Her tone came out sharper than she wanted, and Jo instantly regretted it. What exactly had he seen?

Adam hesitated and then jutted a thumb. "We've got company down there. You'd better come."

"I know. I'm heading down." With both men right behind her, she raced down the stairs.

Sure enough, Regina Anderson was pacing outside the front entrance, her platinum hair flying in the cold Portland wind. The double doors were still boarded over, thanks to Truman's thorough job, so Regina was forced to stand to the side and press her face between a set of promotional posters hanging in the floor-to-ceiling windows. Just inside the store, lined up against the New Release display, was the staff, mouths agape. For a split second, Jo wasn't sure whether to stop and reassure her staff or to rush to meet Regina's fist-pounding request for attention.

"It's okay, you guys," Jo murmured to everyone as she passed. "I'll handle it."

Coming up to the glass, Jo motioned to the side door. But before she could do anything else, Regina was calling her on the phone. She picked up on the first ring. "Hello?"

"Jo! What the hell is going on in there? I've been calling you for hours. You can't be serious with this. Look around—no one has time for this little sit-in of yours."

Jo followed Regina's finger as she pointed to the busy street behind her. It was true; most of what she could see was the scene of a normal downtown street. Sidewalks were full. Cars streamed by, the windows rolled up tight against the damp morning wind. No one seemed to be taking notice of the store.

"Jo?" Regina's biting tone snapped her back into focus.

Jo fixed her face into a compliant smile. "Regina, I understand you're concerned. As you can see, however, most of my staff is gone, and there aren't any customers inside the store. The few of us who are left are okay in here, if that's your worry." Jo knew it wasn't, but she wanted to make a point of sounding responsible. "We've got food and water and are making do."

Regina scowled. "This is ridiculous, Jo. You can't just move into the building like it's a Holiday Inn. We don't own the building, and we haven't the permit for occupancy like that. We'll get slapped with a big fine from the city. You could wind up doing more harm than good."

Jo paused. What harm was Regina talking about, exactly? Because from where she stood, the cost of a city fine was worth the price of saving the store. Wasn't it?

"Regina, some of the employees, myself included, don't believe this is Mr. B's real wish. And we also have no reason to believe that his daughters will deal with the merchandise in the store, some of which are curated first editions, in the manner these things ought to be treated. For goodness' sake, we have first-print Steinbecks in here, signed. And you want us to just close the door and let all those books get hauled out to secondhand stores, or worse, the dumpster? No, Regina, we're intent on saving this place. We intend to stay here until Mr. B's daughters hear us out, or Mr. B himself stops this insanity." Jo felt her blood boiling as she spoke. Why did she have to convince her boss of the store's importance?

"I don't see that happening." Regina yanked her thick Patagonia coat closed against the wind. "You're too emotionally invested," she continued. "I'm telling you, Jo, you can't just ignore what's happening and stage a takeover."

There was something in the way Regina's eyes darted around

as she spoke. Jo couldn't put her finger on it, but the observation struck her nonetheless. Perhaps it was just a result of the early morning hour or Regina's rush to get downtown. But the woman's otherwise steely gaze now seemed to reveal something else: a crack in the facade. Jo watched as Regina spoke, the whites of her eyes flashing wide, the pupils shrinking into cold black dots.

If Jo didn't know better, she'd say Regina Anderson was terrified. But of what, exactly? This was unexpected.

The first time the two women met, six years earlier, Jo very much wanted to hand Mr. Bruebaker's newly appointed CEO a copy of *How to Win Friends & Influence People*. Because while she was professional and courteous, Regina was nothing but sharp edges. Within minutes of shaking Jo's hand, she commented on how she'd uprooted her whole life on the East Coast for her position at Bruebaker's. She claimed that "never in a million years" did she imagine she'd find herself living in the rainy, laid-back landscape of *Portland, Oregon*.

"I mean, how many craft brewpubs does one town need, anyway?" she'd joked as she knotted her designer scarf higher on her neck. "Even the ice cream shops advertise beer flavors!" As she laughed, Jo could tell Regina wasn't convinced she'd made an upward move.

The Pacific Northwest, Jo sensed, wasn't Regina Anderson's happy place. And yet she stayed on longer than Jo imagined, leaning into the job and doing her best to get Bruebaker's in the black. Jo supposed she had to at least admire Regina's work ethic, if nothing else. She supposed Mr. Bruebaker liked this quality as well. His praise for Regina multiplied just as her years working for him did.

The day Mr. B handed over the reins and slowly retreated into so-called retirement, Jo's heart broke a little.

Over the decades, Mr. B had made a point of spending much

of his waking hours right there among the stacks, mingling with customers, inquiring about how readers were liking a certain book, asking if they tried the long list of teas served in the café. He was known to regularly quote lines from his favorite Walt Whitman poems and offer to show off the rare-books room. He took his time with people, always with an air of genuine interest. It didn't take long for him to become a local celebrity of sorts, with bibliophiles and tourists brightening in his presence. Jo spent many days just watching as people reached for his hand and eagerly asked if he might agree to take a selfie with them. The answer, of course, was always yes.

Mr. Bruebaker loved people. And people loved him right back.

But Mr. Bruebaker's two daughters, neither of whom had much interest in the family business, wanted their father to step back from his demanding work schedule. After a minor fracture due to a fall, they insisted he take time off. Hiring a whip-smart female director of a multimedia broadcast company from the East Coast seemed like a smart move to the Bruebaker family. Regina, they said, understood where publishing and media were going. She was eager to guide their decades-old business into an ever-changing landscape—or so she said.

But Regina wasn't a bibliophile. She didn't love books the way a head of a bookstore should. Sure, she'd run other businesses successfully. But she hadn't ever run a book business. This had been painfully evident during her first week on the new job, when she could be overheard asking a salesperson why she couldn't find a copy of Michelle Obama's *Becoming*.

"That's because you're in the fiction section, ma'am," the young woman had responded. "That book is shelved downstairs with the other memoirs." Jo had seen Regina round the corner with her lips pressed into a thin line.

And today, her taut expression on the other side of the glass was no different. Regina didn't want to be standing at the entrance of the bookstore any more than Jo wanted her there. And yet, Jo begrudgingly noted, this woman was still her boss.

"This place means too much," Jo said, standing straighter. "The community will be crushed if we go under. We want it to reopen." She held her breath and prayed her small speech would appeal to Regina's sense of humanity. Surely she could see the sacrifice Jo and her team were making might benefit the entire business. They might even save Regina's job.

Perhaps whatever agreement she made with Suzanne and Jane could be undone.

Regina shook her head into her phone.

"I'm not taking responsibility if Suzanne sends the authorities banging on this door," she finally responded. Just then, it seemed the universe decided to throw Jo and her team a bone. The clouds rolled in and the sky opened up, giving way to rain. Regina hunched over and cursed.

Jo blinked. What should she do? Let Regina in through the side door? Tell her to go away?

With wet hair now clinging to her face and neck, Regina appeared ready to retreat. "This isn't the end, Jo," she said. "My advice is that you vacate immediately."

"I—"

She hung up before Jo could respond. Folding her arms across her chest, Regina turned away to brace against the ugly weather. Jo watched, stunned, as she trotted off in the direction of her waiting car.

A little spark reignited. Bruebaker's just might live to see another day.

Nine

"**T**here's a leak up on the top floor," Truman shouted, bucket and rags in hand. He stood near the stairwell with his shirtsleeves rolled up, waiting for Jo to respond. The others were off in different sections of the store, doing what they could to be productive.

Jo groaned. "It wouldn't be the first time."

The weather outside had turned from a steady drizzle to a nail-driving rain by lunchtime. Soon after Regina left, and Jo gave up on the idea of more sleep, the sky outside took on a steely hue. A percussion of loud drops now came at the windows in sideways sheets. And while rain was a regular event in Portland, today's storm only added to the menacing vibe Regina had brought with her.

With her arms full of newly unpacked fantasy novels, Jo searched Truman's expression. There were shadows under his eyes, his otherwise handsome face lined with fatigue. She wondered how much sleep he'd managed the night before. According to Adam, Truman was up extra early making sure a pot of strong coffee was ready for the rest of them.

Placing the paperbacks on a dedicated shelf, Jo twisted her hands with worry. "Anything up there damaged?"

"I'm not sure. Maybe. I noticed some pooling on the floor, by one of the registers. We've had leaks up there before, but this seems like a new spot."

"Okay, let's go see."

Just then, Adam appeared. He and Grayson were supposedly making a dent in the new orders from a rather large regional book club, who claimed they wanted to support the business by ordering their planned reads for the next six months. Thankfully, their wish list included mostly backlist copies. Because of this development, it was the first of Adam that Jo had seen in hours. She wanted to ask after his progress, but there were more pressing matters to address upstairs. Her pulse was spiking at the thought of potential water damage.

"Hey, Jo." Adam strode over and cut her off at the bottom of the stairs. "Got a second?"

"Hey." She paused, shaking her head. "Not really. Truman and I were just headed to the third floor. The rain is causing some kind of leak. Can it wait?"

He hesitated. "It's just that—"

Jo took another step. They were wasting valuable time. "Adam, unless someone is on fire, it's going to have to wait. Okay?"

He slumped. "Yeah, okay. Fine."

"Good."

Jo moved her feet faster as they ascended the top flight of stairs. Drying out wet books was not something they had time for. She'd already experienced that nightmare a few years earlier, when a pallet of boxes from Random House was damaged in the basement storage area. If the pages weren't completely dried within a short amount of time, not only would they be excluded from the used shelves; they'd have to be thrown out altogether to avoid the risk of mold.

Truman, who'd also been a part of that misfortune, seemed to be thinking the same thing, judging by the pile of equipment he'd dragged along with him.

Please don't be the rare-books room. She held her breath, too afraid to ask out loud whether this was the case.

Arriving upstairs, Jo exhaled. Thankfully, Truman turned away from the rare-books area and headed toward the opposite wall. Because while any kind of damage would be a blow, if the antiquarian treasures went, then they may as well just give up and go home. Those kinds of autographed and first editions were simply irreplaceable.

Instead, Truman led them past the astrology section and toward a sign reading PHOTOGRAPHY. Jo hurried to catch up, their feet echoing on the pale linoleum floors. The top level, with its exposed beams and industrial lighting, often reminded Jo of the interior of a home improvement warehouse rather than a bookstore. But though it lacked in warm furnishings—save for her preferred nook among the bird books—this floor offered many interesting subjects. Divided into proper sections, the third floor housed all things science and math, computing, crafting, art, and more. It was like having the world's biggest reference section for sale, all under one roof.

If she had more time, she'd like to read a book from every shelf and every subject up there. It would almost be like getting the college education she never completed.

"Here." Truman placed his things down and pointed.

Her eyes went from the floor to the ceiling and back again. An ugly brown spot spread along the ceiling tiles like a dark cloud, murky water wreaking havoc on a display directly below. An entire endcap's worth of photography hardbacks were completely soaked through.

"Oh no!" Jo rushed in and began scooping up as many items as she could, the sleeves of her shirt turning damp. Stunning portfolios, pictorial coffee table books, and cardboard rolls of prints were all reduced to wet paper and inky stains. The water bled through it all. With her arms full, she backed away and cradled the damaged objects. Her voice grew small as she scanned the loss. "Such beautiful books."

"I know. I'm afraid many of these are beyond saving at this point." Truman picked up a nearby paperback and thumbed through clumps of damp pages.

Jo recognized a popular title that read *The Methods of Composition and Design*. Its waterlogged corners were soft and mushy. "These books are works of art. I can't believe we couldn't save them."

As the words left her mouth, Jo's throat constricted. The reality hit her. For the first time since Regina's call, Jo allowed herself to recognize the magnitude of their circumstance. These would just be the first to go. If they weren't successful in holding out and waiting for Mr. B to get better, the bookstore might really be lost. Standing there with her sneakers in an inch of dirty water, gripping the pile of trashed books, Jo began to cry.

It had all become so miserably empty and sad. Even in the off hours, when the CLOSED sign was illuminated, one could usually find staff members building displays, teams restocking tables, and cleaning crews mopping the floors.

She missed the usual customers scanning the shelves, their reading glasses pushed high onto their noses, their bodies straining on balanced toes as they reached for a new title. She missed the couples who wandered the aisles together, their fingers entwined, with heads pushed together in shared whispers. She longed to once again see the curious children, with their mouths hanging open at the sight of so many tall bookcases, brimming with possibility. And, perhaps most of all, Jo missed the low chatter of excitement as people shared their discoveries with one another, strangers striking up conversations, patrons and book-sellers trading suggestions of what to read next.

Without any of that, the building felt like a scooped-out husk, fragile and lifeless. "Hey, hey." Truman came over and removed the book from her arms. He placed a hand on her shoulder and guided her over to a nearby bench. Jo sniffed as she lowered onto a dry spot.

"I'm sorry. I don't know why I'm getting so emotional. You brought me up here for a solution, and here I am falling apart." She pressed the heels of her hands to her face and willed herself to gain composure. It was embarrassing.

"It's quite all right. We're all having a hard time." Truman sat beside her, a faint whiff of something like wood polish coming from his clothes. The drumbeat of rain could be heard on the roof above, its sound the only noise filling the vast space. It occurred to her that Truman always seemed to bring a bit of peace wherever he went.

"I thought I'd prepared myself. Or maybe I just thought I could stay busy enough to not really have to think too deeply about what's happening. But coming up here and seeing all of this"—she gestured—"it's just so damn depressing. I mean, have you ever seen the place so void of life? It's like everyone's left and they're never coming back."

"I know what you mean," he said. "In the words of Neil Gaiman, a town isn't a town without a bookstore. I can't imagine what this place, what Portland, might be like if there was no Bruebaker's."

"So true." Jo nodded. It was a good quote. She wondered if Neil Gaiman was a favorite author of Truman's. Whenever she'd asked him what he was reading, he usually rattled off an eclectic list of titles that spread across many genres. Truman, Jo realized, was the one person to whom she had a difficult time recommending reading material. She couldn't figure out his type, or if he even had one. He could be rather opaque at times. And for someone who prided herself on guessing people's reading preferences, this stumped Jo. In fact, it downright bothered her. She was going to have to work on this.

"Is it okay if we just sit here for a moment longer?" A part of her desperately wanted to lean into his shoulder and close her eyes.

"Sure thing."

They sat that way, not speaking, for several minutes. They listened to the rhythm of rain outside and the dripping of water inside, collecting in Truman's bucket. The air smelled of paper and mildew. The temperature was cold, and Jo didn't want to leave just yet, to get up and walk away from the warmth on that bench. Sitting there with Truman, amid the never-ending shelves of waiting books, soothed her. It was as if time stopped, just for them, so they could look back on this one day and remember. Because for better or for worse, Jo knew they might not ever have a moment alone like this again.

"Have you ever thought what your life might look like if you didn't work here?" Jo finally ventured.

"Can't say that I have." He tipped his head back against a pine shelf and let his eyes drift upward. "Have you?"

She shook her head. "Not really. I mean, maybe a few years back when I heard Mr. B was retiring and the leadership was in question. A small part of me worried someone new might come in and clean house, leaving me out of a job. But no, I don't think I ever let myself imagine a different life. I've been working at this place since my twenties. It's in my blood at this point. Besides, where else would I go?"

Truman grunted.

She thought about her sparsely furnished townhome, with its singular couch and rarely used TV on the wall. She thought about the cupboards of her kitchen, containing only enough glassware and dishes for two people. She thought about the clothes in her closets, 99 percent of them suited for work and not much else. Jo wasn't a runner, she didn't do crafts, and she certainly didn't have any kind of a nightlife. The bookstore was her whole world.

She did have a life once. A boyfriend. She'd met Michael in this exact building, on this exact same floor, where he was searching for science books. He had rounded glasses that kept slipping down his nose as he juggled a stack of paperbacks. When he professed his love for space-age lit, Jo was smitten. There was a kind of nerdy charm about him. Michael was every-thing she wanted in a man. He was smart, a Boeing engineer. He could hold a conversation on almost any topic—religion, science, anthropology. The only thing he couldn't really talk about was himself. He wasn't the type for deep connection, and four years ago Jo didn't want to settle for less. She wanted it all, and Michael simply was not offering that.

Now, Jo wished she had tried harder. At least she might have had something to go home to.

Thankfully, she'd had her job to bury herself in and help her ignore the loneliness.

Arnold Bruebaker had plucked her from obscurity at twenty-seven and given her a role that would soon become her entire identity. All Jo ever wanted to do was read books and meet people who liked to do the same. Bruebaker's had delivered on that dream and then some. But if this were taken away, what would become of her?

"Other than books, what else do I really even know?"

"Oh, come on." Truman nudged her. "You know lots of things. Don't sell yourself short. Look at all of these kids you manage, day in and day out. That's something."

She smiled. "You're being nice, but thank you. It isn't too hard. I mean, when we need help, we just advertise for someone who loves books, and then poof, they magically appear. It's this place that makes it easy. Not me."

"Yeah, this place is magical that way. Lots of good people have come through our doors."

Jo liked the way he said "our." He was just as invested as she was. She hugged herself against the cold and let Truman's words soak into her. He was right. Bruebaker's was magical. And it was worth saving. Water leaks and angry CEOs aside, they had to keep going. Thanks to Truman, she once again remembered the silver lining.

"Okay," she said, dusting off her pants. "I'm done sulking. Let's get back to work."

"After you."

Together, they went to find the others.

Ten

Jt turned out Anna's organized list—meticulously outlining each employee's shift—only lasted about half a day. By the time Jo roamed the building, checking in on everyone's status, it was evident most everyone had gone off script.

All except for Jade.

Jo happened upon her first, exactly where the two of them had left off the night before. Only Jade had figured out a way to speed up her order-fulfillment process, lining books up in rows and deftly sliding her scanner over a long line of book covers. When she'd finished this part, she flipped the rows over and repeated the process.

"Wow." Jo clucked her tongue at the sight of so many organized piles. "Much better than my clumsy way of holding each book in my lap. Your method is much more efficient."

"Thanks." Jade smiled. Just like Jo, she too looked as if she slept in her clothes, got up, and went right back to work without sparing any time. Jo pointed to her pair of abandoned eyeglasses and promised to return to her work shortly. With an optimistic spring in her step, she moved on to find the others.

When she entered the gift and souvenir area of the lower level, Jo's nostrils pricked. Stopping short, she screwed up her face and inhaled. *Weed.* Were Jack and Leo smoking inside the store? Irritated, she glanced at the time on her phone. It wasn't even noon and they were already slacking off.

Husky laughter trailed from somewhere behind the occasional-card display. A cough and an amused voice followed. Jo set her jaw and crossed the floor. Who did these guys think they were, anyway?

"Oh, hey, Jo." Leo saw her first, his expression sheepish as he waved a cloud of smoke unsuccessfully from the room. "We were just taking a quick break."

Jack jumped to his feet and began fumbling with a handful of birthday cards. His bloodshot eyes drifted to the floor. Moody indie rock music whined from his nearby phone. From what Jo could see, zero progress on packing up online orders had been made.

"What are you two doing?" she demanded. "You know there's no smoking allowed in the store. You could damage the inventory. What the hell?" Her hands went to her head; she felt as if it might explode. Couldn't these two do anything right?

"Sorry."

"Yeah, sorry. We didn't think it mattered, now that the store is closed. There's no one around."

Jo shook her head. "You're wrong. It does matter. A lot. Forget about the fact you two are down here, goofing off. I mean, the birthday cards? Really, guys? Why are you focusing on the disposable gift items as opposed to the dozens of books that require our immediate attention?"

"We just thought—"

Jo held up a finger. "I'm not finished. There are sprinkler systems all over the place." She said, pointing to the ceiling. "What if you set those off? All this stuff would've been soaked. I've already dealt with one water damage event. I don't need another one."

Her head thumped with what felt like a blooming migraine. Just the idea of this type of accident was too much for her to bear. She'd promised that she'd do her very best regarding the store, to keep it running and making money, but in fact she wasn't. This was definitely not her best. And while it wasn't her fault Leo and Jack brought weed into the building, it was her fault for including them in the plan. They clearly weren't up for the task, with their silly grins and sloppy work. She narrowed her eyes and considered them. Each was hunched over and struck dumb in his rumpled flannel shirt and bedhead. Each had a face full of guilt.

It was clear what Jo had to do.

"You guys are out," she said flatly. "Get your stuff and go home."

Leo's brows shot to his hairline. "What? You've got to be kidding me. We didn't do anything wrong." His face colored as his arms went taut with anger. Jo shot him a look that dared him to challenge her authority.

"We really were working, Jo," Jack offered.

"Not good enough. This mission isn't for you guys. Frankly, I'm not even sure why you wanted to stay in the first place."

"They're here because I asked them to be." Adam was suddenly behind her, coming over to meet them with a look of concern. The sleeves of his denim button-down were rolled up, a cleaning rag tucked into his jeans pocket. His nose wrinkled as he glanced around. "What's going on?"

"They're not taking this thing seriously, is what's going on. Having them here isn't working out. I've asked them to leave." Jo kept her voice even, reminding herself not to lose her cool. She was fuming on the inside, but it wasn't her style to lead with emotion, especially right then.

"Whoa, hang on. You guys are leaving?" Adam's gaze bounced

from one face to the next. A question mark hung on his expression.

Leo shrugged. She watched him turn and drop the last of a hand-rolled cigarette into a water cup. The air was thick with discomfort as Jo waited for Adam to react.

"You guys were puffing on a joint? In here? Dude! Ever hear of vaping? And why not go outside?" Adam said. "What if a spark flew out and landed on something flammable . . . like a book? What then? Do you really want to be known as the two clowns who locked themselves inside Bruebaker's Books only to accidentally burn it down? Come on!"

"They could've set off the sprinklers," Jo repeated.

Leo balked. "We were by an open window."

Jo looked beyond him to the propped-open glass. A misting of fine rain had settled onto the wooden sill. Farther out on the sidewalk, people dashed about, carting groceries and other belongings, heading to parked cars. She thought of all the store owners and wondered how they'd feel if someone were to suddenly shut them down.

And just then, before turning her attention back to Adam and company, Jo spied something that made her heart ache. She noticed the stroller first. It was the same one that she'd noticed once before, gray and worn and top-heavy with bags. A mother and child pushed their way up the street, their heads bent down against the driving rain. Jo saw now that the mother was quite young. And the small child, her heavy-lidded eyes weary under an oversized baseball hat, was no more than four. Where were they going? Did they have anywhere to shelter? Her mouth popped open, wanting to call out to them somehow. But what could she do?

After a second, she noticed a young man jogging after them.

He was tall and lean, a large nylon backpack hoisted on his shoulders. His face was hard. The three paused under a store awning and talked as if they knew one another. For some reason, Jo couldn't stop staring. She had a gnawing feeling but couldn't quite identify it.

"Jo?" Adam was trying to get her attention.

"What? Oh yes." She dragged her eyes back into the room. "We narrowly avoided a catastrophe here."

"So I'm sure the guys won't do it again," he said. "Right, guys?"

"No way," Jack said.

"Sorry. It won't happen again," Leo added.

Jo frowned. Did Adam just sweep into the room and assume control over her staff? Over her decision-making process? Her lips pursed. The shelter-in-place thing may have been Adam's idea, but she was still in charge. She was still his manager. It was important he not forget that.

"Adam, can I speak with you for a moment?" She led him over to the checkout counter and put her back to the others. She was aware of Leo and Jack watching them, wondering their fate.

"Yeah?"

"Why do you want those two here anyway? They're clearly not up to the challenge. Look at their contributions so far—beer and pot. What's next? An underground rave in the basement?"

Adam snorted. "That's actually kind of a cool idea."

Jo scowled.

"But no." He dropped his grin. "You're right. They shouldn't be screwing around."

"I want them gone, and don't challenge my decisions any-more. Send them on their way. They should go home."

Adam rubbed his chin, as if he was debating. He glanced

back across the sales room. "I hear you. I'm sorry for arguing. But here's the thing," he finally said. "Leo and Jack might be lacking direction . . ."

"Is that what you're calling it?"

"They're not perfect. Should they be fired under normal circumstances? Yeah, probably. But look around." His hand made a sweeping motion around the room. "This place is gigantic, and there's way too much work. If we let them go now, we'll be down to a team of six. I don't know about you, but that feels like not enough people to tackle such a big job. Anna just told me we've received close to triple the number of our normal online orders. People are starting to freak out. They're posting messages on our Instagram and Twitter accounts, asking us to please reopen their favorite bookstore. Frankly, the way I feel is, dumbasses or not, we need all the help we can get."

Jo felt as if she were in a lifeboat that was taking on water. Adam was right. They couldn't afford to lose anyone. Not yet at least.

She gave him a hard look, hoping he understood the difficulty in what she was about to say. "Fine. They can stay. For now. But I'm putting you in charge of them. Anything else goes wrong, it's on you. Understand?"

Two fingers snapped out from his hairline in a quick salute. "Gotcha loud and clear, boss."

She grumbled and stomped off. Let Adam deal with their mess. She'd had enough shenanigans for one morning.

As she climbed the stairs in search of Anna, she silently prayed good news would be awaiting her elsewhere. Because at the moment, she was fresh out.

Eleven

*T*wo days later, the Bruebaker's team finally found their groove. Miraculously, the authorities (nor anyone from the city, for that matter) hadn't yet shown up to shut them down. The more time that went by without objection from the outside, the more emboldened the team seemed to feel. By the end of the third day, Jo actually found herself more hopeful than ever. Sales were mounting, and so were her spirits. They might actually be able to save the store after all. Now she just needed Mr. Bruebaker to regain his strength and make his voice heard.

It was because of this newfound hope that Jo found herself outside for the first time in days. With her face angled toward the sun, she snuck a moment alone to enjoy a breath of fresh air in the alley behind the store. The entire team had just finished a group meal of chicken and waffles, thanks to the ambitious plans of Leo and Jack. And everyone had wandered away with full stomachs for a little well-earned rest and relaxation.

Jo had to hand it to the boys. Ever since she'd discovered their idle efforts and then jumped down their throats, the two friends managed to pull themselves together. They'd apologized to Jo on multiple occasions and had done their fair share of lugging boxes out to the loading dock for UPS to take away the heavy onslaught of online orders. They'd even assisted Truman in cleaning up the mess from the upstairs water leak, all without complaints. A small part of Jo worried their tempered behavior was too good to be true. But for the moment, she was pleased with their contributions. Plus, the brunch idea was a huge hit.

Leaning against the weathered brick wall outside, Jo closed her eyes and allowed herself to be comforted by the change of weather. The sun was luxurious, the slight breeze filling her nose and mouth with crisp pine air. And all around her was a kind of stillness she never before thought was possible in the city. On all accounts, Jo was experiencing a true moment of peacefulness.

Her eyes popped back open at the sound of the *thumpity-thump* of hard wheels moving over rough pavement. At first, she assumed the sound was coming from someone's trash bins being put out for collection. The block was lined with boutiques and restaurants. But then she took notice when a young woman was moving in her direction. The woman's head was down, her gaze fixed on the ground. In front of her was a stroller. A cluster of plastic bags bumped around on top, practically obscuring her small frame. In the seat was a child, fast asleep with her delicate head listing to one side under the stroller's sunshade.

Jo's breath caught. The little girl's shoes were so small, too small for her feet. They were baby shoes, not a four-year-old's shoes. They had holes in the front, her toes jutting out. Her mother must have had to cut the front of the shoes off in order for the child to keep wearing them. How did that work when rain soaked the streets and the wind picked up? Jo looked down at her own shoes—simple sneakers, really. She wiggled her toes. They seemed luxurious to her now.

Yep, they're homeless all right. Jo's heart broke for these two. Who was taking care of them? Who was protecting them?

"Excuse me!" she called. The young woman's head snapped up, her light blue eyes meeting Jo's. "Hi there."

The woman came to a halt just a few feet away. She frowned slightly, looking as if she wasn't sure whether to keep walking or not. She was wearing a man's windbreaker that seemed too light for the weather, and a pair of ripped jeans with old running shoes. Her face was clean, but her hair hung in unwashed strands around her heart-shaped face. Jo was startled to realize just how young she was, perhaps nineteen or twenty at most. If her estimate was correct, Jo was looking at a teenage mother.

Wait, she thought, *maybe they're siblings.* She chastised herself for the rush of judgment. It was best not to make assumptions. Everyone had a story. And someone else's wasn't hers to tell. That's what she always said.

But something about this young woman tugged at her heart in a familiar way.

If circumstances had been slightly different, this could have easily been her. When Jo's parents passed away, she was a teenager who was heavy on grief and light on life skills. At nineteen years old, Jo found herself completely alone. There was no extended family, no close friend to take her in. If her parents' house had not been left to her, Jo would've been without a place to live. Without a roof over her head and a small amount of life insurance money, what decisions would she have been forced to make?

Seconds went by. The older of the girls still hadn't moved.

Jo felt her unease turn to worry, a twist in her gut forming. "Are you okay? Do you need anything?"

The girl shook her head, her tight expression softening a little.

Jo tried again. "Do you have somewhere to sleep tonight?"

"Yes," the girl finally said. By the way her lips clamped shut again, Jo assumed she didn't intend to tell her much more.

Jo scanned the bags of things. It was difficult to tell what was inside of them, but she couldn't imagine there was much. She didn't like the idea of the two of them out there like that. Shelter or no, they still seemed to be in need of help.

Raising a finger, she motioned. "Hang on a second. I think I have something I can give you."

The girl hesitated. She glanced over her shoulder, a nervous expression passing over her face. Before she had a chance to protest, Jo spun around and headed for the side entrance to the building. Taking the back stairs two at a time, she ran to the second floor, located what she was looking for, and arrived back outside, breathless.

Thankfully, the two were right where she'd left them.

"Here you go." Jo smiled and extended her arms. She produced the fuzzy blue blanket. Jo was happy to turn it over for the child. She was only sorry she hadn't been able to wash it first. But it had been the last blanket for sale, so it was all she could offer. Still, she hoped the gift would be received.

"Thanks." The girl inched forward and snatched it from her grasp. It was then that Jo noticed a shallow cut just at her cheekbone. Judging by its angry pink color, it was a fresh injury.

"You need anything for that?" she asked, pointing. "Looks like it might hurt a little."

"No." The girl's hand went to her face; her eyes moved into the middle distance, as if she was remembering. Before Jo could form another question, or offer them a meal, the girl placed the blanket over the sleeping child and turned to go. Wordlessly she gripped the stroller handles and steered them in the direction from which they'd come.

Jo sighed. It wasn't much, but at least it was something.

Please let them be okay.

Pulling open the side door once more, she went in search of the others.

"Are you familiar with any of the houseless neighbors who frequent our block?" Jo asked Truman a short while later. He had bowed over a stack of newly packed boxes, labeling each one in big block letters before Jack and Leo carted them away.

"Homeless?" He shook his head, sticking a Sharpie behind his right ear. "Nah. I mean, I've bought a few guys a cup of coffee from time to time. But I don't know any of them by name, if that's what you're asking. Besides"—he stood and scratched his head—"most tend to congregate closer to the tent cities that keep erecting across the river. Our block is usually all tourists and shoppers."

Jo chewed the inside of her cheek. Truman was right. There were definite pockets of downtown that attracted different groups of people. Bruebaker's pocket was high foot traffic, and most of that was made up of people looking to spend money.

"Why do you ask?"

"I just keep seeing the same young girls, that's all. Today marks the third time they've walked by the building."

Truman waited for her to continue.

"Well, obviously I'm hoping the local shelters are taking more people than usual right now, given the heavy rains. Hopefully these girls have somewhere safe to go. It's just that they're so young, Truman. The little one seemed barely out of diapers. It bothers me. That's all."

Living in Portland, it was easy to become jaded over time. Just as in other large metropolitan areas, street life was unfortunately part of the territory. Over the years, it felt to Jo as if chronic mental illness and too few resources had greatly contributed to the growing problem of homelessness. And then there was the simple fact that people were being priced out of decent housing options. Being exposed to this deteriorating landscape day in and day out both pained Jo and hardened her.

After a while, she'd come to accept there wasn't much she could do.

This was a shameful admission. Yet she knew other residents of the city also felt the same way. It was a sad truth woven into the fabric of their daily life. And while people didn't want to accept this social and economic disparity as normal, they did.

"Tell me next time you see them," Truman offered. "I'll see if I can't go out and give them something from our kitchen."

"Thanks."

"Of course."

They went back to work in relative silence for the remainder of the afternoon. Her pensiveness caused Jo to keep to herself more than usual. She moved along the romance and mystery aisles, deep in thought as her gaze swept over one book to the next. She speculated over the girls, the shutdown of her store, and what changes would be born out of the abrupt halt on her routine life. It wasn't often Jo found herself with the luxury of so much quiet time. Perhaps in all of her busyness, she'd allowed herself to become indifferent to the hardships of others. The new silence of the closed door made her see that.

It was time, she realized, to take stock.

Twelve

*B*y the fifth day, sleeping as a group among the shelves in the children's section had become somewhat normal, despite the fact Jo hadn't slept in the presence of other people in years. Never mind that she often opened her eyes in the middle of the night half expecting to see the stuffed animals and colorful books come alive. There was something mystical about the stacks in this part of the store. Perhaps it was the way the moonlight played through the window shades, or the way Jo's imagination sparked near so many illustrated book covers. Whatever the reason, when the sun went down, everything took on a fantastical feel. Sometimes Jo couldn't help but feel like the creatures of C. S. Lewis's *Chronicles of Narnia* might spring forth from the pages and appear right in front of her.

She knew better, of course. But the stress was toying with her mind.

Mr. Bruebaker had apparently stabilized, according to Regina. He was recovering in a nursing rehabilitation facility for seniors near the hospital. To Jo's disappointment, he simply wasn't strong enough to go home or even talk to her on the phone.

More than once, she typed out a text message and sent it to him, hoping he might be able to read her updates.

Text 1: I'm still here at the store with core members of your team!

Text 2: Just wanted to let you know I'm thinking of you. We're still busy at the store, despite being closed to the public.

Text 3: We're not going to shut down until you tell us to! Bruebaker's Books still lives!

Underneath each message read the word "delivered." No response came in return. *He'll read them eventually*, Jo thought. *We've just got to hang on.* And still, the silence continued. Jo kept hoping she'd wake up and realize it had all been a bad dream. But this was never the case. As a result, life hung in limbo. The more time that went on, the more isolated Jo and the others began to feel. For Jo, it felt as if there was no present to connect her past and future. There was only a before and after, but no in-between that felt real enough to be true.

That's why, when a cluster of loud voices came from the street below one dreary Sunday morning, she and the others went flying down the stairs in various states of pajamas and bewilderment.

Stopping short, they arrived at the still-closed entrance. What greeted them on the other side of the windows was a trio of stern faces that Jo didn't recognize.

Jo sucked in her breath. Their shelter-in-place operation was no longer a low-profile event.

"I work for the mayor's office," a neatly dressed man hollered into the glass. Jo's gaze traveled over his starched shirt and polished black shoes. "We need to talk."

She shifted. This was a bad sign.

The building that housed Bruebaker's was, in fact, a city-owned property. While the City of Portland owned more municipal buildings and vacant lots than retail locations, the bookstore was an exception. Jo wasn't totally clear on the details, but she knew enough to understand that not even Mr. B had total say on what happened to the building in the end.

Because of this, she needed to hear this man out. Just as she'd done during Regina's visit, Jo motioned for the man to call her on the phone. In a loud voice, she dictated her number from the other side of the window. Giving a thumbs-up, he began dialing. The others in his group stood by stiffly as they waited.

A nervous ripple of commotion traveled through the room as Jo's cell rang.

Jo shushed them. "Quiet, you guys." Adam drew in close, assuming the role of wingman to Jo's trembling frame. She wished she wasn't so anxious, but getting a surprise visit from the mayor's office wasn't good. If it was, the faces staring back at her wouldn't be frowning.

"Ms. Waterstone," the gentleman in a starched button-down spoke into the phone. "I'm Sam Turnbull, acting deputy mayor for the city. I'm here on behalf of Mayor Fink."

"Nice to meet you." Jo's voice went up at the end, making her response sound more like a question than a statement. "What can I do for you?"

"This is a very unusual situation, Ms. Waterstone." His brow furrowed, his thin mouth dipping down at the corners. He was on the young side, perhaps in his thirties, with smooth skin and a full head of well-styled hair. His face, however, was masked with blatant disapproval, as if Jo were a young delinquent.

"Oh yes. It is." Jo had no idea if he was referring to the shutdown of the store or the fact that they were forced to speak through a boarded-up entrance. Either way, she wasn't sure she wanted an answer.

"Don't give in to whatever he wants," Adam hissed into her ear. "He's just here to intimidate us. Why else would he show up with his cronies?"

Cronies? Jo would've laughed if she wasn't so nervous. This wasn't a crime film. Adam's imagination was clearly taking off with him.

"What you can do," Sam said, "is discontinue this protest of yours and go home. Mayor Fink has requested everyone vacate the store—per the Bruebaker family wishes—until further notice. This is to avoid any unwanted discord downtown. His office is not acting, as you say, *on the side of fascism*."

Jo blanched. His tone was considerably sharp, accusatory. "What does that mean?"

"Oh no," Adam muttered, suddenly taking a step away from Jo's side.

Sam pointed with his phone. His face told Jo he was not playing games. This was serious. "Why don't you ask your boys there which one of them was all too happy to speak to the press about it?"

Confused, Jo turned and cast Adam a questioning look.

His eyes went to the floor. "I, uh . . ."

Leo and Jack stood behind him, trading guilty looks.

"Adam?" She covered the phone with her palm. What was going on?

Like a dog who'd been caught chewing the furniture, he slowly lifted his eyes. "I tried to tell you. More than once, actually." He feigned innocence. "But you were always too busy. Sorry, but it was taking too long. I had to take matters into my own hands."

He didn't.

"You sent in that manifesto." Jo nearly dropped the phone. Adam's admission landed like a punch in the gut. The air in the room suddenly felt as if it had been drawn out. And now there was backlash in the form of the deputy mayor.

Jo realized, as she stood there absorbing this new information, that she'd been a fool. Here she thought they'd been doing just fine on their own, working in unison to save the business. And in one fell swoop, Adam went and did something reckless, jeopardizing each and every one of them. More than that, he'd broken Jo's trust.

"Hello? Ms. Waterstone?" Sam's irritation was growing. "Time is of the essence here. Mayor Fink wants an answer."

Jo turned her back to Adam and willed herself to stay calm. She would deal with her staff later. Right then she needed to figure out a way to get the deputy mayor and his intimidating entourage to leave.

"Yes, sorry. I'm here. I understand our presence at the store has likely caused some concern. And I understand your need to come down here and make sure we're all okay. And"—she gestured behind her—"as you can see, we are."

Sam shook his head. "That's not why I'm here. Yes, of course, I'm glad to know everyone is all right. But you shouldn't be here. You *can't* be here. I see from all the nails and wood that you've taken great lengths to board up the place, so I won't have my men dismantle this. But you need to pack up your things and vacate. Today. This is a matter for you to take up privately with the business owner, not a platform for a public protest in a city-owned building. Do you understand? Mayor's orders."

Jo looked beyond Sam, sizing up his so-called men. They appeared to be plainclothes security, probably from the mayor's detail. Had Sam come expecting trouble? It struck her that he hadn't gone so far as to bring the police to her door. Perhaps Sam didn't want to add fuel to Adam's fascist fire, something else for the media to catch wind of and report. Or maybe it was the fact he didn't want to spend tax dollars by sending officers to settle a business dispute. Even so, Jo suspected a protest, political or not, wasn't something Mayor Fink wanted. Lately, with rising crime and increased houselessness, the city and its leadership had enough trouble on its hands.

As Sam tapped his foot impatiently on the other side of the glass, Jo's mind raced. She had to think fast.

"We can't leave yet; we're just making progress." Anna tugged on Jo's sleeve.

"Yeah, can't he just let us stay? We're not hurting anyone," Grayson urged.

"This is total tyranny," Adam muttered. Jo sent him a hard look, and he slunk away.

Jo's stomach flopped. Where did her loyalty lie? She was in an impossible situation. Bruebaker's could be heavily fined, or worse. Yet the rest of her staff stood firm—all except for one.

"Hey, dude." Leo sidled up to Adam. His color had paled. "I can't afford to get arrested or anything over this. I, um, already have a prior."

"You do?" Truman's eyes widened.

"Yeah, nothing serious. Just a thing that happened at a bar one night. A misunderstanding. But still . . ."

Jo huffed. She knew this guy was trouble. Murmurs erupted. Cracks in the team were beginning to show.

"Sam, I understand your position." Her voice wavered. On one hand, it would be so easy to give in, to pack up the little inventory they'd been able to sell and gather, and walk away. Whatever the bookstore's fate, at least Jo could say she tried. Couldn't she? But another more nagging part of her felt her feet rooting to the floor. This place was her home, her church, and her sanctuary. Thanks to decades of loyal patrons, it had become an institution. How could she possibly give that up? Was she really going to let some young guy dressed in Brooks Brothers take all that away?

Steeling herself, she straightened. "It's just that I can't do what you're asking."

Sam's eyebrows shot up. He moved closer to the window and peered in. "You can't?"

"No. I'm sorry, but I can't leave. Bruebaker's means too much to this community. I promised I'd try and save it, so that's what I'm going to do. If any of my staff want to leave, they're free to go. But I'm staying right here."

Her knees shook a little as she said it. This was the most defiant she'd ever been in her entire life, and she wasn't sure she liked the feeling. But she knew what she was saying. She was saying her truth.

"Yes!" Adam cheered, his feet doing a little hop. He might be excited now, she thought, but Adam had another thing coming once she got a hold of him. She'd deal with him later.

"What?" Sam's jaw hinged wide. Jo waited as he processed the meaning of her words. Clenching a fist by her side, she waited for whatever threat might follow.

"I'm staying."

Sam fixed a hard gaze in her direction. "This is not going to work out in your favor, Ms. Waterstone. The mayor doesn't want to use force, but he will if he has to. I suggest you talk this over with your staff and revisit your decision. I'll give you until this afternoon."

Before Jo could respond, Sam ended the call and turned on his heel.

So much for negotiations, she thought. All that remained in his place was the heavy shadow of an ultimatum.

Jo reached out and steadied herself on a nearby shelf. She had no idea what to do next.

Thirteen

$\mathcal{A}$fter Sam Turnbull and his security guards drove off in their unmarked SUVs, the main sales floor exploded in tense chatter.

"Jo, I'm sorry. Let me explain." Adam scrambled in Jo's direction, apologies and excuses tumbling from his lips.

"Just don't, Adam. I can't with you right now." Her ears were so full of blood that she hardly heard a thing he said. Instead, she gave a terse nod to Truman—a gesture that was silent but conveyed a hundred words—and stormed off in the direction of her office.

It was only with a slam of her door that Adam finally retreated, leaving her alone in the basement. He clearly knew his mistake, and she was going to have to talk to him about it. But at the moment, Adam was the last person Jo wanted to see. Well, maybe Leo was the last person—then Adam. But either way, those guys were being careless. It was all fun and games until someone came back with an injunction and a set of silver handcuffs. Then where would they all be?

Out of a job and out of prospects—that's where.

Jo had to read the article. With her nose pressed close to the computer screen, she rubbed her temples and attempted to focus. The first time through was to find out what Adam had written in his fifteen-hundred-word op-ed piece, published in that morning's edition of the *Saturn*.

Unbelievable.

Scanning the essay again, she saw that it read like a love letter to Bruebaker's Books, noting all of the important reasons so many bibliophiles and tourists alike cherished the store. Adam claimed the business was "worth saving, worth risking financial instability, and even worth risking the job." It was quite admirable, if you didn't count all the undertones of self-congratulation.

Then, about three paragraphs into the piece, Jo nearly choked when she read the word "fascist." Adam turned the point of the article, and his aim, toward the government. His words were like arrows, shooting accusations and claiming infringement on civil liberties if the mayor stepped in. Jo shook her head. Somewhere along the line, Adam lost the thread. The result was a hostile letter to the public to help save Bruebaker's, even if that meant "standing up to the Man."

And at the end of it all, he'd tied Jo and the rest of the team up with him in an ugly bow by mentioning them in the article.

How could he? Jo thought, letting her screen go dark as she sat in her office and grumbled. She'd trusted him. She'd supported him. And this was how Adam repaid her? By calling Mayor Fink a fascist? Why? Jo dropped her head into her lap and groaned. How was she going to get out of this one unscathed?

As if on cue, her phone buzzed. The blood drained away when she read Regina Anderson's name illuminated on her screen. Word traveled fast. Jo needed to answer for it, whether she wanted to or not.

"Damn!" She pinched the bridge of her nose. She really wasn't in the mood for another fight.

"Hi, Regina." Jo plastered on a smile, even though her boss

couldn't see her face. She hoped the politeness would be conveyed anyway. "I was just about to call you."

This, of course, couldn't be further from the truth. Yet she played the part of dutiful employee anyway. She was too depleted for anything else. Her back ached from fulfilling an umpteen number of orders for days on end, her knuckles raw with cuts from packing boxes, and the insides of her eyelids burned from lack of sleep.

Exhaustion was currently winning on all fronts.

"Jo!" Regina barked into the phone. "Are you out of your mind?"

Jo cringed. "That depends. What's up?"

Jo knew the woman had her Google alerts set to any news mentioning the bookstore. This was usually the only way Jo learned about headlines involving the business. Regina was almost compulsive with her propensity for forwarding links.

"This ridiculous *Saturn* article. That's what's up. Whose idea was it for your nutjob sales associate to pen an op-ed piece in an alternative, antiestablishment newspaper right in the middle of what was supposed to be a very quiet operation? Come on! Could you get any more controversial? We're in the midst of a crisis, and you guys are down there stoking the fire!"

Jo held the phone away from her ear and cringed. This was not at all the day she envisioned when she'd woken up that morning. Suddenly, Jo yearned for the simpler days of rain leaks and beers for dinner. How naive she'd been, merely a week earlier, to think those might be her biggest setbacks.

"I understand," she said. "I had no idea that Adam was going to submit an article to the press. Well, I mean, I knew, but I didn't think—"

"That's right." Regina cut her off. "You didn't think. I can't believe I allowed you and your band of misfits to continue down there. What a mess. We've got to unravel this whole thing. The first thing that needs to happen is for this guy to be banished. Officially."

Jo's lips pursed. Yes, Adam's actions had been immature and selfish. This much she knew. And now he'd called a lot of unwanted attention to their supposedly clandestine project of saving the store. Yet, however misguided his actions were, he'd acted from his heart.

What she wanted, she realized, was to protect Adam.

This was surprising.

Regina plowed ahead, not bothering to wait for an answer. "I hate to say it, Jo, but I told you so. You and this crew of social activists you've tangled yourself up with have reacted with your emotion instead of your brains. And now, I'm going to have to be the one to clean up the mess."

Jo decided to switch gears. "Have you talked to Arnold?"

Silence.

Jo frowned. "Regina?"

"No. Not yet. The old man is much too fragile. I didn't want to cause undue stress. Besides, he's retired, Jo. I'm the one who has been put in charge. I'm the one his family hired to take on the big challenges. And I'd say this is one big challenge. Wouldn't you?"

Jo wasn't listening anymore. Her mind was too busy spinning. Why hadn't Regina spoken to Mr. Bruebaker? Was she truly worried about his tenuous condition, or was it something else? Because if Jo had to guess, she'd say it was perhaps that Regina feared the bookstore's founder, the one who'd poured his entire life into the business for nearly half a century, might be endeared by the great lengths the team was going to in order to save the store. Regina feared Mr. Bruebaker might actually side with Jo, and then she'd be in a dilemma with his daughters. This, she decided, was Regina's greatest fear. Because loyalty ran deep. And when it came to loyalty, Regina Anderson had none.

"Hmmm. You've given me a lot to think about. And I need to touch base with my staff to find out how much of the online order fulfillment has been accomplished so far. If we're going to close down, I really should determine where we stand with the out-standing orders and inventory and such. Can we talk again in a little while?" Jo held her breath. She hoped Regina wouldn't read between the lines and realize Jo hadn't committed to anything quite yet.

"Fine. Make your assessment and get back to me as soon as possible. And, Jo?" she said.

"Yes?"

"I don't want to hear another word about that Adam character."

"Yes, right. Got it."

With jittery nerves, Jo exhaled and hung up the phone. She had to be quick if she wanted to reach Mr. Bruebaker. Because at the moment, it was her only move left.

She tried his cell phone, but it had been turned off. She looked up the rehab center Regina mentioned and dialed the number. Miraculously, a nurse answered at the first ring. Jo's breath hitched with hopefulness.

"Hello," Jo said. "Can you connect me with Arnold Bruebak-er's room?"

"Are you a family member?"

Jo frowned. Should she lie? Would his daughters be in the room with him and get her into more trouble? She decided to tell the truth. "I'm a close friend."

"I'm sorry," the nurse said. "His family asked that he not be disturbed. He's still recovering. You're welcome to leave a message, and I'll give it to them."

"No." Jo sagged. "No message. Thanks."

What she had to say wouldn't fit into any message. She needed to speak with her boss. But she also worried over causing him more undue stress. There had to be a way to reach him but not cause drama. The question was, how?

Fourteen

Wandering back upstairs, Jo struggled over what she might say. How much should she tell the others? Mr. Bruebaker was forever available for regular advice, to tell Jo whether or not she was making the right decision. She counted on his honesty. Without it, she felt starkly alone. No longer was anything certain or permanent.

The realization jarred her.

Judging from the noisy rumblings coming from the break room, the team was looking to her for guidance. The only problem was, she didn't have any.

She'd relied on Mr. Bruebaker's wisdom. Despite stepping back from the day-to-day operations and hiring an executive to fill his place, he'd always kept an open channel of communication for Jo.

"How's my favorite bookstore manager today?" he'd always ask over the phone.

"Doing great, Mr. B," Jo would reply, smiling as she imagined him sitting in his breakfast nook with the daily newspaper spread out before him.

"Fill me in, kid. What's happening this week at the store?" Even though Jo was now middle-aged, she still got a kick out of Mr. B referring to her as a kid, like when they'd met so many

years ago. Perhaps it wasn't very politically correct or professional, but to Jo it was a lighthearted term of endearment from
her much older boss. That was just how he spoke. It was part of
what made him Mr. B.

For the last few years, she'd assumed the weekly calls were
strictly for his benefit, to keep him in the loop and to ensure he
wasn't left out. He enjoyed hearing about the lineup of new author
events and the customer activity in the store. Jo often believed
their phone chats to be the highlight of his day.

After all, his daughters, Jane and Suzanne, had moved away
from their father years ago, choosing the sunny shores of Florida
over the Pacific Northwest. After their mother passed, they'd
begged their father to join them on the opposite coast, claiming
the change of scene would do him good. But Mr. Bruebaker
wouldn't hear of it. The last thing he wanted to do was leave the
community he'd come to know and love.

For this reason alone, Jo had become his lifeline to the one
thing that meant the most to him. She'd become family.

Jo's feet slowed as a new thought occurred to her. Maybe all
this time it wasn't she who was comforting Mr. Bruebaker. Perhaps, she realized, it was the other way around. Because right then,
in the absence of hearing the old man's reassuring, gentle voice, Jo
was afraid. She was weary of Adam's ongoing antics, overwhelmed
by the sheer quantity of newly delivered inventory—which hadn't
been stopped in time—worried for the welfare of her young
staffers and the potential risk they now faced, and desperately in
need of support.

Jo was sinking, and her regular lifeline was nowhere to be
found.

Lost in her own thoughts, she wasn't aware of Truman, who'd
wandered out to find her. She also wasn't aware, until she noticed

the concern in Truman's eyes, that tears were sliding down her face. He had once again caught her in an embarrassingly vulnerable moment.

"Hey there."

"Hey."

Jo blotted her damp cheeks. She willed herself to gain her composure. Truman didn't need to see this. No one did. She was supposed to be the confident manager in charge. If she couldn't stay strong, she couldn't expect the same from the others.

"You okay?" He came over and stood awkwardly, his hands thrusting into his pockets. It was clear he wasn't sure what to do.

"Yeah, sorry. You just caught me having a moment. I'm fine. Everything is fine."

His voice softened. "Is it?"

"Well, maybe not everything," she admitted. "I mean, other than an unexpected visit from the deputy mayor, harsh words from Regina Anderson, and a controversial article authored by one of my employees . . . yeah, it's all fantastic. Why do you ask?"

This time they both chuckled. It was a welcome release, letting the pressure go from an overinflated balloon.

"Quite a fix we've all gotten ourselves into, huh?" Truman rocked back, his gaze going out the window, like he was checking for more unexpected visitors. Jo noticed he still looked awfully tired. The shadows under his eyes had taken on a bluish tint, the lines at his mouth deep from worry. And yet, as she studied him in the quiet midmorning light, she had to admit he still had that handsome, rugged quality about him. He always had, she supposed. It was just that she'd never really stopped to give this much thought. He was just Truman, the helpful guy you called when something needed fixing.

A warmth spread over her now. Jo felt a mix of gratitude and adoration for her friend that she couldn't ignore. The urge to tell him came in a rush.

"Truman," she said. His eyes drew back into the room.

"Yeah?"

"Have I ever told you how important you are to this place?"

His toe kicked at something on the floor. "Oh, that's not necessary. I'm just doing my job, that's all."

Jo shook her head. He may have wanted to stop her, but she was compelled to keep going. "No, that's not all. Other than me, I can't think of anyone else who's spent so much time in this building, who's been genuinely invested in the well-being of the place. If I've ever taken your help for granted, I'm sorry. Because truly, I can't imagine going this far without you." *And I like being with you*, she wanted to say.

"Thanks." He met her gaze and then looked away. Perhaps she'd embarrassed him.

"You're welcome."

"So what's next?" He checked his watch, a worn black band hugging his wrist the way it had done for as long as she'd known him. She wondered if it was sentimental or if Truman was one of those people who didn't like change. Either way, she could relate. It seemed they had more in common than she'd realized.

"I suppose what's next is going and talking to the others. Adam kicked a hornet's nest this morning, and I'm sure everyone's anxious."

"Yep. They're all in the break room. If you're up to it, I'd say it would be a good idea for you to go give some reassurance."

"Ha! That's funny, Truman. What if I'm the one who needs reassuring?" She offered an unsteady grin. "Between you and me, I don't exactly know what I'm doing."

"Ah, sure you do. You're the big boss in those kids' eyes. Just go in there and talk to them. You'll know what to do after that."

Turned out the reassurance she'd needed was coming from the person standing next to her. Wordlessly, she nodded and made her way toward the back of the store. Truman mumbled something about rechecking the leak upstairs and left her to do the next part on her own.

"You know where to find me," he called, mounting the stairs.

"I do."

The break room had been turned into a war room in Jo's absence. Arriving in the doorway, she was surprised to discover big sheets of butcher paper taped up along the walls. Anna and Jade were armed with sizable markers as they furiously jotted down ideas being verbally tossed around the room. Adam was perched on the table, his brown boots on the chair, an apple in his hand and a look of excitement about him. As usual, Grayson was stuffing his underfed face with leftover pasta from the refrigerator. It was as if he was making up for lost time, vacuuming up all the unwanted food whenever he could.

Her heart broke a little for him.

Watching him, Jo decided he needed a copy of Laura Hillenbrand's *Unbroken*. The fictional story of how Louis Zamperini and his fellow copilots crash in the Pacific during World War II and end up floating on the craft for forty-five hundred miles was a powerful one. Zamperini survives on virtually no food for over ninety days. It was just the kind of inspiring tale to show Grayson the power of the human spirit (even when food is scarce). She made a mental note to search it out for him later.

Still unnoticed, Jo leaned against the doorframe and observed. For the most part, the group appeared to be working together to find a solution to their growing list of problems. One sheet of paper read "Bookshelves," another read "Press." Bullet points dotted the space underneath each category, listing jobs to be done. On top of all of this, everyone was getting along.

If she weren't so dumbfounded, Jo would've been impressed.

The one element in the room that wasn't surprising, however, was the scene of Leo and Jack conspiring in the corner. They were up to something; she could sense it.

Typical, Jo huffed.

With quick, even strides, Jo crossed the room. She was on the two of them before they noticed. Jack was hunched over his phone, sniggering that he'd posted the deputy mayor's photo to something called the *Butthurt Report*. They both examined his screen and laughed.

Jo fumed. Their immaturity was going to get them all into more trouble.

"What's this about a prior arrest record?" Jo planted herself next to Leo.

He startled. "Oh, hey, Jo." His eyes darted around the room. "Yeah, um. It's no big deal. Just a mis—"

"Right, a misunderstanding. I heard you the first time. You know the company asks you to disclose stuff like that on your job application, right?"

"Uh-huh." He looked to Jack for help, but his friend shrank back.

"So you lied then? On your application?"

"Kinda. Yeah, I guess."

"Okay then." She folded her arms. Catching the two of them in the corner had struck her in just the wrong way. She was exhausted, and these guys were making it worse. This interaction was the last straw for Jo. She decided it was time to get tough and show she was the leader, not the other way around. "Thanks for making this easy for me. You're no longer an employee of Bruebaker's. You're also no longer a part of this thing. Time to go home."

His eyes narrowed into slits. Jo watched him slowly process the fate that had just been handed to him. And then she watched as he tried to signal to Jack that he should follow.

"Let me save you some time," she said. "Jack, I think you should go too. This just doesn't seem to be the right place for you guys. No hard feelings. Just time to move on. Okay?"

Grayson gasped. Another couple of people whispered something inaudible. Jo never fired employees in public. This was new.

But they were all in enough hot water as it was.

Leo threw down an empty Gatorade bottle he'd been holding. He sneered in Jo's direction. "Fine. We'll go. But we better be paid for our time. We've been slaving away in this building for nearly a week. Bruebaker's is going to have to compensate us. Big-time."

"Uh-huh. We'll see," Jo replied flatly. "Right now I need you to gather your things and meet Truman at the side door. He'll let you out." *He'll escort you out, is more like it.*

Jo turned and headed for the door. The boys lobbed complaints from the back of the room. The term "Debbie Downer" was mentioned. Jo rolled her eyes. She didn't care. Getting rid of those two would be a huge relief. What she did care about, however, was exiting before anyone noticed the trembling in her hands. Her uncertainty over what to do next wasn't something she wanted the others to see. Because if she wasn't moving forward with confidence, why should they?

Fifteen

Jo's fingers skimmed along a row of spines: tall ones, short ones, thick ones, and slim ones. All of the books were neatly lined up, like soldiers reporting for duty, only each uniform was different. Jo marveled at each book's individuality, its creativity. Their artful covers represented all the shades of a color wheel, their fonts inviting and large. Seeing them reminded her there were still so many yet to read.

Someday I'd like to open each and every one of you.

The collection in front of her made up a tidy assembly of titles marked "American Classics" in the used-books section of the store. Thanks to Anna's scrolling handwriting, a pile of recently acquired literature was now organized. Library carts lined the outer walls, waiting to be wheeled to the appropriate spots on nearby shelves.

Given the large amount of newly delivered inventory they weren't able to head off, plus the litany of online orders, there was still an immeasurable amount of work to be done. But for the first time since their occupation began, Jo was content to view their progress.

It was finally time for a break.

Spying a favorite title on the shelves, Jo reached out and plucked it from its spot. A blanket of comforting warmth dropped down over her.

Hello, old friend.

Turning the hardback over in her hands, Jo admired an unblemished copy of *To Kill a Mockingbird*, by Harper Lee. It must have been an older edition, judging by the quality of the binding. Jo suspected Anna had removed its papery dust jacket, leaving the cover bare and exposed. This wasn't an unusual practice in the store's used-books section. She understood why. It was lovely. The pad of her index finger slid slowly along the embossed gold lettering that danced atop a dark blue background. It was so simple, so beautiful.

Just under the title was a charming illustration of an umbrella-shaped tree. The tree's branches arced and swayed, bending over the silhouette of a modest country house. Both the tree and the house were dark, save for a golden light peeking out from a bottom-floor window. A matching golden moon hung in the sky above.

Mesmerized, Jo ran her hand over the front cover again and again. Its existence was deeply soothing.

Scout Finch was a character to whom Jo could relate as a young girl. Jo couldn't place it at the time she'd first read the book, during her middle school years, but looking back, she could see the parallel between her life and Scout's. Like the book's young protagonist, Jo spent her childhood running around their sleepy neighborhood with little barrier between the lives of the adults and children. Maybe it was because Jo was an only child, and her older parents regularly involved her in grown-up conversations. Or perhaps it was because Jo's youth was void of today's distractions—no cell phones, no mass gun violence, no one caring if she was out climbing trees and exploring neighbors' yards until after dark. Parts of Scout's story—the innocent curiosity of a child—represented elements of Jo's younger self. Other parts of the story, however, included hard-ships she was yet to discover.

Compelled to look inside, she sank down among the stacks. She hardly noticed the cold, hard floor beneath her or the fact that everything was now covered in dust. Careful not to disturb the perfect row of books, her head came to rest on the solid frame of a tall wooden case. Out of habit, Jo lifted the pages to her nose and inhaled. A flash of memories projected behind the lids of her closed eyes:

The scent of well-worn hymnals tucked lovingly on the pews of her childhood church.

The color of her mother's sunspotted hands as she sat under a lamp in her bedroom and read aloud from *The Secret Garden*.

The glow of yellow highlighter ink, marking the dull pages of a high school textbook.

The comforting heft of Jo's tote bag as she walked the few short blocks back from the local library.

These pages represented all of the smells of her youth, her home, her work, and the place she never wanted to leave. These books represented so much. Hugging the hardback to her chest, Jo took a long breath.

She decided right then and there that she didn't care about Mayor Fink, about Regina, the press, or even the disagreements she'd had with some of the staff. The only thing she cared about was preserving the one place that meant so much. She had to save the store.

After all, books were what Jo turned to when the world failed her. They'd been there for her when her parents died, one after another, when she'd been lost and living all alone in her early twenties, when she was searching for her first true job, and when her romantic relationships fell apart.

Books were the one thing Jo could consistently rely on. Other people—lots of people—felt this way too. That's why Bruebaker's was always full of contented, happy faces. Books were the balm to soothe the soul. And she'd be damned if she'd be the one to help take that away.

Making her way back to her office, Jo decided her next move. If Regina and Mr. B's daughters weren't going to listen, she'd make them. With her phone in her hand, she scrolled the screen until she found the number she was looking for. It was time to take their mission public. And Jo knew just the reporter to call.

Several hours later, Jo found herself shoulder to shoulder with Anna and Adam on the sidewalk outside. Lewis, the one reporter she knew from the *Oregonian*, had answered Jo's call and was eager to do a story on what he was coining "The Bruebaker Movement."

"I'm so glad you phoned," he said to Jo as he arrived, winded and wide-eyed. "I'd actually heard about the op-ed piece and was super curious."

"No problem," Jo answered. She shoved her hands in her pockets. This was the right next move, wasn't it?

The sudden attention was both exciting and horrifying, a sensation she could only compare to the time she rode Adrenaline Peak at the nearby Oakfield Amusement Park, which once took Jo and her date on a seventy-two-foot vertical lift before plunging them into jaw-dropping speeds. The same combination of jangled nerves and tingly anticipation flooded her now.

As best she could, Jo was embracing the moment.

The rain had moved out, leaving the spring afternoon air crisp and damp. At once, everything had a fresh feel, including Jo's outlook. The sun came out, creating a fog of steam on the wet pavement. Only a few vehicles went by, a delivery truck, a taxi. A young woman in an apron rounded the corner and slipped into the side entrance of a bakery. Two men in utility maintenance gear strode by, their walkie-talkies buzzing at their sides. The city was otherwise peaceful.

Lewis, however, seemed as if he intended for his piece to be anything but quiet. At least that was the impression he'd given on the phone earlier that day.

Just before his arrival, Jo rounded up the team and expressed her desire to keep going with their mission.

"I've thought it over," she said. "While I don't agree with how Adam went about announcing our actions to the world, I do understand the power of positive press. If we hope to have any chance of staving off the mayor's office, and Regina for that matter, then I think our one big shot is to make this thing even more public than it is. If we get our customers and our fans on our side, then maybe it will help our situation. Of course, this still means we keep a united front. But let's see what kind of support we can drum up while we can. Okay?"

She'd been met with stunned approval. Everyone was happy to stay.

Buoyed by hope, she phoned Mr. Bruebaker's room. Still unable to reach him, she conceded and left a brief message with one of the nurses, asking him to call her when he could. What else could she do but keep going? If her boss hadn't asked her to leave, she wouldn't—not yet.

In the meantime, Jo decided to embrace the attention. She and her team had been given a platform, and they were going to use it.

So there she was in front of the store, nodding along with Adam's all-too-eager input—he'd been instructed that any name-calling or disparaging remarks about the mayor's office was off-limits—and showing a united front. She was, after all, defying all kinds of orders by participating. Yet, as she listened to Adam explain the importance of preserving the beloved institution of Bruebaker's and all it represented to the community, she was infused with a new kind of exhilaration. Her insides were buzzing. It was good to stand up for something she so whole-heartedly believed in.

Noticing the broad grins on the faces around her, Jo understood the members of her team mirrored her sentiment. They were doing something meaningful. And they were doing it together.

"So, Joanna"—Lewis held out a recording device and fixed an attentive stare in her direction—"you're the bookstore's manager?"

"You can call me Jo, Lewis. And you know I'm the manager from when you covered the store's anniversary a few years back."

"I know." He smiled. "Just making sure nothing's changed. So let's get right to it. Does your job description include sheltering in place to protect the store during a crisis?"

She emitted a small laugh. "No. Not exactly."

"So why are you here, when the daughters of your ailing business owner have asked you to close up and send the employees home?"

"Well . . ." She hesitated. "I'm here because Bruebaker's is an important fixture in this community. Where else can you go to experience an entire city block full of books and fellow book lovers? It's an institution that deserves to be saved. And I guess you could say I'm here because of my committed staff members who agree with this sentiment. I'm here, in large part, because of Adam."

Jo turned and gestured to her right. Adam beamed.

"I see." He leaned toward Adam. "So you convinced your boss to stage a protest?"

"No, man. It's not really a protest. It's more of a demonstration. You know, by remaining on the property, by putting our personal lives on hold, we're demonstrating our commitment to the store. This place is iconic. Everyone in Portland and beyond knows that. I mean, can you imagine people coming here in the future and finding a giant void where this place used to be? Can you imagine the cosmic shift in our culture if that happened?" Adam's speech sped up as he spoke, his passion evident. Jo watched as he stood a little taller, his eyes clear and focused. She couldn't help but feel a morsel of pride. This kid she'd previously doubted wasn't really a kid at all. His methods may have been unorthodox for Jo, but at that moment, in the middle of his response, Jo understood this was a passionate soul who had a purpose. Adam was the real deal.

Lewis let his hand fall a little as he ruminated on Adam's question. After a couple of seconds, he shook his head. "No. I can't say that I can envision a Portland without Bruebaker's Books. I've lived here nearly two-thirds of my life, and the bookstore is usually one of the first places I take visitors to see. It's an experience just to wander the different rooms and discover titles I never knew existed. My favorite is the growing display of Pacific Northwest authors. I always leave with at least two or three new purchases. This place makes me want to read more, that's for sure."

The group pumped their heads in agreement.

"What about you, Anna?"

"What about me?"

"Well, Jo tells me you're also a premed student. I have to imagine that this demonstration, as Adam puts it, has put a pause on your studies. What about school? Are your parents supportive of what you're doing?"

Jo saw Anna's face drop ever so slightly, the corners of her pink lips dipping down. This was a sore subject. Jo wouldn't blame Anna if she wanted to brush off the question. She felt her hackles go up. She glanced at Lewis, gauging how far he'd go with his probing, but he didn't seem to notice.

"Well, I've put my classes on hold, so there's that. And as for my parents, they are cautiously supportive."

Jo jumped in. "Anna's been integral in helping us understand how to move most of our business online for the time being. She's quite savvy in ways that I'm not. She's also an incredible researcher. Really, without her we'd be lost."

"Hmmm. Interesting. And as for everyone's overall mental state? Is staying in the building, day after day, wearing on anyone? Any cabin fever yet?"

"No." Anna shook her head. "We're all like family." She cast Jo a brief glance. They'd agreed not to make mention of Jack and Leo and their dramatic exit.

"Wow." Lewis's brows lifted. "Sounds like you guys found a way to make this work."

"Yeah, I guess we did." Jo and the others exchanged glances. He was right. So far, they'd made it work.

"So what about the threats from the mayor's office? Has Mayor Fink said you'll be arrested if you stay?"

Jo shifted. Just the word "arrest" sent a wave of heat flashing through her. She needed to get a handle on where this was going. The interview was clearly starting to turn. She wanted to put an emphasis on the benefits of keeping the store open, not the ramifications of doing so. "We're in talks with his office. The situation is fluid. That's all we know right now. I'm grateful a line of communication has been opened up. But nothing is definitive beyond that."

"I see." Lewis scrunched up his mouth. Jo wondered if he'd hoped for more drama. "So what's your ultimate goal, if you're allowed to continue?"

"Our goal," she said, "is to find a way to reopen the store. We want Mr. Bruebaker's daughters to revisit their decision to close."

He nodded. "Sounds like you're committed."

"We are."

Now, Jo thought, *if we can just keep going.*

He rattled off a few more questions pointed at Anna and Adam, about what it was like to work in such a famous retail spot. Jo listened to their thoughtful answers.

As Adam answered a final question, her phone buzzed with an incoming message. Discreetly pulling it from her pocket, she peered at the screen. There was one new text message from Mr. Bruebaker. Finally.

Hello. This is Arnold's nurse at the rehab center. He's asked me to send you a message. Arnold says, "Keep fighting the good fight. I have faith."

Jo beamed. The feeling of sparkling fireworks erupted in her chest. Mr. B finally reached out, and he approved!

All this time, Jo had not even been aware of the niggle of fear lurking within her. What if Mr. B woke up and agreed with his daughters? What if he didn't condone what the staff was doing? What if he himself wanted to close the store? Jo hadn't allowed herself to even acknowledge this fear up until now.

With this message, however, a small current of dread dissolved. In its place emerged a fresh wave of adrenaline. They were only warming up. Now she was ready to fight this thing to the fullest.

Thank you, Mr. B, she thought.

Discreetly, she nudged her staff. It was time to go back to work. Their boss had just given his blessing.

Sixteen

When the second article published, featuring Jo, Anna, and Adam, the crowds really started to gather.

Jo was on the second floor with Jade, digging through the alphabet as usual. They'd been hard at work curating titles to feature on their still-lively social media feed and fulfilling a slew of new orders Anna collected. Jo had taken on the frustrating task of mending a faulty barcode scanner when voices from the street below caught her attention.

"Did you hear that?" She turned with her ear cocked. Jade, who was on all fours trying to retrieve a handful of paperbacks from behind a shelving unit, paused to listen. She crawled over to where Jo sat and rested beside her.

"I think it's probably that guy and his dogs. He goes by every morning, shouting at them to follow. He can get kind of loud." Jade brushed her bangs back from her face, her skin glistening with perspiration. The building's air-conditioning was acting up again, and the crew found themselves constantly opening and closing the windows based on how much rain was getting inside the store.

Jo heard more voices. "I don't think so. It doesn't sound like him. This sound is different." Holding her back as she rose, Jo stretched and made her way to the bank of windows. Sure enough, down on the sidewalk was a small crowd of men and women holding signs—protest signs.

Jade came to stand next to her. The girl squinted, trying to read what was written on the colorful squares of poster board. "Oh, wow," she said.

"What is it all about?" Without her glasses, which she'd once again forgotten in her office, Jo couldn't make out more than blurry shapes.

"Well, I can't be totally sure from this angle. But I think we should go down there," Jade said.

"Why?" Jo tensed. The last thing she needed was another problem to fix. Let whatever was happening out on the street be someone else's worry. Perhaps the police would come break up the gathering.

Jade, who was not one to be pushy, shifted uncomfortably. "I'm pretty sure those people are here because of us. One of the signs has the word 'Bruebaker's' written on it."

Oh, wow.

Sure, the articles had garnered some attention. Adam had been buoyant over the past day, routinely reading aloud the on-line comments published on both publications' websites. What the staff at Bruebaker's was doing had created a buzz in the community. All kinds of responses poured in; some die-hard fans of the bookstore cheered on Adam and the team, while other more skeptical people scolded them for taking matters too lightly and thumbing their noses at authority. She'd been naive to think the reaction to their so-called movement would remain removed from them, out in the virtual world. Of course people would come, she thought. This place was a big deal.

When Jo and Jade arrived at the front doors, Truman was there to meet them. He stood with a hammer dangling at his side and a nail sticking out from his teeth. A broken shelf was on the ground. Apparently, the commotion outside had pulled him from his work.

"What's going on?" she asked, peering out the side window. A woman gripping a sign caught sight of her through the glass and hollered. Startled, Jo stepped back. "What's she yelling?"

Truman plucked the nail from his mouth and chuckled. "It appears you have some fans."

"I do?" She had no idea what was so funny about this. If anything, the gathering outside was a little unnerving.

"Indeed. They've been out there about thirty minutes now. They're all yelling to 'Save Bruebaker's.'"

Both Jo and Jade raised their brows.

Jo eased toward the windows again and surveyed the scene. There were about nine people in all, gathered at the entrance and holding up signs:

HONK IF YOU LOVE BRUEBAKER'S!

SAVE OUR BOOKS!

SUPPORT INDIE!

A car sped by, and the driver jutted his thumb into the air with approval. The group cheered and waved. A minute later, another couple of people came jogging up the sidewalk carting similar signs. They greeted the others with fist bumps and smiles. Jo was speechless.

Their little endeavor was creating waves.

At the sound of the commotion, Adam, Grayson, and Anna came running. The three had teamed up to "work more efficiently" and had spent their morning in the nonfiction rooms. Jo couldn't help but notice that after the newspaper interview, when both of them were given the chance to make their voices heard equally, Adam and Anna seemed to form an unspoken truce. Or maybe they were getting along better with Grayson wedged between them, acting as a kind of buffer to any additional tension. Either way, the bickering among staffers had ceased, and for the most part, everyone who remained was getting along.

"What's going on out there?" Anna asked, peeling off her sweatshirt. Jo looked on as she rolled her neck around a few times. The task of book cleaning was apparently taking a toll on her as well.

"Seems a few people have shown up to offer support." Truman rocked on his heels, grinning. His gaze slid over to Jo.

"Wow. Really?" Anna asked.

"Cool," Grayson murmured.

Adam strode right up to the glass and pressed his face close. Jo believed if he could walk right out and join the group on the sidewalk, he wouldn't hesitate. These were his people. It was like watching a moth to a flame.

"This is epic!" he said, still with his face at the glass. "They must've seen our interview!" He rapped on the window in several hard knocks. "Hey! Hey! Thanks, you guys!"

The small gathering saw him and cheered again, this time louder.

"Wow! Incredible!"

Jo could practically see Adam's feet lift off the ground.

"Well," she said, "I have to hand it to you, Adam. You said getting some press would do our little movement good. You were right. We've got cheerleaders now."

"I know, right?"

With the corner of her eye, Jo caught sight of Grayson sidling next to Jade. He must have said something funny, because Jade nodded and laughed. For the briefest moment, they seemed suspended in time, like in a slow-motion film. But then they turned away from each other, each looking awkward. When Grayson turned, the corner of Jade's mouth lifted.

Good for them, Jo thought. *These kids should have some happiness from this situation.* But if she was being entirely honest, her chest felt empty at the same time. How long had it been since a man had looked at her like that? The thought burned inside her, so she pushed it away.

"So what do we do now?" Anna turned and asked the group. "Are we supposed to go out there and talk to them? Or let them inside?"

Jo was shaking her head before Anna could even finish her question. "Oh no. We can't risk opening the doors. I think we let them do their thing, and we continue to do ours. Remember, we still don't know how much longer we'll be allowed to stay. According to my latest text from Regina, she's still trying to smooth things out with the mayor's office. I'm guessing this is because she was impressed with our continued sales numbers. But God help us if Suzanne or Jane show up. Good press aside, I'd say our time here is still pretty limited. And there's more work to be done with making sure outstanding deliveries to the store are paused, and packaging up recent orders. Let's all just keep going. Okay?"

Everyone exchanged quick glances. It was hard to concentrate when a growing group of revelers was just on the other side of the glass. Finally, Adam left his perch at the window.

"Jo's right. We can't really celebrate if our job is only half-done. We need to keep going."

"Okay, but before we go, I have to take a picture." Grayson

pulled out his phone and opened up his camera app. "Jade? Wanna do a selfie with me?"

Clearly embarrassed, she glanced around. "Um, sure. I guess."

The two stood in front of the window. Grayson held up his phone to capture the crowd in the background. At the last minute, he threw an arm over Jade's rounded shoulders. Her cheeks pinked, and a flash went off.

Truman looked over at Jo and winked.

Jo brightened. She didn't know what she liked more, witnessing a tender moment between her young employees or the secret exchange between her and Truman. Either way, Jo couldn't help but smile.

"Okay, now everyone!" Grayson ushered the group over, and together they posed in front of the protest crowd.

"Cheese!" they said in unison.

This was really something. Jo had no idea what would happen next. For now, it was just a happy moment for them to pause and be proud.

Seventeen

Once the streets cleared out and another few hours of work were under their belts, the team agreed it was time to unwind. Beers were uncapped, chips and salsa came out, and Grayson cranked up the volume of what he called "hipster cocktail party" music from his phone. The mood inside Bruebaker's was a festive one.

Anna read off some of the latest posts about the store on Twitter:

> I'll never forget the first time my grandma took me to @Bruebaker's. I was a nerdish kid, and for me, it was the event larger than visiting @Disneyworld. My grandma is now gone. At Bruebaker's, I still feel her with me as I go down the aisle and pick books off shelves. #savebruebaker's

> I met my wife at @Bruebaker's, and we spend every anniversary among the stacks. I can't imagine not having that tradition. #savebruebaker's

> My first job was @Bruebaker's in PDX. Best employer ever. Shout-out to Mr. B! #savebruebaker's

Underneath the hashtag were hundreds of tweets, all in tribute to the store. Jo knew the store meant something to the patrons, but this was quite something to see online. *Wouldn't it be great if Mr. B's daughters saw this too?* she thought.

Later on, after the others took turns using the building's only shower, Jo sat in the window seat on the third floor and checked her emails. Among a flood of press inquiries, seeking a quote on the now very public Bruebaker Movement, was also a message from Regina requesting a status update on the inventory and rough projections on affected sales. She and Jo had come to an understanding of sorts, and true to her word, Jo briefed the CEO at regular intervals. For this reason—and likely because Mr. Bruebaker had made his opinion known to her, however quietly— Jo was allowed to continue, at least for the time being.

Jo clicked on her barely used Facebook app. Over the past two weeks, she'd felt more cut off from the outside world than she ever had. And while Anna was good about keeping her abreast of the news headlines and growing support on social media, Jo was curious just how visible their endeavor was elsewhere online.

She had created a Facebook account years ago when everyone was making their profile, connected with a bunch of friends from high school and beyond, but she wasn't one to post her life online. Frankly, with what little life she had, she doubted she could compete with her old friend Lianne's visits to Paris and French Polynesia, or Helen's family of four "and growing." While she loved her life, she knew most people out there would consider it humiliatingly boring.

The app loaded. Her timeline filled with little red numbers: 25 new friend requests, 202 mentions in comments, 78 private messages.

Jo's heart thumped. What the hell was going on? Why was she
getting all the attention? She opened Messenger:

Hey, Joanna! Is that really you in the Oregonian?

Long time no talk, Jo. Read about you online. Are you
really living inside a bookstore?

Hi, Jo! Wow, I wish I still worked at the store. That article
makes me miss everyone. More power to you guys!
#savebruebaker's!

Jo had to laugh. It was absurd. Even her high school teacher
from the Bay Area had reached out. The larger news outlets had
picked up the article and run it as a feel-good story. Strangers
from all over had sought her out and were messaging her notes of
encouragement and goodwill regarding the store. Only a few
were from naysayers, criticizing her reckless behavior.

Jo was stunned. She knew people loved Bruebaker's, but this
was wild. She had no idea so many people knew about her in-
volvement. And frankly, she wasn't sure how she felt about all the
attention.

For most of her adult life, Jo kept a low profile, surrounding
herself with a small circle of friends from work. She wondered if
any of the others were experiencing this same level of newfound
attention. To Jo, it was surreal.

I wish Mr. Bruebaker could see this, she thought wistfully.
Much to her disappointment, she still hadn't been able to reach
him over the phone. And every time she decided to leave the
store and show up at his bedside, Truman questioned the timing.
"These kids need you here too," he'd said. "I'll cover for you if
you like, but just choose your timing, that's all."

He was right. It seemed like every day there was a new pressing development, and her guidance was evidently needed. A big part of Jo feared that the moment she exited the building, Sam, Regina, or the mayor would come knocking and she wouldn't be there to quell the situation. Maybe she'd go find Truman again and see what he thought about her sneaking away the following morning.

Truman, she mused.

Still at her computer, she placed her cursor in the search bar. She hesitated. After a second, she typed in "Truman James." The screen refreshed as she chewed her lip. It was possible Truman wasn't even on social media. He didn't really seem the type. But still, she was curious.

Surprisingly, his face immediately popped onto her screen. Jo blinked. There was a photo of Truman, in his younger years, tan and waving from the bow of a sailboat.

Huh, she thought. *I didn't know he sailed.*

Jo looked around before clicking on his face. Viewing Truman's personal page sent a kind of buzzing adrenaline coursing through her. She also felt a tad guilty. It was as if she were doing something wrong, poking around in his private life. Yet she couldn't help herself. She wanted to know more.

Now, an hour later, she unwound in the shower, welcoming the soothing rivulets of water running down her back. Taking her time, Jo reflected on what she'd learned. Truman, it seemed, *did* have a life outside the store.

He had lived with a woman several years back—an Ellen something or other. Jo met her briefly at a company holiday party. The only thing she could recall was the woman was tall and wore a green dress. That was it. Scanning Truman's Facebook page, Jo noticed there wasn't any mention of that woman now. The only

photos—which were scarce—were of Truman at the San Juan Is-
lands and a handful of shots at an outdoor barbecue with his sister
and her husband. Other than that, Jo hadn't been able to glean
much more information.

When the water suddenly dropped in temperature, she was
jolted from her thoughts. Grumbling, she reached out and
turned the handle. It figured there wouldn't be enough hot water
to support six showers in a row. Eyeing the empty container of
body wash balancing on the tile ledge, she understood many
things were running low.

Two weeks was a long time to set up house in a commercial
building. She was beginning to miss the creature comforts of
home: her overstuffed sofa, her patio facing the perfect patch of
afternoon sun, and her tidy bathroom, to name a few.

But low supplies and stiff muscles aside, it had been a good
day.

Plucking up her small towel, she shivered and shook out her
hair. Behind her a row of damp towels hung along the wall. If Jo
didn't know better, she'd say the cramped shared bathroom
looked like it belonged to a family.

Her heart snagged. This was something she hadn't had in so
very long.

Wrapping herself up tight, she regarded her reflection in the
steam-covered mirror. Underneath a wet mop of hair, a contented
face smiled back at her. She wasn't really so alone after all.

Eighteen

At 7:30 a.m., Jo was up and dressed. She tried to ignore the fact that her clothes needed laundering and her eyes burned from another rough night's sleep. She'd been anxiously anticipating the scheduled conference call with Regina and Sam Turnbull. The mayor's patience, it appeared, had run out.

Jo paced her small office and debated over what she might say to convince everyone to give her more time. It had been two days since the first protester appeared at the storefront. And what had started out as a fun show of support had quickly morphed into a scene the mayor didn't want to see. The gathering had grown too large. Sidewalks were clogged, and traffic on their block was increasing. The mayor claimed he had no other choice but to get involved.

"Ms. Waterstone." Sam's voice came over the line first.

"Hello." Jo lowered into her seat and tried her best to sound more professional. She didn't know why this young man unnerved her so much.

"Hello. I already have Ms. Anderson on the line, and Mayor Fink will be joining us momentarily. We're all concerned over what appears to be escalating tension downtown."

"Yes, I understand." She kept her response brief to hide her shakiness. Why had Regina been on the call first? Had the two been speaking this whole time, conspiring how to shut Jo's team down once and for all? Suddenly Jo felt very out of the loop.

"Hello, Regina."

"Good morning, Jo." Regina's tone was cool and even. There was no way for Jo to know whose side she was on at the moment. Ever since her in-person visit the week prior, the two women had only corresponded via email and text. In the old days, Mr. Bruebaker—bless his soul—had stepped in between Jo and Regina and acted as a kind of mediator. He'd also been the one to keep on good terms with the mayor. Without him now, Jo felt exposed.

"Good morning, everyone," a new voice boomed over the line. Jo straightened at hearing the mayor's firm greeting. It was as if the teacher had walked into the classroom and the disobedient students stopped messing around.

Maybe if she dove right in, stated her case like Adam had encouraged her to do, then she'd have a fighting chance. Her goal—the team's goal—was to be permitted to continue. They were nearing day nine of the shutdown, and despite being dirty and tired, they very much wanted to keep going. Mr. Bruebaker was counting on them.

Apparently, so were the protesters outside.

Jo opened her mouth to speak, but Regina beat her to the punch.

"Good morning, Mayor Fink. Regina Anderson here. Thank you so much for taking the time to speak with us." Her tone warmed. Jo narrowed her eyes. This woman had multiple faces.

"Yes, well, you Bruebaker people haven't really left me with much choice. Seems you've started a dustup over there."

"Oh yes." Regina emitted a light, fluttering laugh. "Well, we've certainly got some passionate people who love their books."

Jo shook her head. Regina's tone said everything. She was going to side with the mayor.

"Ah yes. I'd say you're right. But passion aside, this is no time to make waves. We've got a real problem now. We're already in the midst of a campaign to service and relocate our unhoused population who've established overcrowded and unsafe tent cities along main thoroughfares. Given that I've tasked them with the job, the police department is stretched thin as it is. And now, on top of this, neighboring shops are being affected by the sudden crowds and the noise created by the news of your store. Customers are being scared off. It isn't good for the greater business community."

What about our business? Jo wanted to ask.

Mayor Fink continued. "And while the police chief and I are working in tandem to safeguard all of our citizens during this, um, situation, staged events like yours only make our job that much more difficult."

Jo blinked. She would hardly call their takeover "staged"— more like "spur of the moment." Fighting to keep her cool, she bit her tongue.

"Yes, of course. I understand completely," Regina said. Jo wanted to reach through the phone and smack her. What a kiss-up. If only Mr. Bruebaker could witness his CEO turning her back on the company and its employees.

"I've been briefed on the happenings over there at Bruebaker's," the mayor continued. "I've known Arnold for many years. He's a great asset to this community, and I consider him a friend. Out of personal respect and in consideration of his fragile condition, I've given this whole thing some leeway. But it's become rather public, and it's drawing unpredictable gatherings downtown. While your goal is a lofty one, Ms. Waterstone, I'm not sure I can let you continue."

Jo's breath hitched.

"Yes," Regina broke in. "I think we can all commend Jo on her dedication to the bookstore. Her staff is equally passionate. But Arnold's daughters have some real concerns, business concerns that go way beyond passion. I'm sure when she set out to make her point, Jo didn't foresee the additional complications that would come from all of this."

Jo's jaw clenched. Regina's veiled disapproval was made to sound like a compliment, but Jo wasn't fooled. Regina wanted them to shut down just as much as the mayor did, perhaps even more.

"Well . . ." Jo's mind whirred as she tried to think of what to say. She desperately needed more time.

Before she could continue, the door to her office swung open with a bang. Anna and Adam burst inside, wild-eyed and flushed. Jo's gaze flicked from one to the other. She placed a palm over the phone. "What's going on?"

Wordlessly, Anna slid an open laptop onto the desk in front of her. Adam waved his arms and gestured for Jo to take a look.

She frowned, unsure where to place her attention. The mayor was busy asking Regina logistical questions, and Jo didn't want to miss what they were saying. On the other hand, she'd never seen an otherwise calm and collected Anna so animated. Jo tried to process what was going on as her employees pointed excitedly to the computer screen.

Conceding, she focused on the laptop.

The first thing Jo noticed was a headshot of the famed Stephen Knight in what appeared to be an online article. Stephen was the bestselling author of over twenty-five thrillers, seven of which had made it to the big screen. He was a celebrity in the writing community and a regular patron of the bookstore. Every one of his book tours always included a sold-out event at Bruebaker's.

But what about the author was so urgent? Jo struggled to piece the details together. She really needed to get back to her phone call.

It wasn't until Anna thrust a finger under the article's headline that Jo understood.

"Stephen Knight Applauds Portland's Efforts to Save Bookstore; Mayor Fink supports employees' unconventional measures to preserve the city's cultural touchstone."

Her heart was racing now. Jo skimmed the quotes from the author. He called the bookstore staff "brave" and referred to the mayor as "progressive" and a "true patron of the arts."

What in the world?

Jo blinked back the shock and peered closer. Each line sent her pulse skipping into double time. She could hardly believe what she was reading. Not only had their little story made it into national news, but perhaps one of the most well-known writers of the modern day was touting their efforts. And, more importantly, as Anna so brilliantly pointed out, Stephen Knight was also praising the mayor.

Bingo! This was exactly the kind of ammunition Jo needed.

"Thank you!" she mouthed to Anna and Adam.

Returning her attention to the phone conversation, Jo waited for the right moment. Regina and Sam were discussing different scenarios for winding down the work and sending people home. Finally, Jo decided she couldn't wait any longer. She now had to share her news.

"Mayor Fink," Jo began. She could barely contain the excitement in her voice. "I'm sorry to interrupt, but have you seen the front page of the *Times* today?"

"Jo," Regina said, "I hardly think—"

Jo squeezed the phone. "Mayor?"

Clearly confused, the mayor hesitated. "No, I, uh, I haven't. It's been a busy morning, as you can imagine. What about you, Sam?" he asked. "Perhaps you've seen it?"

"No, sir." Sam had gone quiet, but Jo detected a *click-clacking* of computer keys in the background. The deputy mayor was playing catch-up.

"Well, let me be the first one to say congratulations, sir," Jo continued. "It seems Stephen Knight is applauding you for your true patronage to the arts. He's calling your support of Bruebaker's—and I quote—'a fearless act in a challenging time.'"

The line fell so silent Jo feared it might have gone dead.

But then, the mayor's voice: "Really?"

Jo pumped her head. "Really. The story's gone national, sir. People from all over the country are praising your courage to support the survival of the most famous bookstore in the country. That's really something. Wouldn't you say?"

A satisfying grin spread over her face. Wheeling around in her chair, she waited for her news to sink in with the mayor and high-fived Anna and Adam. Both of them did a jig.

There was no way Mayor Fink could shut them down now. The story had already built up too much momentum. Plus, Jo thought, she'd played right into the man's ego. Mayor Fink may have been many things, but humble he was not. His expensive suits and ultra-whitened teeth said as much in every press conference and photo.

"Do you want me to announce on the company's social media that you've withdrawn that support, sir?"

"Well then. I, uh . . ."

Sam cleared his throat. "The story's made the front page, and it appears to be getting a lot of traction. I'll have to check with our office to see if the publication has contacted us for a comment."

"Well," the mayor mused, his tone lightening. "Isn't that something? I quite like Stephen Knight. Wonderful writer. Yes, Sam, please find out. I imagine the *Times* would want a response from our team."

Jo leaned back in her chair, relief coming off her in waves. She could practically hear the mayor grinning on the other end of the line.

Regina, on the other hand, had gone mute. Jo imagined her boss's rigid fingers searching out the article online, silently fuming over the fact she'd been left out of such a big story. As Jo read more, she saw that indeed everyone from Mr. Bruebaker on down had been mentioned. But not Regina. It struck Jo as odd. Wouldn't the company's CEO be called for a statement as well?

Why hadn't she said anything? Regina always received Google alerts regarding the bookstore. A sour taste coated Jo's mouth. Had Regina tried to bury this? Jo realized, with fresh disappointment, that this was entirely possible. Regina had never been on board with Jo's plan in the first place. Why would she start now?

"Let's table this conversation until tomorrow," Mayor Fink announced. "I've got a call with the governor scheduled and a presser to prepare for. I suppose getting positive attention right now isn't the worst thing for the city. Jo, Regina, Sam? Okay to pick up where we left off later?"

"Sure."

"Yes, sir."

"Fine with me."

"Okay, Sam will set something up. In the meantime, stay well, everyone. And, Jo, we're letting your crew stay for now, but under no circumstances are you to allow anyone else into the store. Do not open the doors to the protesters. It could bring on an entirely new complication. Am I clear?"

"Yes, of course. No problem." Jo pumped her fist under the desk.

"Fine. We'll talk again soon." With that, he hung up the call. The line went dead.

Springing from her seat, Jo let her phone tumble onto the desk. "The mayor's agreed to give us more time!"

Together, the three of them hooted and hollered, their hands clapping as their feet danced around the room. Despite everything, luck was still very much on their side.

Nineteen

*T*wenty-four hours after Jo made her promise to Mayor Fink, she broke it.

The following afternoon, she found herself carefully sneaking the struggling young mother and child from the streets through the side entrance of the building.

Jo had spotted the twosome once again in the alleyway and decided to introduce herself. She learned the young woman's name was Sierra, and the four-year-old—who was indeed her daughter—was called Rain. It didn't take a genius to recognize the two were tired and dehydrated, and although neither came out and said it, they were drifting.

This wasn't okay.

Something sharp pulled at Jo's heart, as if it were attached to a taut string. At once, her protective side kicked in. These young things were in trouble.

Before she could think it through, Jo was convincing them to take a load off in the warm confines of her private space.

Under no circumstances are you to allow anyone else into the store. The mayor's words rang in her ears as she ushered the pair over the threshold, but she quickly dismissed the warning. This was a special circumstance. Surely, she had to do something.

"My office is just down these stairs," she said. The young

woman's face was masked with uncertainty as she gripped the handles of the worn stroller. It was dark and cool inside the stairwell. Jo wondered if its vacancy frightened her. Offering a reassuring smile, Jo spoke again. "Why don't you pick up your little girl and follow me? No one will touch your things if you leave the stroller off to the side here."

Thankfully, the mother agreed.

"We can't stay long," she said, untangling her daughter's soft legs from the confines of the stroller seat. "I have to be somewhere soon."

The sleeve of her dark sweatshirt rode up as she did so, exposing the thinness of her wrist. A ring of purple-and-blue bruising circled it. Jo stared. Someone was definitely hurting this girl. Peering closer, she inspected the child. There weren't any marks that she could see. While this was a good sign, her gut still twisted with discomfort. She had no way of knowing what these two had been through.

Once inside, Jo paused halfway down the short flight of stairs. She wondered how much the young woman might tell her. "Where do you need to be? Is it somewhere close by?"

Because the mayor just informed me he's clearing out the homeless camps and people are being shuffled out into oblivion.

"Just somewhere," Sierra answered. She wasn't willing to share much more. In the shadowed half light of the stairwell, her solemn features took on a darker shade, giving Jo a sinking feeling.

"Well, you're welcome to come out of the rain for a bit. I bet your girl here would like to see some of the children's books we keep."

The child blinked back at her, nonplussed by the idea of being somewhere new.

Jo sank a little more. This poor girl had likely been dragged around half the city, judging from the worn-out look on her face. Jo was even more determined then to fill their bellies with a warm meal. Her mind ticked over the contents of the upstairs refrigerator—some leftover noodles perhaps, if Grayson hadn't gotten to them first. And maybe some of Truman's juicy red apples to go.

It wasn't much, but it was better than nothing.

"I have a private bathroom down here. You two are welcome to wash up, use the shower, if that sounds good. There are just a few of us staying here right now. But they're all upstairs working. No one will disturb you."

"Did you say you're living here? In this big store?"

Jo gave a half laugh. "It sounds rather strange, I know. But yes, there's a handful of workers sheltering in place inside the store for now. Believe it or not, we're protesting its imminent shutdown. We've managed to make up living spaces while we're taking care of inventory and such. It's only temporary, thank goodness."

Sierra's brow dipped.

That was stupid. Jo pressed her lips together; she'd said the wrong thing. Temporary housing was probably all Sierra knew at the moment, and Jo had likely come across as ridiculously privileged in her response. Chastising herself, she fixed her face forward and kept walking.

"Well, here we are," she said as they approached the door. "It's a bit cramped, but like I said, you're free to wash up and change your clothes or whatever."

Sierra kept a tight grip on her daughter with one arm and clasped a bulging shopping bag with the other. She seemed uncertain as she surveyed the small room. The child continued to stare, her expression weary and reserved. Jo wondered if she could even speak.

Sierra hoisted her daughter higher onto her hip and winced —another red flag. This young woman was in bad shape.

"Are you all right?"

"Fine." Sierra's tone hardened. But her eyes hinted at something else much more fragile. It took everything Jo had not to reach out and offer a comforting hand.

"Okay, well, I thought I'd just run upstairs and see what we have in the kitchen. Are you two hungry?" She bit down on her lower lip in an effort to keep twenty more questions at bay. It was important to tread lightly. Each word out of her mouth felt like a potential risk. Sierra was clearly scrutinizing her actions, distrustful of Jo's motives. She could hardly blame her. Jo was a stranger who lured a mother and daughter into a dark basement. She could see how this would set any woman on edge.

"Is there anyone you'd like to call?" Jo pointed to her phone. Perhaps the ability to let someone know she was safe might put Sierra's mind at ease. "You could let them know where you are."

Sierra was shaking her head before Jo could even finish. "No."

Another red flag. Jo's memory flashed back to the young man on the street. She hadn't seen him since that first day, when he'd argued with Sierra under the awning. Sierra apparently wasn't interested in making her whereabouts known. She wondered what she could do to help.

But first she wanted the mother and daughter to be comfortable.

"Okay, well, the bathroom's just in there. I think there's a clean towel folded above the toilet. Help yourself."

Sierra said nothing.

Jo's feet shifted as she lingered in the doorway. When she'd approached Sierra in the alleyway, she'd hoped the young woman would give her something to go on, some kind of sign that might confirm her instincts. But Sierra and her daughter remained guarded.

"Right. I'll just head upstairs now." Jo shut the door and immediately heard the lock click behind her. She made a mental note to ask Truman for his spare key, just in case things turned south.

Stop it, Jo. She was being paranoid. It would be all right. The young woman just wanted some privacy, that's all. Besides, it was Jo who sought them out on the street, not the other way around. Forcing herself not to go down a rabbit hole of grim assumptions, she went in search of food.

"You did what?" Truman blurted out. His stunned face made Jo shift with unease.

They were together upstairs in the kitchen. Truman had his hip propped against the Formica counter as he cradled a mug of hot coffee. Jo felt color rising to her cheeks. She'd done something rash.

"I didn't plan it." She spooned curry sauce into a bowl of noodles and pushed the food into the microwave. "They looked so lost, Truman. And the mother appears to have been hurt by someone. I had to help her."

"Is she badly hurt? Maybe the ER would be a better place to send her."

Jo shook her head. "No. It's not too bad. Plus, I doubt she'd take herself to the hospital."

Truman uncrossed his ankles and set his coffee on the counter. Jo didn't know why exactly, but she feared a lecture coming on. "That's really nice of you. Of course you want to help. It's only natural. But did you think about directing them to the closest family-assistance center instead? There are other places far more equipped to aid people in need than we are. Normally, we're in the business of helping people find books, not shelter."

Jo opened a cabinet and closed it again, willing the heat in her face to subside. Too many people were questioning her decisions, her judgment. For once, she'd love the freedom to do as she pleased without having to answer to anyone. But of course, that wasn't realistic. They were a team working for a common goal. Still, she couldn't help but bristle. "I get that, Truman. I really do. But nothing about what we're doing here feels normal anymore. I mean, can you really blame me for wanting to lend a hand to a mother and her child who are in jeopardy?"

Truman opened his mouth as if to object, but he stopped.

Jo turned away, feeling her eyes prick.

"No," he replied, stepping closer. His tone softened. Jo could tell he was measuring his words. She even wondered if he might reach out and wrap her in a hug. But instead he hesitated.

"I don't blame you at all," he said. "You have a good heart, and you want to help. I guess I'm just looking out for you, for all of us. The mayor gave strict instructions that no one else was to be let into the building. Inviting that young mother and her little girl inside sort of breaks that rule, doesn't it?"

Jo nodded. "Yes." It was exhausting to keep her emotions in check all of the time. Truman had a point, maybe. Here she'd been the one insisting that Adam and the rest of the staff keep a united front. The six of them weren't supposed to go off and make big decisions that might affect the whole team. Truman was gently reminding her what was at stake. If the mayor—or, God help them, Regina—found out about additional people entering the store, they might be shut down altogether. Jo was now torn over what to do next.

The microwave dinged, bringing her back to her senses. She

continued gathering up utensils. "I haven't promised anything other than a meal and a shower."

"Okay."

"I wouldn't be able to sleep tonight if I just let them pass by another day. I'll call the women's shelter and see if I can encourage Sierra and her daughter to head that way. But let them have a moment to regroup downstairs. Okay?"

Truman held up his hands. "I'm not telling you what to do. I'm merely pointing out the risks. You asked me for my opinion, remember?"

"Yes, thanks. I understand. And I appreciate you keeping this between us, for the time being. The others have enough going on. No one needs the added stress."

"Agreed."

Snatching up the plate of hot food, Jo turned to go.

"Wait." Truman stopped her.

He's changed his mind, she thought. Maybe he would hug her after all. A tiny seed of hope planted itself in her chest.

"Take these." He rummaged through a brown bag and produced an unopened box of sugar cookies. "Maybe her little girl would like something sweet."

Tucking the box under her arm, Jo smiled, pushing past the disappointment. "Thanks, Truman." She slipped out of the kitchen.

Arriving downstairs, Jo could hear the shower running from the other side of the door. Testing the knob, she discovered it was still locked. She hesitated, patting Truman's extra key in her sweater pocket. After a minute, she chose to leave the food by the door. *Let them have their privacy*, she thought.

There was no rush. She'd check on them later.

For now, they were safe.

Twenty

Jo stood in the center of her office and stared. Whatever she'd hoped to find an hour earlier was now gone. No Sierra. No Rain. No note or goodbye. Just an empty room, save for a dirty plate and two forks stacked neatly on top. Jo moved to the bathroom and peeked inside. Nobody was there either. Steam still clung to the mirror; a damp towel was folded back in its place.

Jo couldn't help but feel a small lump of unease.

"What are you doing?" a female voice asked.

Jo jumped in the air, her nerves zinging. Her hand went to her heart. "Oh, Anna. You scared me. I didn't hear you come in."

Anna stuck a pen behind her ear and frowned. "Clearly. You looked like you were a million miles away just then."

"I guess I was." Jo quickly pushed the plate to the side and stood in front of her desk. Now that Sierra had come and gone, there wasn't any reason to explain. Best not to mention the incident at all. Her face rearranged into a smile. "Now you, on the other hand, look busy. What's the pen for? Have you been labeling more boxes?"

"Yeah. I didn't realize how much stuff was waiting to be unpacked from last week's delivery. The boys are still up there, organizing a few stacks. I thought I'd come down and see if you chatted with the mayor's office again. Any news?"

Oh no! With everything that had gone on, Jo completely lost track of time. There had been a scheduled phone call after lunch. She'd planned on it but then let time slip away from her. Glancing at her phone, she noticed two missed calls and one text message.

Regina: Hello? You weren't on the call. Please give a status update.

"Oh damn. I missed the meeting. Lord only knows what Regina said in my absence. I'll have to call her back and find out." Jo ran a hand over her face. It was only 2:00 p.m., but so much had transpired since breakfast that she felt as if it had been days since she'd told the team she expected the mayor's cooperation. Everyone was still buzzing from the *Times* article. Jo supposed she'd gotten too cocky and set her concerns over the mayor's office aside.

She should have been paying better attention. Instead, she'd redirected her focus to a young woman and child who didn't appear to want her help. Peering up at Anna, she wondered if her employees had noticed.

"Well, hopefully we can keep going," Anna said. "We're actually doing well after two and a half weeks. Sales are up big-time. I'm pretty proud of us, if I do say so myself."

Jo smiled. Anna was so steadfast.

"That's wonderful. And what about you personally?"

Anna's face scrunched. "What about me?"

"Well, what I mean is, how are you holding up? You're missing school, and you hinted that your parents aren't thrilled about your whereabouts. Have you spoken to them recently? I'm sure they're worried."

"Oh, it's fine. I mean, yeah, I'm bummed I wasn't allowed to finish online. I'll have to actually meet with my counselor at some point. But to be honest, it's kind of nice not having to constantly discuss my 'long-range plans' with my parents." She hooked her fingers in the air. "With this occupy movement, everything's been put on hold. Including the pressure from my mom and dad. They just assume I'll pick up where I left off when this whole thing blows over. Those are their words, not mine."

Jo knew Anna's parents were conservative and traditional and expected their well-educated daughter to finish up at Portland State and be accepted at OHSU. Anna complained in the past about them not understanding her passion for her job. They claimed the indie book crowd was a pointless distraction from Anna's life goals.

More like their *goals*, Jo always thought.

She'd met the Singers only once. She still remembered how Anna's father offered a firm but discriminating handshake and asked after the location of the "good science books." Anna's mother—an older, shorter version of her daughter—mutely followed behind with a look of uncertainty. Working retail was apparently not what the Singers wanted for their aspiring young doctor, not by a long shot. But Anna was determined to forge her own path. Jo found this admirable.

"So, what do your mom and dad have to say about you living here, in the bookstore?"

"Um . . ."

Jo raised a brow. "Anna?"

She shooed the air. "It doesn't matter."

"I bet they're not pleased."

"Not really." She tried to act nonchalant, but Jo could see it bothered her. If only the Singers could see in their daughter what Jo saw—an invaluable member of the Bruebaker's team who lit up when she described the new literature to curious customers. Anna was a tireless researcher and imaginative with new ways in which the store could improve, present circumstances included.

And yet, Jo couldn't help but sense that Anna might be hiding behind her position. In her eyes, Anna was plenty smart and capable of much more than being a shift manager for the rest of her days. She wondered if Anna's reluctance to move forward with school was more than just her loyalty to Bruebaker's. There was something about the hitch in her voice when she talked about the future that gave Jo pause. It was as if she was afraid to fail, afraid she might not meet her parents' high expectations somehow. Perhaps taking on so many hours at the bookstore was more about Anna's unwillingness to move on than it was about her love of literature.

Jo couldn't be sure. And she certainly didn't want to lose Anna. But she also didn't want to see so much talent go to waste. This girl would have a bright future if and when she decided to take the leap.

"Well, you've been amazing, Anna. I hope you know how much I value your being here. I couldn't have done this without you."

Anna blushed. A strand of smooth dark hair hugged her face. "Thanks, Jo."

"Of course. But please don't sell yourself short either. From where I stand, you have a lot to give. Medical school might be the thing that launches you even further toward success. I bet you'd be a wonderful doctor. Of course, only if that's what you want."

"Thanks."

"But," Jo ventured, "I'm also sensing you might be using your work here at the store to procrastinate going to med school."

Anna was quiet for a moment. Her gaze went somewhere far away. Jo worried she might have said too much. What Anna did with her personal life was her business, not Jo's. But she also didn't want to be the reason this bright, shiny star diminished. There was a whole world waiting out there for her. Jo wanted her to realize this.

"Maybe," Anna said, "I just want my plans to be my choice, you know? I don't want to move forward on a path if it's just to please someone else. Right now everything about my future feels kind of foggy."

"I understand." Jo knew what she meant. She'd felt that exact same fogginess after her parents passed and she'd yet to land a job at the bookstore. Hearing Anna express her worries brought back memories of so many sleepless nights with the bedside lamp on, pouring all of her hopes and dreams into her journal.

Anna's situation tugged at her heart. "My only advice is to make sure you're being true to yourself. I bet your parents just want you to be happy, that's all."

"You're right. I guess I need to figure out what it is I want. I've sort of been putting that off lately."

"I understand. Moving forward into the unknown can be a scary thing."

She nodded. "Thanks, Jo."

Jo placed a reassuring hand on Anna's shoulder and gave a light squeeze.

"Go ahead, go upstairs. I'll be up in a minute, after I call Regina."

"Okay." Anna headed for the stairwell, and Jo was grateful not to have to explain why strangers were using the shower. While she didn't believe Anna would mind, Jo also didn't want her to think decisions were being made without her input.

Casting her previous concerns aside, Jo settled into her chair and dialed Regina's number.

"We had an agreement, remember?" Regina's greeting sliced through the line, causing Jo to wince. It took her a minute to catch up.

Was this about Sierra and her daughter? Had Regina viewed security footage or driven past the building, spotting Jo opening the door to the homeless?

Keeping her breath steady, she smoothed her tone. "Hi, Regina. To what are you referring?"

"You promised to update me regularly and not go dark! Do I really need to remind you?"

"Oh." Jo's shoulders relaxed a little. Of course. This was only about the missed phone call, nothing else. "Gosh, Regina. I'm so sorry. It wasn't intentional. We just got busy. Orders are still coming in. You're right, though. I did promise. It won't happen again."

"Good."

"So I'm assuming you had the call with the mayor's office. Anything new?"

"Other than the swelling group of protesters outside the storefront? No. Not really. To be honest, I think the mayor has much bigger fish to fry. Seems like the campaign to clean up the city has brought on more unsolvable obstacles for Mayor Fink. The governor is now involved. His focus is split. With that said, we're not out of the woods yet."

"Yeah, I read some of that online. But you're saying he's not making us vacate the store yet either."

"Correct. So it looks as though you and the others can remain in place and continue your efforts with the online sales. That's your only decent negotiating point with Suzanne and Jane. They're not happy about your protest, but they aren't complaining about the steady stream of sales either. That could all change tomorrow, however. So don't get too comfortable."

"Oh, wonderful." Jo let out a whoosh of breath. She'd been hoping this was the case, given Mayor Fink's reaction to the influx of good press. But still, she wasn't totally sure.

"Yes, I suppose." Regina wavered. "We have another problem, however."

"We do?" Jo's anxiety was beginning to seesaw. Every time this woman opened her mouth, she found herself bracing for impact. There were so many things that could go wrong, and yet she still didn't follow where this was going.

"Your employee, Leo Tomlinson—did you let him go?"

"Yes," Jo said hesitantly, wondering how on earth Regina knew—or cared—about him.

"Well, he claims Bruebaker's held him over during this shutdown, without pay and without job security, and now he's threatening legal action."

"What?" Jo was on her feet, her chair thrusting backward. This was unbelievable. "He can't be serious. I let him and his party buddy go because they were creating problems. This is a joke. They volunteered to be here right from the beginning. I have witnesses to prove that. Plus, Leo has a criminal record that he failed to disclose when he was hired. Did he mention that?"

Jo was steaming. True, she'd fired Leo and Jack in an abrupt manner. But they didn't belong there. Weren't they the least bit embarrassed over their behavior?

"No, he didn't mention anything about having a record. I'll inform our lawyer. Still, Jo, this isn't good. I haven't informed Suzanne about any of this. She doesn't need the added stress. The last time we spoke, she seemed a bit . . ."

Jo froze. "What, Regina?"

"I don't know. Maybe it's nothing. It's just that Arnold isn't doing well. Suzanne sounded exhausted. I'm guessing she's explained to him that she hopes to close the business eventually, that it's better for everyone in the long run. That's got him defeated, I suppose."

"Uh-huh." Jo wasn't even listening anymore. Her ears filled with a white noise as she pictured her beloved mentor being brought down by the demise of his lifelong dream. The store was Mr. Bruebaker's legacy. If he thought it might not continue, then perhaps he felt like giving up too. Jo felt as if a vise were squeezing her heart. She couldn't let this happen. She *wouldn't* let this happen.

Because as much as she wanted to save the bookstore for the sake of the community, Jo wanted to save it for Mr. Bruebaker more.

Twenty-One

"**J**ade, look how far we've come!" Jo patted a tower of books ready for pickup with pride. "I'd say that's progress. Wouldn't you?"

"Yes, totally." Jade was equally pleased. The two women had been working tirelessly for the past two days, sorting, labeling, and packing up inventory as fast as their muscles allowed them. Never mind that every fiber of Jo's being screamed with exhaustion or that her brain was still going a hundred miles an hour, ticking over all the things yet to be done.

Because while Jo had been given the green light to keep working, the deputy mayor also hinted there'd been complaints. Community members were starting to take sides. Not everyone, it seemed, shared the sentiments of the *Times* article. Jo couldn't imagine why anyone would care if six employees volunteered to remain in the building. What harm were they causing anyone? Yet there'd been backlash all the same. Local business owners didn't appreciate the growing crowds of protesters, the trash they left behind, or the chaos created at nearby storefronts. There'd been reports of vandalism.

As a result, two separate groups of campaigners had now formed on the streets outside: one in support of the Bruebaker Movement, and one against it. It was as if the two camps had appeared out of nowhere. But both were visible and vocal. Both were determined. The only thing they had in common was their focus. Whether they liked it or not, Jo and her team were at the center.

This development filled Jo with a new sense of dread.

"It's political now," Sam stated during a recent phone call. "Small-business owners are starting to bare their teeth. With this movement of yours nearing two weeks, people are getting restless. They want to get back to normalcy. They need to earn a living. And the fact that Mayor Fink is allowing Bruebaker's to continue like this isn't making anyone happy."

Jo hung up the phone, stunned.

The tide was turning.

Thirty minutes later, Jo was sitting in the fiction section, channeling her nervous energy into the organizing of more books. Jade was one aisle over, diligently doing the same.

"So," Jade ventured, her tone cautious, "Anna told me Leo is getting a lawyer and he might be suing. Is that right?"

Great. Jo's jaw clenched. She hadn't wanted to share this unfortunate piece of news with her staff. As far as she knew, only Regina was privy to Leo's course of action since he'd been let go. She walked over to where Jade was cleaning. "Anna told you?"

Jade nodded. "Leo texted Adam about it. Adam told Anna, and she mentioned it to me. Why? Is it supposed to be a secret?"

Jo pushed air from her nose. The paperback in her hands was set to the side as she removed her eyeglasses and rubbed at her forehead. "No. I don't know. Leo's ego is bruised, that's all. I'm still hoping he'll calm down and come to his senses. It's fine that you guys know. You were all here when Leo left. But maybe just keep this information between us for now. That company lawyer is trying to contain the situation. Is that okay?"

"Yes, of course."

Jo offered a weak smile. She appreciated Jade's loyalty.

"Does Mr. Bruebaker know?"

"No." Jo's gaze went to the window. She'd compartmentalized her concern for her boss over the past couple of days, but her unease over his worsening condition was growing. *He'll get better,* she kept telling herself. *This is just a bad patch.*

A tiny voice told her otherwise, but Jo refused to give it power. She wasn't ready for Mr. B to be anything less than he was. She wouldn't let him.

Maybe he'd have a chance to get back into the store, to feel like his old self, once things settled again. But what would settled even mean? Things were changing. Would she be able to control any of it before it was too late?

Deciding it was best to switch topics, she turned to Jade. "I've been meaning to ask you for help with something."

"Sure, what do you need?"

"Well, it's not really me that needs help. There's a mother and daughter that have been hanging around. I think they're homeless. The little girl, she's around preschool age, and I was thinking the next time I see her, I'd like to give her some books."

Jade's gaze deepened. She likely thought Jo's idea was coming out of nowhere. "Okay."

"So, since you're so good with kids, I thought maybe you could pick some titles out." Jo kept her voice light, hoping Jade wouldn't see right through her veiled attempt to get the others on board. Jo had worked in the store for over two decades. Clearly she was capable of recommending books to a child. But perhaps Jade, with her desire to become an educator, would take on this task anyway.

Plus, Jo thought, *if I ever feel the need to let Sierra and Rain use my office again, I don't want to be sneaking around to do it.* She didn't like keeping secrets.

"Sure, no problem."

"Wonderful. Thanks, Jade."

That night, Jo lay in her makeshift bed and willed her noisy thoughts to quiet. A mere two weeks earlier—which felt like a lifetime at this point—she hadn't any idea the luxury she possessed in not knowing what was to come. Business had been up, spring tourism was on the rise, new author events filled the store calendar, and life was predictably on track. Now, as she punched her thin pillow and prayed for sleep, Jo couldn't believe all the ways life had changed. And yet, spending an indefinable amount of time in a dated commercial building, scrambling to save a precious institution, was nothing compared to the mounting anxiety she had over lawsuits, protests, and, perhaps the most painful of all, Mr. Bruebaker's sudden decline.

All of this was unexpected. None of it was welcome.

What bothered her was the fact she hadn't been paying attention. It took a call from Regina to alert Jo about her boss. This fact alone seeped under her skin like a slow-burning acid. Jo was supposed to be the one who knew Mr. Bruebaker best; she was supposed to be the one in weekly, if not daily, communication with him. She should have been looking out for him on a personal level in the absence of his daughters. She always had before. So why did she miss all the signs of late? Was she really so wrapped up in her role as martyr that she failed to notice the person that needed her attention most of all?

Kicking a borrowed sheet from Jade off her legs, Jo stewed. Her best wasn't good enough. She needed to do better.

The question was, how?

Perhaps she should pack up in the morning and leave. The team knew the tasks needing to be finished; they were fairly autonomous at this point. Jo could just walk out the side door, locate her parked car (was it even still there?), and make the twenty-minute drive to Mr. Bruebaker's rehabilitation facility. A brief visit wouldn't pose a risk; hopefully Suzanne and Jane would understand that. She could check in with the caregiving staff, make nice with Mr. Bruebaker's daughters, and spend time lifting his apparently dampened spirits. This was all doable. Wasn't it?

Reaching for the small pile of personal belongings beside her bed, Jo fumbled around in the dark. Ever since Jade suggested the team sleep in the one room with window shades, Jo had a difficult time finding her things. There was always someone napping or sleeping off a long shift of work. The room became the place employees tiptoed around in, careful not to disturb the unmoving bodies scattered about the room. Finally, she found what she was looking for. Clutching her phone, she tapped the screen and read over a list of notes she'd been keeping.

Progress report on nonfiction, remind Adam of signed Dani Shapiro memoirs.

Phone meeting with legal.

Spreadsheet to Regina.

Ask Grayson to dump the trash and recycling—too full!

Write thank-you note to Stephen Knight.

Anna to refresh social media account, discouraging gatherings.

Squinting against the blue glare of her screen, she punched in a new note.

Plan trip to check on Mr. Bruebaker.

Placing down the phone, she rolled onto her back and stared up at the darkened ceiling. She wondered if Truman might give her some advice on whether or not to leave the store. She'd found him to be a good sounding board over the past weeks. She'd come to appreciate his level of discretion too. She'd certainly cried enough in front of him, confessing her fears and her uncertainty. So far, he'd kept both her breakdowns and the matter of Sierra and Rain to himself. He was a good listener.

Of course, she'd always noticed this about Truman, the way he lingered in the break room, nodding along as the younger employees shared stories of weekend escapades and inconsequential tiffs with other workers. As far as Jo knew, he never participated in gossip or broke anyone's confidence.

These were all things she'd taken for granted in the past. And now that their world had become immeasurably smaller, Jo saw these qualities as true gifts.

Had she returned the favor? She wondered.

What else had Jo overlooked? What, or who, else had she taken for granted? This thought unsettled her just as much as everything else. Jo used to pride herself on her ability to observe. That's how she'd become so skilled at recommending titles to people. She *noticed* them.

But lately, Jo feared she'd stopped noticing. She'd been so busy grasping at ways to save the familiar that she'd lost her grip on what was important.

Tomorrow, she told herself, *that will change.*

Twenty-Two

Jo woke the next morning full of intention and plans. At 6:30 a.m., with the others still fast asleep, she crept downstairs to start a pot of strong coffee.

The Portland sky was still dim, the morning sun reluctant to chase away the lingering rain. Cradling a steaming mug, Jo went to visit the first floor. It would be hours before the protesters appeared, and she wanted a moment to revel in the peacefulness that inevitably wouldn't last.

Making a brief stop in the poetry section, she plucked an old favorite from the shelves. It had been far too long since she'd found a corner of her own to curl up and read something of interest. The only thing she'd read lately was the onslaught of emails filling up her inbox. Perhaps the fact that no one was around meant she could indulge in a little alone time. Lowering into a seat, she decided to take advantage.

Flipping the pages at random, she landed on a poem in Mary Oliver's beautiful book *Felicity*.

Things take the time they take.
Don't worry.
How many roads did St. Augustine follow
before he became St. Augustine?

Jo drank in the words. Something within her lightened. She couldn't help but feel as if this poem was meant for her. How many nights had she gone to bed, tired and frustrated, deeply wishing for things to move faster? It had been weeks in that big, empty building. While Jo always dreamed of living in a house where bookshelves were walls and stories became sustenance, the reality of her situation was far less romantic than she'd imagined. People were restless, work was draining, and Jo's list of concerns seemed to multiply by the day. All she wanted was to restore life to the way it used to be. That included the well-being of Mr. Bruebaker, the well-being of her staff, and the happiness of the customers who once flooded the space.

She'd woken up that morning unsettled. Mr. Bruebaker needed her. Her beating heart told her she wanted everything at once to fall into place or she might fold into a tight ball of anxiousness and alarm. But Mary Oliver's written words soothed her fears like a balm.

Things take the time they take.

Don't worry.

Jo exhaled. Her fingers brushed over the book. The artful cover was like a dreamy oil painting she'd want to hang on her wall at home. How could something so simple be so moving? Mary Oliver's beautiful and poignant message reminded Jo she was doing her best and this was enough. It would take time to fix the things that needed fixing. And, just like the spring weather traveling outside the window, renewal would happen. But it would happen in its own time, not hers.

Sipping her coffee, Jo decided she'd wait for Truman to wake up and then ask him for his thoughts. She then gathered up her book and her drink and made for the basement. There were still emails to answer and some tweaks to be made to a spreadsheet

Regina had requested. It was as good a time as any to check some of these tasks off her list. Besides, Mr. Bruebaker likely wasn't awake yet anyway. The hour was still quite early.

Descending the stairs, she detected a strange sound.

What is that? Jo froze. She craned her neck. Squinting, she tried to determine what it was. Her first thought was that there were rodents in the building. Jo shivered. She'd take spiders and snakes any day of the week over small, squeaky creatures with long rubbery tails. Just the thought caused her to pick up her feet, her head swiveling around to check for any movement in the dark.

The faint *tap-tap-tapping* continued. Willing herself to stay in one place, she leaned forward. It sounded like it might be coming from the walls. Were rats in the walls? Was a bird outside in the alley, building some kind of nest under the awning? But no, the tapping was more rhythmic, more solid. *It sounds*, Jo thought, *human.*

Someone was tapping on the outside of the side door. Rushing back up the steps, she pressed her ear to the door. "Is someone there?" Out of caution, she decided against turning the handle. It was still early, and no one was around. Whatever or whoever was on the other side might not be safe. "Hello?"

A muffled voice sounded on the other side. It was slight and female. "I'm looking for Jo."

Jo frowned and pressed her ear closer. "Who's there?"

The voice hesitated. "It's Sierra and Rain."

Her hand was on the lock within seconds. Flinging the door wide, Jo met two frightened faces. Sierra and Rain held hands, wearing the same clothes they had days before. Jo looked beyond them to see if they were alone. The alley was empty, save for a few dumpsters brimming with trash. The two girls had nothing with them. There wasn't any stroller or bags of belongings in sight. Something was wrong.

"Are you all right?" Jo searched their faces. Rain was mute as usual, her long lashes drooping down from what Jo guessed was a lack of sleep. Sierra's features were tight, stricken. Her blue eyes were glassy and rimmed red. Jo assumed she'd been crying. Before they had a chance to answer, Jo ushered them inside and shut the door. It was cold out there, and no doubt the girls needed some warmth.

"Come into my office, and you can tell me what's going on."

Silently, they followed.

Jo looked over her shoulder as they went, noticing the fierce grip Sierra had on her child's tiny hand. Jo quickened her steps.

"Sit, please." She pulled out her roller chair and pointed. "Did something happen?"

Sierra appeared uncertain at first, her gaze unsteady. Seeing that they were truly alone, she conceded. She lowered into the chair a bit too gingerly and then hoisted Rain into her lap. She winced with pain.

A lump formed in Jo's throat.

"I didn't know where else to go." Sierra's voice was meek, somehow different from the last time she and Jo spoke. It was as if her hardened shell had sloughed away, leaving a frightened young woman in its place.

"Okay."

"We'd been knocking for a long time. I almost gave up, but then you opened the door."

"Well, you're lucky I happened to be coming downstairs while you were still out there. I'm not always in my office so early in the morning."

Sierra shifted as Rain buried her head in her mother's neck.

Jo watched as the little girl closed her eyes and tried to rest. She wondered how long they'd been up.

"We, um, just need a place to hang out for a little while. Our regular spot is, um, it's just sort of cramped right now. I saw a light on in one of your windows, so I thought maybe . . ." Her voice drifted off.

"Yes, of course. It's fine. You can hang out here for a bit. But, Sierra . . ." Jo hesitated. She wasn't sure about pressing her. "I have to ask. Are you in any danger? Is someone hurting you?" She held her breath, praying for honesty but also praying her hunch was wrong.

Sierra wavered. Her chapped lips rubbed together, as if she was deciding how much to say. She played with a rip in Rain's thin jacket.

"I'm okay," she finally said. "Just having some bad luck. That's all. You said we could come back if we needed to. So here we are. Just for a little while. Then we'll be on our way."

Jo rubbed her hands together. Sierra's answer was far from satisfying. She really hadn't told Jo anything. But Jo had a knack for reading between the lines. These two needed a safe haven for the moment. "All right. I understand. Why don't you two shed some of that wet clothing, and I'll see what I can find you upstairs? Okay?"

"Okay."

Jo snatched up a few of her personal things and left the girls to the sanctuary of her office. As she jogged to the upper level, Jo's mind raced. She couldn't send those two back onto the streets unless she knew what they were up against. But before she did anything, she was going to have to tell her team.

Swallowing back her trepidation, she arrived on the second floor. The others didn't know it yet, but their group of six was about to grow. For how long, Jo had no idea.

Twenty-Three

The bookstore was just coming to life by the time Jo found the others. The aroma of toasted waffles floated out from the break room, the low chatter of voices punctuating the otherwise-still space. Jo could hear Adam whistling—a habit he had while pouring his daily cup of coffee.

In the absence of any female voices, Jo assumed Jade and Anna were in the bathroom they'd taken over on the third floor, brushing their teeth and getting ready for the day. It struck her then, as it had when she'd noticed the bulk of used shower towels, that one day she'd miss living in close quarters with what, for the most part, was a family. These were her people, for better or for worse. And despite the lack of fresh laundry and proper bedding, a big part of her would be sad when this experiment of theirs was over.

Arriving at the break room unnoticed, she took a second to observe the scene. Did employees at other companies feel the same about one another as the Bruebaker's team did? As if they were a family of sorts? She wondered. But then again, employees at most businesses didn't sleep on mats in the children's section or cook chicken and waffles in the break-room toaster oven. The six of them had become a tight bunch. They were there for a common purpose.

Jo only wished Mr. Bruebaker was there right then to witness it. The camaraderie would make him proud.

Mr. Bruebaker. She planned to go visit him that afternoon. But with the unexpected visit from Sierra and Rain, she couldn't exactly leave the store. Perhaps she should have thought this through better.

"Hey there, boss." Adam approached, a mug in one hand, a plate of syrupy Eggos in the other. "Up early?"

"Yes. I had some emails to catch up on."

And there's a mother and her child hiding out in my office. I think they're in trouble, but I'm afraid to tell you.

"That's why you're the big boss." Adam grinned. "Always working."

"Ha. Yeah, right." Jo fidgeted, wondering if Adam should be the first to learn her predicament. But he turned and plopped himself down in a chair and proceeded to stuff his face with breakfast. She decided it was important to tell Truman first.

"Hi, Jo." Grayson came next, with a towering waffle plate similar to Adam's. Only his included a yogurt carton and two bananas stacked on top. Jo marveled. The kid was a bottomless pit.

"Hi, Grayson. Hey, I thought I heard Truman in here. You know where he went?"

"Oh yeah." Grayson tipped his chin toward the door. "He went off in search of his Gorilla Glue. Guess a bookshelf got moved and broken. I'm supposed to help him in a minute."

"Ah. Okay, thanks." Spinning on her heel, Jo dashed back in the direction of the basement. Truman's supply closet was on the way to her office. If he went downstairs and heard unfamiliar voices, there might be a problem. The last thing Jo wanted was for Truman to think she was hiding the truth from him. Or worse, that Sierra and Rain had somehow broken in. With her heart in her throat, she hurried to locate him. It was important he learn her side of things first.

Winded, she arrived at the bottom step and ran into Truman's broad chest with a smack. "Ooof!"

"In a hurry?"

Jo's first reaction was to laugh. She saw, however, that there was nothing humorous about Truman's expression. A big V formed where his wiry eyebrows came together, and his mouth was set in a firm line. *He knows*, Jo thought. Searching for the right response, she inched backward.

"Truman, I—"

"I see you've got company." His tone was flat.

Her shoulders slumped. "That's what I was coming to tell you. I was down here earlier when they knocked on the door. I didn't know what else to do. I was hoping maybe—"

"Hoping maybe you could hide them away from the rest of us?"

She shook her head. "No, of course not. It's just that the timing isn't great, and I needed to make sure . . ."

"Make sure what?"

Jo's mind turned to mush. How was she going to explain bringing in strangers to the building—not once but twice—after she'd agreed not to? Of course Truman was angry. This made perfect sense. And yet it didn't. As far as she could recall, he'd never let his temper show. In fact, Jo couldn't even recall a single time when Truman let his emotions show whatsoever. Sure, he'd comforted her over the past weeks when she'd crumpled into a weepy mess. But he'd never revealed his own feelings. About anything.

And now, standing there ruminating on this observation, it was Jo who turned angry. Who did he think he was, anyway?

She'd worn her heart on her sleeve and gone above and beyond to help everyone in that building. Truman, on the other hand, had shown no emotion. It was maddening. Sure, sometimes Jo let her emotions get the best of her, and as a result, she'd probably done things that didn't make sense. But Truman would understand this if he wasn't so unbelievably passive.

"It's my office, Truman. I would think I could do with it what I want. I am the store manager, after all."

He studied her for a brief moment and then brushed past her toward the stairs. "Do what you want, Jo. Looks like you have anyway. But don't say I didn't warn you."

"Warn me about what?" she called after him.

He glanced over his shoulder before disappearing. "Everything has a consequence, whether you like it or not."

He left Jo alone to fume.

What the heck just happened? Had Truman really just judged her for being helpful? Of course she knew everything had a consequence. Good grief, he didn't need to suddenly be so condescending. She wasn't a child. Yes, she'd technically broken an agreement and once again opened the building doors for someone other than a staff member. But surely the others would understand. Wouldn't they?

Twenty-Four

"So," Jo began, "I've called you all together because there's something I want to discuss." She scanned the room. It had been half an hour since her testy encounter with Truman in the stairwell, and as far as she could tell, he hadn't yet told the group about what he'd discovered.

Jo was grateful for that at least. He wasn't getting too involved. It was up to Jo to resolve matters as she saw fit. Perhaps she'd been too hard on him. She didn't know why she'd gotten so defensive; she was just caught off guard. That was all.

She was beginning to relax when Adam opened his mouth.

"We already know what you're going to say," he said.

"You do?" A pinprick of anxiety danced along the surface of her skin. Just as soon as it appeared, her softness toward Truman evaporated. He hadn't kept her secret after all.

"Yeah," Adam continued. "You're going to say that Leo is suing the company, and we might all be called as witnesses or whatever. We know. He's pissed off, and he's not being quiet about it."

"Oh." Jo pursed her lips. In all the chaos, she'd failed to circle back around with Regina over the Leo debacle. Was that guy really following through with his threats? What a nightmare he turned out to be.

A dull murmur rippled around the table as the staffers traded comments on Leo's actions. From what Jo could gather, everyone was genuinely surprised at Leo's level of vengeance. No one hated Bruebaker's. It was like saying you despised Disneyland, or sugar.

Jo held up a hand, urging everyone to be quiet. "No, that's not what I was going to tell you. Leo's situation is unfortunate, to say the least. And it couldn't come at a worse time. But I suppose you all know that."

"So what did you want to talk to us about?" Anna asked over her open laptop. Her eyes kept drifting down, and Jo assumed she was checking in on news of the Bruebaker Movement. A kind of cultlike following had cropped up online in the form of a Facebook page. The last time Anna briefed her, Jo learned the page had over eighty-six thousand followers. This was quite something, considering the long-standing bookstore account had just over two hundred thousand. Of course, many of the followers were likely news outlets and competitors watching to find out the fate of the bookstore. Anna wasn't sure who ran the account, but it got her attention for sure. It was proof that thousands of people were interested in the action of the team and wanted to somehow be a part of their efforts.

"As you guys know, Regina Anderson and I are in almost daily communication with the mayor's office. The fact that we've ruffled some feathers in the small-business community hasn't helped our situation, and the mayor isn't pleased. But so far we haven't been asked to leave. So that's a positive!"

"Why do I feel like something bad is coming then?" Grayson asked. Jo noticed he was sitting close to Jade, who looked on and nodded in agreement.

"It's not something bad, per se. At least I hope you don't view it that way. It's just a, um, a decision I made without you guys." Her gaze flicked over to where Truman stood, arms folded, face blank. Whatever he was feeling, he clearly wasn't letting it show. Jo couldn't decide if this was a good thing or a bad thing, but it irked her nonetheless.

"What kind of decision? Are we giving up on the nonfiction section? Because in our defense, we've been busting our butt up there, restocking the shelves with the newest releases and boxing up older titles. There's still a lot more to do, but we're getting there."

"No, Adam. Not at all. I've seen what you four have done, and it's awesome. Nothing is changing about our tasks." She was botching this. Reaching for a chair, she pulled it out and sat down. This little speech of hers was making her more nervous than she'd thought. Her old self used to make all kinds of decisions alone, not worrying about the input from the staff. But that was then, before she'd allowed herself to get close to anyone. Now, she realized, she cared very much about what they thought.

"I know that we've promised to keep a united front. And we've also agreed to make decisions regarding the store a group discussion. And I also know I told you that under no circumstances are we allowed to bring anyone else inside the building."

"Right."

"Okay."

"Has something changed?"

Jo nodded. "Yes. I broke that rule and brought two people into the building. Twice. A mother and a daughter who are living . . . well, I don't know exactly where they're living, because they won't tell me. Anyway, they're young and frightened. I befriended them, and they're currently eating lunch in my office. My point is"—Jo took a deep breath, trying to judge the pulse of the room—"I think they might be in trouble, so I invited them to stay."

The room fell silent.

Jo collapsed against the chair. Anna was blinking back at her with her mouth agape. Adam's eyebrows dipped, and Grayson was cocking his head. So many times she called these kids out for being immature or uncooperative, or plain irrational. And here she was, taking people in off the street, hiding them inside the building at the precise time when letting people in jeopardized the thing they were all there for—saving Bruebaker's.

"Wow, that's like . . . a surprise." Adam scratched his head. He looked around the table, trading glances with Anna and the others.

"Yes. It is. I apologize for not asking you all to weigh in before I asked these young girls to come inside. It's just that the situation was, well, fluid. I wasn't sure how it would all play out. Just before coming to talk to you guys, I contacted the local women's shelter and the offices of family services. I was left feeling rather discouraged. There's too much demand in the city right now because of the mayor's campaign to clean up the tent cities. As you can imagine, officials and nonprofits are scrambling to provide alternative and safe accommodations. But there's just not enough to go around. I couldn't turn those two back onto the street. I'm not sorry I helped them. I'm only sorry I didn't seek your approval first."

Jade broke the silence. "I think it's nice of you to help them."

"Yeah," Grayson chimed in. "Me too."

Adam didn't look as convinced. She'd come down hard on him after he submitted his story to the press. She'd chastised him for his rash behavior and voiced her disapproval for not running his plan by the team before he acted. And now here she was, seeking exculpation for doing nearly the same thing. Her actions, should they be found out, might very well affect the whole team as well. And she hadn't asked for their input until after the fact.

She wouldn't blame Adam for losing respect. Jo was supposed to lead by example. At the moment, her example was proving inconsistent.

"Adam, Anna, what do you both think?" Jo didn't bother to include Truman's name in her inquiry. She already knew where he stood—mostly.

"Are they healthy? No drugs or anything?"

Jo thought for a minute. She hadn't exactly probed, but they didn't look unhealthy. "I think so."

"Okay," said Anna. She snapped her laptop shut and rested her elbows on the table. "So, from an emotional standpoint, I get it. None of us want to see someone, let alone a mother and her kid, turned away. But on a logistical level, I fail to see how this could work. I mean, like you said, the mayor doesn't want us expanding our numbers. We could get in trouble. And also, we aren't exactly overflowing with supplies here. The food is getting low—and takeout is expensive—and we may have used the last of the sleeping mats. It just sounds tricky. That's all."

"Good points, Anna."

Adam's mouth twisted from one side to the other, as if he was working out his answer. Jo both wished for and feared his response. She wrung her hands under the table and waited.

"I'm not gonna lie," he finally said. "I'm bummed out. I mean, look at all the grief you gave me over the article and the decision to keep Jack and Leo on a while longer." He held up his hands. "I know, I know. Bad example. Leo turned out to be a total dick. But still, you get my point. Not to be disrespectful or anything, Jo, but you went and did close to the same thing you reprimanded me about. You broke the united front."

A space hollowed out in her gut. He was completely right. She deserved the judgment, perhaps from Adam most of all.

"I'm so sorry," Jo answered. "I should have spoken to each and every one of you before I did anything. You're entitled to be upset. But please know I'm doing this because it feels right. Even if that means I have to hide the truth from people on the outside. I obviously don't want to get us into more hot water. So . . ." She placed her palms on the table. "You all need to decide. Is this something you can live with or not? Can you accept all of us occupying the building—the newcomers included? I'll understand either way. I'm going to leave the room now and try to get you more information on the two girls. Maybe that will help. Either way, you guys talk among yourselves, and let me know. Take your time." With that, she pushed up from her chair.

Truman caught her eye and dipped his chin. She'd come clean, and he approved.

Jo sent him a look that said "thank you" and strode from the break room. Making her way toward her office once more, she uttered a silent prayer. With any luck, they'd see things her way. If they didn't, however, she was going to have to follow their lead. They were a team. They were the Bruebaker Movement. For the sake of everything Jo knew and loved, she desperately needed them to stick around a little while longer.

Twenty-Five

"**Y**ou need to tell me more about your situation," Jo said. She perched on the side of her desk, while Sierra and Rain nibbled on plates of bagels and cream cheese. Jo wished she had the ability to whip up something heartier, like eggs and bacon, for the pair. She guessed it had been a while since they enjoyed a hot meal. But then again, with Sierra's refusal to reveal where the two of them had been sleeping, it was hard to know. Sierra was embarrassed to say, or she was protecting someone. Either way, Jo was troubled.

"Like what?" Sierra broke off a chunk of bread and handed it to her daughter. Rain sank her teeth in and smiled. Her cheeks were pink and damp, probably from being subjected to a good face scrubbing in the bathroom.

This is a good sign, Jo thought. Sierra was noticeably trying to care for her girl, at least in small ways.

"My team is most likely going to want something to go on. Our position here is precarious; we've only been allowed to remain in this building under strict guidelines. So while I'm happy to help, I also need you to be honest. Do you understand?"

Sierra nodded up at her from the floor, her legs folded underneath her slim frame. Rain scooted closer, pressing her face into her mother's faded hoodie. She reminded Jo of a little magnet, attaching itself to a stronger force. It turned out Rain could speak after all. Jo had heard the two whispering just before she entered the room.

Jo pushed hair from her face. She needed to get to know this little pair better.

Glancing down, she noticed the two children's books lay at Rain's side, untouched. Jo had brought copies of *The Very Hungry Caterpillar* and *Chicka Chicka Boom Boom* from the upstairs sharing basket. These were well-loved books, set out to encourage parents and children to open the pages and read together on the rug. Jo liked to think of these books as seeds, planted in the eager hands of children, their love of stories blooming right there in the store.

Instinctually, she wanted to provide Rain with this same experience. Other than a plastic troll doll, she hadn't seen the child playing with much else. But the small books remained untouched on the floor. Rain regarded them only briefly, a mixture of confusion and disinterest on her tiny face. It was as if the preschool-aged reads were too foreign or too boring to approach. Jo's heart sank. She'd yet to meet a child who wasn't captivated, even if merely by the illustrations.

Rain, it appeared, was indifferent.

This thought sat on Jo's chest and stayed there, dense and uncomfortable. What other assumptions had she made that were wrong?

Sierra was going to have to shed some light.

"I used to live in Idaho," Sierra finally said. She placed her bagel down and brushed crumbs from her jeans. "Went to high school there. But then Rain was born, and we had to leave. First we lived in Medford, then Gresham, and now Portland."

"Okay, and who is we?" Jo was careful not to push too fast. She could tell by the way Sierra drove her attention at a bloodied hangnail that the young mother was uneasy. A hundred scenarios played out in Jo's brain. Had there been criminal activity? Was Sierra on the run from someone? Was there abuse? Perhaps revealing too many details would get the two of them into further trouble.

"Me, Rain, and Casey. That's my, um, boyfriend."

"I see. Is Casey also Rain's father?" Jo asked, trying her best to keep her tone light. It was perhaps too intrusive, but curiosity got the best of her.

Sierra shrugged like she wasn't sure how to answer. But Jo caught a shadow darken her expression. "No. Not by blood. But he cared about me and her when no one else did."

"Ah." Jo was starting to put the pieces together. There was no way Sierra was a legal adult by the time Rain was born. She looked far too young. Because of this, Jo had to assume there'd been friction at home over the teenage pregnancy. It wasn't difficult to read between the lines. Sierra was a runaway, in one form or another.

"So the three of you moved around a lot?"

"Yeah. Casey works construction. Well, he used to anyway. His cousin said there'd be a job on a site here. But that kind of dried up fast. Things were fine for a while. Until they weren't. Portland hasn't really worked out the way we thought."

"And your parents or family back in Idaho? Are you in contact with them?" *Do they know you're alive? Wouldn't they want to know you're out there on the streets?*

Sierra shook her head. Her jaw set. "No. We don't speak. I don't plan on going back there either."

"Okay. What about Casey? Does he know where you are right now?"

"No."

Jo mulled this over. Something told her that was all the questioning Sierra could tolerate for one morning. Jo's suspicions were confirmed. The two girls were out of safe options, and they needed a secure place to stay, even if it meant a commercial building in the middle of downtown. All of this would be reiterated to the others. Surely they would understand.

Jo left Sierra and Rain to the rest of their snack and told them she needed to go make some calls. Her concern for Mr. Bruebaker still hung in the back of her mind.

Would he be in better condition today? Jo closed her eyes and hoped.

Making her way to the main level, she settled onto a window seat. She'd expected to hear some news from Regina by then. Their interactions had become more regular lately. Plus, Jo hoped for some news before visiting with Mr. Bruebaker. A positive update would do everyone some good, Jo included. But there weren't any new voice mails, and her inbox had been cleared. Checking the time, she saw it was just before nine o'clock in the morning. Everyone else downtown was likely just starting the day.

Everyone except for the group upstairs. Jo felt as if she were awaiting a jury to deliberate a trial outcome. It was agonizing not knowing what they might be saying about her.

What she needed was a distraction. She could thumb through the order printouts and go right back to pulling books in the fiction section. There certainly was enough to do there. Or maybe she should go to a far end of the store so the others wouldn't think she was hanging around, eavesdropping on their conversation. But the thought of going too far from Sierra and Rain wasn't appealing. What if they came looking for her? What if the staff went looking for them?

No, she decided. It was better to stay close by, just in case.

Viewing the city streets, she was struck by the stillness. Other than a few pieces of trash floating by in the wind, everything appeared rather lifeless. If Jo didn't know better, she'd think she'd fallen into one of the dystopian novels they sold in the young adult section. The landscape had an eerie feeling. The usual band of protesters and counterprotesters, shoppers, and tourists had not yet arrived for the day. Hardly any cars passed. Even the city pigeons that sometimes flew in and picked at debris seemed to all have flown off.

In the absence of any activity, Jo felt as if she were the only one left.

Her gaze traveled around the store, noticing the racks of postcards and bookmarks, and tables of new releases. Grief tugged at her heart. So many wonderful things, and yet there wasn't anyone around to buy them. Jo missed the steady hum of voices, which once moved freely throughout the aisles. Gone was the happy buzz of energy; gone was the sense of joy.

How sad Mr. Bruebaker would be if he walked through the front doors now, Jo thought. How terribly disappointing it all was. Dedicated staffers aside, the life had been sucked out of what was once a magical destination.

Would it ever be the same again?

For the first time, Jo forced herself to envision her life should the store not reopen. Two decades of her life had been spent inside that building, forming bonds with the employees and customers, meeting authors and discovering new reads. Jo had everything she could ever want right there.

Besides, it wasn't as if she could walk down the block and work at some other indie bookstore. With the exception of a very few used bookshops, Bruebaker's was it. There wasn't anything else out there like it. And, as far as Jo was concerned, nor should there be. Bruebaker's and its founder were special because they were both one of a kind. Nothing, in Jo's opinion, could possibly replace them—ever.

Thinking of Mr. B, she took out her phone. She dialed her boss's number. When an unfamiliar female voice answered, she frowned.

"Arnold Bruebaker's phone," the woman said. "Can I help you?"

"Who's this?"

"This is Eunice, Mr. Bruebaker's caregiver. Who is this?"

"This is Jo. I work at the store. Can I speak to him, please?"

"Just a minute." There was shuffling and then what sounded like a hand covering the device. She could hear mumbling and another woman's voice in the background. Jo's frown deepened. What was going on?

"I'm sorry, Jo. I'm going to have to take a message."

"Why?"

"Mr. Bruebaker can't come to the phone. I'll tell him you called though."

Jo felt her heart rate double. "Wait!" She was practically shouting now. "What do you mean, he can't come to the phone? Is he in physical therapy or something?"

There was more muffled mumbling. It sounded as if two people were arguing. But neither voice sounded like Mr. Bruebaker. "We've been told not to disturb him with anything regarding the store. He's had another episode, and it's best he remains stress free right now."

No, please no. Jo was on her feet. "What do you mean he's had another episode? I need to know what's going on."

Suddenly a new voice came across the line. "Hello, Joanna."

Jo swallowed. Only one other person called her by her full

name. Jo pictured her standing in her father's room, with her curly auburn hair and her narrow reading glasses.

"Hello, Suzanne. Is everything all right?"

Suzanne sighed, her voice older and wearier than Jo remembered. "Dad's had what the doctors are calling a small brain bleed—"

"He's had another stroke?" Jo's hand went to her heart. "Tell me, Suzanne. You know he'd want me to know."

"Yes," she said. "The doctor is calling it a minor event. He's apparently been under a lot of stress. Probably because of everything going on at the store. You know how he gets. He can't let anything go. Luckily a nurse was here when it happened, and she called for a doctor right away. There wasn't much the facility could do, other than hydrate him and make sure his vitals were stable. There's nothing we can do to reverse a stroke. He may require some different treatment to strengthen his right side. In addition to this, we hope to protect him from having another one. That means low stress. Sorry, Joanna. But we don't think you should be calling him about the store—which we've instructed you to close—right now. It's too much on him."

Jo tried to swallow, but her mouth turned dry. She didn't care about Suzanne's request; she just needed to know about Mr. B. "He's okay though, right? Does he have all of his faculties?" Ugly images of oxygen tubes and bowlfuls of pureed food filled her memory. She'd seen what happened to her own father. Age and illness robbed him of all his dignity.

"Yes, he's fine. He can still speak and eat and shuffle around. He just needs rest. Lots of it. Okay?"

Jo sniffed. She wasn't aware she was crying until just then. "Yes, okay. I won't bother him. But, Suzanne?"

"Yes?"

"Please tell him I'm thinking of him."

"I will."

Jo hung up the phone and stared out the window. She didn't bother to wipe her tears. All of this time, she'd been silently waiting for Mr. Bruebaker to come to her rescue, to regain his health and deliver the weight of his full support. The idea of this not happening was crushing.

Twenty-Six

By the time Truman found her, Jo was shuffling around in the bookstore's abandoned café. She was thrusting fistfuls of expired baked goods into a large trash bin, muttering aloud. Not wanting to eat the inventory in the event they reopened, she and the others had originally opted to leave the café alone. Now, as she noted the green flecks of mold covering a tray filled with muffins, Jo deeply regretted the waste. There wasn't any other choice but to throw them out.

Darn it! Jo yanked another fistful. In her haste, she dropped half the contents onto the floor. She kept going anyway. It didn't matter if she was efficient or even effective. At that moment, all she sought was the satisfying action of hurling things into the trash. She needed to take her anger out on *something*. At present, it was the muffin section.

"Wow, you're not messing around up here." Truman strode over to where Jo stood, paper napkins and pastry liners littering the ground at her feet.

"Someone needs to do it," she huffed, blowing hair from her face. She was only partially aware of how insane she must look. Her clothes were haphazard, and her hair was most likely wild and frizzy. She was standing near a small mountain of trash, and there was a good possibility the limited amount of mascara she wore had now streaked down her face. But none of this mattered. What mattered was finding a way to channel her anger before she gave up and punched something.

Truman must have sensed this, because he kept his distance. "You, uh, okay?"

"Fine. Fine. Just working."

He sank his hand into his pocket, the loose change jingling again. Jo wanted to scream at him to stop. Lately it felt like he was always hanging around, judging her. It would've been better if he'd come down there to work, to roll up his sleeves and join her. That would have made Jo feel better. But instead, he kept his hands in his pockets and observed her wordlessly. It was making her crazy.

"So the gang has been talking."

"No kidding. Tell me something I don't know." Immediately, she regretted her biting tone.

He rocked back on his heels. "Okay . . . well . . ."

Jo stopped midthrust and placed her hands on her hips. "Oh God, Truman. Just spit it out. Stop dancing around the subject. I get it. I broke everyone's trust and created waves. First Leo with the lawsuit, then Sierra and Rain, and now Mr. Bruebaker."

Her chin began trembling before she could control it. Truman's eyes went wide.

"What are you talking about? Did something else happen with Mr. Bruebaker?"

"Yes." Jo wiped her eyes with the back of her arm. "Apparently the bad news and stress became too much for him. He's had a second stroke."

"Oh no! That's awful. Is he okay?"

Jo slumped against a bookshelf and nodded. "He's okay, I think. I mean, it's all relative. But he's resting. I don't know the full extent of it. His daughter is calling it a 'minor brain bleed.' She says all the drama with the bookstore proved to be too much, and I'm not even allowed to speak with him."

"That's awful." Truman took a hesitant step forward, his hand reaching out as if he wanted to console her. Jo ignored him; she didn't deserve anyone's pity. His hand dropped back to his side.

"The worst part of it is that it's true."

"What's true?"

"All of it!" She couldn't keep her voice from cracking. "Suzanne is right to keep me away. Look at all the events I set into motion that led up to Mr. Bruebaker's failing health. First I informed him that a band of his employees had gone rogue and locked themselves inside the store. Next I failed to keep it under wraps, and the story went public, attracting protests and drama with the city officials. Next came a potentially harmful lawsuit and then my risky decision to take on more people. No wonder Mr. Bruebaker's daughter wants me to stay away. Everything I touch turns into a complete disaster."

The sob she'd been holding back escaped in a violent rush, sending Jo sinking to the floor. Openly crying now, she sat amid the litter. It didn't matter if she was covered in crumbs. She didn't care that Truman was witnessing her most humiliating moment. All she cared about was preserving the well-being of Mr. Bruebaker and the wonderful life he'd given her through his store. Now all of that was slipping away. And Jo feared she was to blame for all of it.

She'd failed everyone.

She'd failed herself.

There was nothing left to do now except cry.

"Hey, hey, come on now." At once, Truman was down on his

knees, his breath warm on her cheek. Jo felt his strong hand on
the small of her back, which no doubt was damp from perspiration. Her nose was running, and her eyes were most certainly
swollen and red. If she had more energy, she would run away.
And yet she lingered, allowing her shoulders to drop just a little.
Truman's sudden comfort was like a balm on her aching heart. Jo
considered him. Maybe he didn't despise her after all.

"I'm sorry, Truman," she said, searching his gaze. "I didn't
mean to cause problems. We've been here nearly a month now
and not once have I asked you how you'd handle things. I guess I
got so caught up in managing one crisis after another that I failed
to see the bigger picture. I've just been putting one foot in front
of the other without always seeking anyone else's input. I don't
blame you for being mad at me."

"Jo, I'm not mad at you."

She swallowed. "You're not?"

"No," he said, gently shaking his head. "You're being too hard
on yourself. Sure, I wasn't happy to discover you'd invited people
inside without telling anyone. But that was more out of concern
than anger. When you came upstairs and told everyone what you
did and why you did it—well, how could I not be impressed? You
lead with your heart, Jo. You always have. I know you wouldn't
have brought those two young girls inside if you didn't have good
reason. The others know this too."

"They do?" Jo couldn't believe it. "They're not upset?"

"Nah." Truman leaned back beside her, his shoes kicking away
loose papers on the ground. Jo noticed how their shoulders were
nearly touching. His head tipped against the long shelf behind
them. "You still have some questions to answer, but no. They're
not mad. Jo, you have to look at this stuff more objectively. Mr.
Bruebaker's health, the protesters, the bad employee, none of

those things were your fault. You did not set those things in motion. They would've happened with or without you."

"Yes, but I could have handled all of it better. I could have reacted better. I'm sure Leo wouldn't be suing the company had I not let him go the way I did. And I was the one who kept Mr. B involved as much as he was, asking him to make his voice heard with Regina and Suzanne and the fate of the store. He didn't ask to bear the burden for any of that, and yet I put all of it on his shoulders anyway. And look what happened." She sniffed, fighting back the salt in her throat.

"Yes, but the old man sounds like he's in good care. And we'll be okay, Jo. Despite all the crap that's been thrown at us, look at all of the good things that have been accomplished as well."

Jo blinked. There was good? "Like what?"

He cocked his head and raised an eyebrow. "Really?"

"Yes, really. I need you to tell me, Truman."

"Okay, fine." He clearly wasn't someone who vocalized his emotions; no one would describe Truman as a touchy-feely type of guy. But she needed to hear him say it out loud. If he saw something positive about their current situation, Jo wanted to know what it was. "For one thing, look at how many dozens of boxes are now filled with new book orders. You all did that in an incredibly short amount of time. Whatever the fate of the bookstore, large portions of the inventory will not have to be returned or destroyed because of you and your staff. Think of all the authors you're supporting. That's amazing."

She allowed herself a small smile. "Yeah, that part is good."

He continued. "And speaking of the staff, look how tight everyone has become. Well, with the exception of the two knuckleheads that left. Think about it. Don't you remember how Anna and Adam used to roll their eyes at one another and argue? In the beginning, there wasn't a ton of respect between those two. Now they're thick as thieves. They'll make good leaders for the rest of the staff should the store open up again. And I'm pretty sure Grayson would be starving and evicted if we'd sent him home. Look at him now. He's gained at least ten pounds, and he's thrilled about being part of the team."

Jo laughed. Truman was making light of Grayson's ravenous appetite, but it was still a good point. That kid had been awfully happy lately. Jo also suspected his joy might have something to do with Jade, but she kept that to herself.

"And then there's me," he said, his voice drifting off.

Jo peered closer. "What about you?"

"Well, I guess I've never said it before, but the past weeks have been good for me too."

Jo paused. This was perhaps the most surprising admission of all. She'd always assumed Truman stuck around out of a sense of duty and loyalty to Mr. Bruebaker. She had no idea he'd benefited from the experience in some way. If anything, Jo assumed the entire thing had been a hardship.

"You probably already know this, but I live alone." He hesitated, his mouth twitching.

Jo nodded and waited for him to go on.

"I don't have a spouse or a family. Hell, I don't even have a dog. I've always poured myself into my work. I like it here and, for the most part, have been happy to spend my days in the store. But being here day after day, eating, sleeping, and working alongside the five of you, has made me feel . . . well . . ." He fidgeted. "It's made me feel like I'm a part of a family. A dysfunctional one, but a family all the same. And I like that. It's been fulfilling." He folded his arms across his chest, as if to protect himself from scrutiny. But he didn't need to. He'd just said the most beautiful thing Jo had ever heard. Her heart felt as if it was expanding in her chest, making room for all the emotions Truman shared.

Without thinking, she leaned over and laid her head on his steady shoulder. Wanting the moment to last, she closed her eyes. She very much wanted to tilt her face up and kiss him. Did he feel the same? "Thank you, Truman."

"For what?"

"For being my friend."

The two of them remained that way, side by side, for a long time. Contentment, it appeared, was still attainable after all.

Twenty-Seven

"**D**on't be nervous," Jo said, ushering Sierra and Rain from her office. "They just want to meet you, that's all." She tried to offer a reassuring smile to the unsure-looking mother and daughter, letting them know it was going to be all right. After the team talked it over, they'd found Jo and Truman and announced their decision to let Sierra and Rain remain in the building temporarily. No one knew what this meant, exactly. Especially since Jo didn't know how much longer they'd be allowed to remain either. But Adam reminded everyone: "Bruebaker's has always been about inclusivity, so why would we stop now?"

For this, Jo was eternally grateful. He'd chosen to rise above whatever grudge he may have held and accept this new circumstance with maturity and grace. Truman was right. Adam really had proven himself to be a leader. She made a mental note to swiftly promote him should the store survive.

Sierra and Rain trailed close behind, hand in hand as Jo led them through the main level. Their footsteps slowed, however, once the stairwell opened up into the expansive sea of literature titled "Bestsellers." Jo watched as their gazes widened, awestruck at the sight. She paused and waited for the two of them to take it all in. Rain perked, as if the tiny cogs in her brain had been set spinning. Jo wondered if it might be too much stimulation, the sheer volume of colorful books on display overwhelming. But then the corners of Rain's mouth turned up, and her soft cheeks pushed back to reveal an expression of joy. Jo warmed at the sight. It was so lovely to witness the setting through a child's eyes, especially one who'd likely rarely entered a bookstore.

"Wow, that's a lot of books," Sierra said. She angled her head and scanned the towering shelves. If she was impressed, Jo couldn't tell. Sierra had one of the best poker faces she'd ever seen. This girl was used to shielding her emotions.

Jo would have to think about which title might be best suited for her.

"Yes, we have over a million volumes in the store. I can give you a tour later on if you want."

Sierra shrugged, noncommittal. Jo wondered if she even liked books. Perhaps she was like Rain, who so far had been a tough sell. But judging by the little girl's reaction now, Jo was hopeful to turn that around.

"Okay, here we are," Jo announced as they arrived in the break-room door. Inside, Anna, Adam, Jade, and Grayson were waiting. Jo wasn't sure where Truman had gotten off to, but it didn't matter. He'd already given his blessing.

Jo cleared her throat. "Everyone, this is Sierra and her daughter, Rain."

The three of them entered, and Jo pulled out chairs. Feeling the need to keep her hands busy, she set about gathering up more snacks and drinks. Her stomach flipped as she moved about the room. It was strange how invested she'd become in Sierra and Rain's story. After all, she hardly knew them. But there she was, fussing about the kitchen and trying to put them at ease. She hoped the others wouldn't ask too many questions. But that part was up to them. Jo ceded control.

After everyone went around the table introducing themselves, Adam was the first to speak. He placed his elbows on the
table and looked Sierra straight in the eye. "So we only have one
rule," he said. "And that's anyone who stays here also should try
to help out. Does that sound okay?"

"Sure," Sierra answered, keeping her expression flat. Jo
wondered if she had any idea what Adam was talking about.

"That's great, because it's a big building, and there really
aren't enough of us to get everything done as it is. Jo probably
told you that our time inside Bruebaker's is limited. We've been
spending it working and sleeping and then doing it all over
again the next day. Maybe you'd consider pitching in in some
way?"

Jo tensed. She was rather taken aback by Adam's directness.
Perhaps he was doing his best to have them fit in, to become part
of the team. Still, she knew Sierra was still in a bit of pain. Of
course she still wouldn't admit this, but Jo wasn't stupid. She saw
the way the girl winced when she moved too quickly.

But Sierra surprised Jo with her answer. "Yeah, I can help
out. I don't really know anything about bookstores, but I worked
in housekeeping at a motel for a few months. I can clean bathrooms and stuff. If that's the kind of help you're talking about,
I've done it before. Rain won't be a bother either. She just follows
me around."

"That's cool."

Jo watched them exchange a look that seemed to say they understood one another. She was amazed. Adam's approach worked.
Just because the two girls were down on their luck, he wasn't going
to be patronizing or distrustful of their situation. Instead, he was
going to treat them like equals. Up until that moment, Jo had
only viewed the girls as vulnerable and broken. But Adam wasn't

having that. He addressed them as if they were capable and qualified to join the group. Jo liked that.

"Um, we also have one other rule," Anna broke in. She smiled nervously in their direction. "The last two guys who worked here were asked to leave because they were smoking in the building. We don't want that to happen again. Okay?"

Wow. Her employees were really taking this thing seriously. Jo knew the movement was their top priority. But she saw now that her staff really took ownership of every aspect, right down to the code of ethics.

"Yeah, that's fine. I don't, like, have anything on me if that's what you're asking." Sierra appeared unruffled by the exchange. Jo wondered if she was used to answering similar questions at places she'd stayed before. She also wondered if Sierra was telling the truth. Hopefully she was.

"Okay, good." Anna seemed satisfied. She looked around at the others and nodded. "So maybe Jo can get you two settled, and then one of us can show you around."

"Okay."

"Um, Jo?" Jade gave a little wave. "We could use more help in the fiction section. Word is getting out to other book clubs to stock up in case we don't reopen, and we have more orders than I can fill."

Jo pumped her head. Pairing Sierra (and probably Rain) up with Jade made for a nice combination. Jade was nothing if not patient, and this quality would come in handy when training someone new. A spark of gratitude glimmered for Jade. Her willingness to be of service was a marvel. "Yes, right. Good point, Jade. Bathrooms will just have to wait. I have to make some more calls this morning, so maybe Sierra can fill my spot for a short bit. Come on, girls, let me show you where you'll be sleeping."

With that, the group dispersed, and everyone filed out of the break room.

If she was honest, Jo could hardly believe it worked out so smoothly. She'd been anticipating more pushback. But why? Why had she doubted Anna, Adam, and the others so much before? They'd risen to the occasion time and again, and Jo was pleasantly surprised every time. Then another thought hit her. Had she shown up for them in the same manner? Did they expect the same from her? She wasn't sure, but something told her she needed to do better by them. They deserved it.

Twenty-Eight

For the next twenty-four hours, life inside Bruebaker's remained fairly routine. Sierra and Rain were still there and hadn't made any mention of leaving. If the team was concerned over the offer of temporary shelter morphing into more, they didn't voice it. Other than adjustment to the additional bodies taking up room in the building's makeshift living spaces (Anna was forced to create a formalized shower schedule to alleviate overcrowding in Jo's tiny bathroom), everyone seemed to stay on track with their workload. Jo made repeated visits to the second floor, trying to appear casual as she checked in on Jade's progress with her new helpers. For the most part, Sierra had resigned herself to being a silent assistant, doing the task assigned to her of gathering up ordered books. Rain could usually be found sitting alongside her mother, playing with a set of building blocks Jade pulled down from a shelf of an education display.

"I'll pay the store back," Jade said, waving the opened packaging in the air when Jo walked by. "I saved the price sticker so I'd remember."

Jo was quick to correct her. "Oh no. That won't be necessary. If anyone is reimbursing the bookstore, it's me. You're an angel for thinking of it. Thanks, Jade."

While Rain's disinterest in books was disappointing, Jo was

thankful at least something in the store was keeping the little girl occupied. She looked on as Rain sat with her legs splayed to either side, a line of brown blocks in front of her, creating an imaginary train. Rain's cheeks puffed out as she made little *choo choo* sounds, moving each block along an invisible track on the cement floor. Jo thought about the tracks that ran through the far end of the Pearl District. Perhaps the girls had been living somewhere in that area. She had an urge to ask but then decided against it. Sierra would tell her more when she felt like sharing.

For the moment, it appeared Sierra was content to keep her hands busy. Jo watched as she secured a clipboard and transported paperbacks to a waiting rolling cart, stopping to make sure the barcodes matched up with the correct titles on her list. At one point, Jo overheard her sounding out the letters to her daughter.

"Can you say the alphabet with me, Rain?" she asked. "Do you remember how to start?"

Rain paused, a fistful of blocks in her hand, and shook her head.

"Okay," Sierra said. "It starts with the letter *A*. Remember?"

Jo warmed at the scene. And while she would have liked to stick around and watch, she also couldn't quiet the ticker tape of worry running through her brain. Regina wasn't returning her calls, and Suzanne had been less than forthcoming with new information. If Jo didn't know better, she'd think the two women were conspiring against her. Without contact to the outside world, Jo was left spiraling with her own thoughts. Why would these women want to cut her out of the loop? Was it because they blamed her for Mr. Bruebaker's newest development? Had they both discussed their disapproval of Jo's actions? Was the mayor in on it too?

Jo couldn't be sure, because they'd simply left her twisting in the wind. Of course, none of the staff knew this. It wouldn't do anyone any good. If anything, it would create a level of paranoia and mistrust. And that's the last thing Jo wanted to see happen. Well, close to the last thing.

Until someone told her otherwise, Jo's goal was to save the store. Even though she couldn't talk to Mr. Bruebaker, she knew in her heart this was what he'd want too. *One day soon*, Jo thought, *I'll walk out of here and go be with him. I'll sit down and share all of the good that's gone on inside these walls.*

Somehow she needed to find a way to reach out. But doing so could come with real consequences. Her options were dwindling to remaining with the team and fulfilling the movement, or abandoning their efforts by leaving the store for a period of time. She just wasn't sure she could have it both ways.

Truman knocked on the door to her office later that afternoon with a concerned expression. He was panting slightly, as if he might have run down the flight of stairs to find her. "Have you looked outside lately?"

"No." She pushed back from her desk and searched his face. "Why? What's going on?"

"Well, I'm not sure exactly, but something or someone has caused things to escalate. The police have arrived, and it looks like they mean business. I think you better come see for yourself."

Oh no. Jo had the urge to lean over and bury her head. She could not take any more bad developments. And yet, Truman was right. She did need to know what was going on.

"Okay." She sighed heavily. "I don't want to, but let's go."

With Truman leading, Jo trailed after, steeling herself all the way.

The audible pitch of chants and rally cries reached her even before she rounded the corner on the main level. In the days preceding, a few voices could be heard as small groups gathered out front and waved their signs enthusiastically in the air. It also wasn't uncommon to overhear an exchange between the two different groups, who tended to congregate on opposing sidewalks. All of this had become what Jo saw as the new normal—people of Portland expressing their freedom of speech over the landmark's abrupt shutdown and the now-controversial existence of the Bruebaker Movement.

But today was noticeably different.

"What's all that noise?" Jo cocked her head, and she followed Truman toward the front of the store.

"People. Angry people," he said, still panting slightly. Jo tried to keep up with his long strides; her pulse quickened.

Suddenly Adam, Anna, Jade, and Grayson were also there, with expressions of concern.

"This isn't good," Adam said, coming to her side. His brow furrowed as he approached the windows and peered out.

Even before she could process what she was seeing, Jo understood the energy outside had largely shifted. It was as if a dry crackle of electricity floated through the air, ready to spark into something potentially dangerous at any moment.

Looking out, she surveyed both groups—the bookstore supporters and the protesters—which had multiplied overnight. Signs and fists jutted into the air in an angry rhythm, shouts and jeers propelling in all directions. Jo searched the crowd, struggling to understand how and why things had grown so out of control.

"What's going on?" she asked. Truman stood by and scratched his head. Jade hugged her middle and murmured in astonishment.

"We don't really know," Adam said. "I mean, yeah, word was

obviously starting to get out about activity down here. And one man from a small business—an electric bike shop, I think—was interviewed by the local news, expressing frustration over all the activity and his suffering business. Seems his front window was broken and merchandise was damaged. But this is madness. It's like everyone's had enough, and they are pushing back."

Jo scanned the signs.

NO MORE SPECIAL PRIVILEGES FOR BRUEBAKER'S!

SMALL-BUSINESS OWNERS DEMAND EQUAL RIGHTS!

MAYOR FINK STINKS!

On the perimeter of it all was a cluster of police, standing by as if they expected a ratcheting up of tension. Jo stepped back and swallowed. This wasn't at all what any of them wanted. And yet, it was happening anyway.

"What else did the bike guy say?"

"That the bookstore isn't the only valuable asset downtown, and why does his business have to suffer?"

"Was that it?"

Adam shook his head. "No. There's more. He kind of went on a tirade about the special privileges the city officials were giving to Bruebaker's because it was a status thing, and who did we think we were anyway, blah, blah, blah."

"Wow."

"Yeah," Adam said. "Totally unfair, if you ask me. Anyway, something switched, because all these people have now shown up to support one side or another. And, um, now suddenly we have cops."

A pit formed in Jo's gut. This brand of uprising was never her intention. Her focus had always been on preserving the store, being there for their book community, not making a political statement. She knew Adam, with all of his boisterous talk and article writing, had only hoped to inspire people, not make them angry. It was as if they had created a monster that insisted on growing, despite their good intentions.

Anna's phone buzzed in her pocket. Jo glanced over with a raised eyebrow. "Are you going to get that?" She wondered if the reporter from earlier might be reaching out once again. Anna was the group's point person for all things media.

"No." Anna shook her head. Jo noticed her color was rather pale, her shoulders high and tense around her ears. Something was off with her.

"What's the matter?" She inched closer to where Anna stood, lowering her voice. "Are you feeling all right?" A pulse of worry seized her.

"I'm fine." Anna kept her mouth tight. "It's just my parents. They won't stop calling."

"They're anxious about you being here." Jo understood. Anna wasn't sick. She was stressed out.

"Pretty much," she said. "I think they saw the news, and they want me gone. They just don't get it."

The news. The pit in Jo's stomach hardened as she scanned the outside scene once more. Sure enough, a cameraman and a reporter with a tall portable microphone stood at the corner, capturing the crowds.

Oh God, she thought. *Mr. Bruebaker.*

Jo was suddenly torn about where to first focus her attention. It was important to support Anna, to pull her aside and find out whether or not staying was going to jeopardize her situation at home. None of this was worth a rift among family members. But another part of Jo was breaking into a cold sweat over the idea of Mr. Bruebaker catching wind of the situation. Suzanne had been very explicit: Her father had stroked out due to stress over the store. Jo wasn't to upset him with more drama.

If Mr. Bruebaker caught a glimpse of a television news channel from his hospital bed, it would surely make his blood pressure skyrocket. The scene outside was exactly the kind of drama Suzanne was talking about—and then some.

Jo's entire body filled with pulsing dread.

At a loss for words, the team stood by the windows and watched. Truman was jingling his change again, and Adam kept dragging a hand over his face. Jo looked on with horror as someone hurled a water bottle into the crowd; another shouted back with a threatening fist. This was no longer about cheering on a handful of book nerds as they tried to save a store. Whatever this was had grown into something much bigger.

Jo had never wanted to turn back the clock so badly as she did in that moment. Her gaze traveled from the impatient-looking police to the raucous crowd across the street and then to the bookstore fans lining the sidewalk. Her mind raced in a dozen different directions, trying to determine the best course of action. She knew she was supposed to be in charge, to manage. But she had no idea whether to speak to the staff, the mayor's office, Regina, or Suzanne first. Each was equally important, equally urgent.

And that's when she saw him.

Jo's breath hitched as her eyes locked onto the one thing she couldn't control. Just to the right of the crowd was a tall, wiry body. There, peering into the windows with his hands cupped around his face, was the young man Jo recognized as Sierra's boyfriend, Casey. And by the way he was leering directly at her through the glass, Jo understood this guy was nothing but trouble.

"Where's Sierra?" Jo spun around, her heart hammering in her chest. How did Casey know to find them there? All of her uncertainty seemed to melt away as the fear took over.

"I think she's still upstairs with Rain. They were taking a break in the Beatrix Potter room."

"Don't do anything until I get back!" she shouted over her shoulder. Her feet carried her as fast as she could go, up the stairs and down the hallway to the children's section. All the while her mind continued to spin. Sierra hadn't somehow told him where she was going, had she? Would she jeopardize Rain's safety just when they'd found sanctuary? How else would Casey have found them?

"Sierra?" she called, entering. "Are you in here?"

Two blonde heads poked out from behind the early-readers display. The girls were on their hands and knees, a puppet fixed to each of their hands.

Sierra frowned. "What's up? Are you guys back to working again? We just thought everyone was taking a break."

Rain gripped her puppet and regarded Jo's panting with big eyes. Jo suddenly worried her news might startle the child.

"I need to speak with you in private," Jo said, trying her best to send a silent message. "Maybe Rain could stay here and play for a few minutes while you help me with something over there." She angled her head to the other side of the room and willed her heart to calm down.

"Yeah, sure." Sierra lifted from her crouched position and gestured for Rain to stay put. She followed Jo behind a set of narrow bookshelves and crossed her arms. Her wall was coming back up; it was clear by her rapidly hardening expression. Jo wondered if Sierra thought they might be asked to leave.

"I saw him," Jo blurted out, once she saw that Rain hadn't followed them.

"Who?"

"Casey. I saw him out on the sidewalk, trying to look into the store windows. Does he know you're in here?" Jo peered close, scrutinizing Sierra's reaction. It was important to know the truth. And while she didn't want to upset Sierra, it was also important to find out whether or not Casey was there to cause trouble.

Sierra blanched, her arms tightening. "No. God. No, I didn't tell him, if that's what you're asking. Me and Rain took off in the middle of the night. No one knew where we were going. *I* didn't even know where we were going until we got here. I promise."

Jo pursed her lips and studied Sierra's face. She didn't know this girl very well, but she could tell Sierra was being truthful.

What Jo had witnessed over the past couple of days was a scared mother who wanted to protect her daughter. Whatever hold Casey did or didn't have on her, it didn't seem like enough to make Sierra want to be found. That much was clear. Sierra even hinted at this late the night before, as she and Jo sat at the kitchen table watching Rain gobble up a bowl of cereal.

"Well . . ." Jo wavered. "It may have simply been the large crowd outside that drew him here. Maybe he was just curious about the commotion. Regardless, I'm uneasy about his sudden appearance. I think if you really don't want to see him, then you best keep out of sight."

"Yeah." Sierra looked down and toyed with a frayed edge of her sweatshirt. Jo didn't like the faraway feeling she was getting. Why hadn't Sierra looked her in the eye?

"Sierra? Am I wrong? Are you thinking you'll go back and find him?"

"He's not so bad, you know?"

"Who, Casey?" Jo asked.

"Yeah. He's not so bad. He took us in when we had nowhere to go. He accepted Rain as if she were his daughter . . . and let's face it. This bookstore thing isn't exactly permanent."

Jo swallowed. This wasn't what she expected to hear.

"Okay, I see." She pursed her lips. What could she do? "Well, I obviously want you and Rain to be safe. But it's also your life and not mine. As you know, the staff and I will be in a real pickle if it's found out we've let more people into the building. If you go back to him, I ask that you do it privately. I also ask that you two steer clear of the windows. At least for the afternoon. We'll just take it one day at a time and see what happens. Okay?"

"Okay." Sierra offered a tense smile and wandered back over to where Rain was quietly waiting.

Jo watched them for a minute before she went in search of the others. It was going to be a very long day.

Twenty-Nine

"Have you spoken with Mr. Bruebaker?" Jo couldn't take the silence any longer. After having witnessed enough of the agitated protesters and nervously paced the confines of her office for close to an hour, she finally broke down and phoned Regina. When she picked up after half a ring, Jo didn't bother with pleasantries. Being cut off from the outside world was taking its toll.

"Hello to you too," Regina answered. "No. I haven't spoken to Arnold." Her tone was measured, reserved. If Jo didn't know better, she'd say Regina was distancing herself from the store.

"But," Regina continued, "I have been in contact with Suzanne."

Ugh. Jo stifled a groan. *Of course you have.*

"She's not pleased, Jo."

"Well, none of us are, obviously. I was gutted to hear Mr. Bruebaker suffered another stroke."

"No, that's not what I mean," Regina countered. "Well, of course we were all saddened to learn about his episode. That's a given. But I also wasn't too surprised. I mean, he sounded so worn out the last time we spoke. It's no wonder all of the chaos at the store was too much for him to take. He's a frail man in his eighties, for goodness' sake."

"Uh-huh." Jo narrowed her eyes and squeezed her phone. Why did Regina have to act so condescending all the time, as if Jo hadn't a clue about the man she'd known for over twenty years? Besides, the Mr. Bruebaker she knew used to run circles around everyone else. Regina was making him out to be much more fragile than he was. Jo didn't like the direction the conversation was taking. "What are you referring to then? What's got Suzanne upset?"

"The mess downtown, of course! It's all over the news. Suzanne and her sister might not be overly involved with the family business, but they're horrified at the recent turn of events nonetheless. The girls are doing their best to keep this away from their father, but it's been tricky. He's not a willing patient, if you catch my drift."

Oh, I catch it all right. Jo seethed. How was it that Regina was simultaneously condemning things at the store and distancing herself from the business she was supposed to be running? Her passive-aggressive manner was more than Jo could bear. But then again, it had always been that way. It boiled Jo's blood to think of how Regina had sidled up to Suzanne and Jane so easily, making her out to be the bad guy in the whole scenario. If Mr. Bruebaker had anything to say about it, Jo knew he'd come to her defense.

She had to remind herself that he couldn't do this. Jo was on her own.

And yet, she and her team were making big sacrifices to preserve the integrity of the store. Without them, there would be nothing left.

"Yes, well. I understand Suzanne's desire to protect her father's health," Jo said. She did her best to ignore the blood pumping in her ears. None of these decisions were what Mr. Bruebaker would want. Someone had to stand up for him. "But

I don't see how keeping him in the dark is helpful. The store is his life's blood. He needs to feel connected. Otherwise, you might as well leave him in a room to wither away."

Regina was silent for a second. It was impossible to know what she was thinking.

Not willing to wait for a response, Jo plowed ahead. If she was going to go down, it may as well be in flames. "And this chaos, as you call it, with the store . . . well, I can assure you none of us here condone any of the protests or disturbances out on the streets. People are restless, and that's not our fault. Not everyone holding up a sign is angry with us, you know. A good lot of them are upset with the people who run this city."

Had Regina bothered to come down and see what was going on for herself, perhaps she'd agree with Jo's point. But it was as if the woman was trying to find ways to discredit the team's actions.

"That may be," Regina finally chimed in. "But remember, much of this started when you and your staff decided not only to defy orders and remain in the building but to go public with your actions. I can't say I didn't warn you, Jo. If you recall, I was the first one to show up to try and convince you otherwise. I had to shout through boarded-up doors, for goodness' sake. I suspected this thing would go south sooner or later. Turns out I was right."

What? Jo wanted to scream. This woman was too much. No doubt she'd repeated that same speech to Suzanne as well. It wouldn't come as a surprise to learn Regina was trying to get Jo fired even before this whole thing started. The two of them never saw eye to eye. Why would that change now?

"I need to go," Jo said. Her finger itched to press End. "One of my staff members is calling me." She didn't care if it was a lie. She couldn't stay on the phone with Regina any longer. If she did, Jo was pretty sure she might break something.

"Fine," Regina said. "But we're not done here. Let's talk again first thing in the morning. I have a call with Sam Turnbull at 8:00 a.m. I'll ring you after that."

"Fine." Jo hung up before she heard any more. Shoving her phone into a drawer, she stomped upstairs in search of Adam. She very much hoped he'd kept the stash of Jack and Leo's beers. Because all she wanted to do at the moment was numb her brain. She needed Regina all the way out of her head.

"Tell me what's really going on with your parents." Jo sat across from Anna in the break room, her feet kicked up onto a chair, the arches of her socked feet aching. An icy beer bottle was in one hand, and two others sat empty on the table between them. As tired as she was, Jo was enjoying the late-night chat with Anna. Thankfully the streets had cleared out for the evening. A bit of calm was restored. The others had gone off in search of sleep an hour earlier. The two women took their time, draining their beers and reflecting on the insanity of the day.

"Oh, I don't know." Anna swallowed her sip and sighed. "They're just unhappy."

Jo shook her head. "No, you do know. These are your parents. Tell me what they're saying to you. I can tell by the way your phone's been blowing up that they aren't going to let this thing lie."

Jo could tell Anna had been conflicted all day. Her employee's otherwise sharp and organized attitude had been distracted, to say the least. With each hour that passed and with each buzz of her phone, Anna seemed to almost shrink with defeat. She'd excuse herself to go listen to her voice mails and then return minutes later, somehow smaller. Jo found herself relating. Anna's rounded shoulders and hunched frame mirrored exactly how Jo felt after a conversation with Regina.

It was one thing for the company's executive to question the employees, but quite another for Anna's own parents to make her feel insecure. Anna was an incredible young lady, and she deserved to feel supported. Or maybe Jo was jumping to conclusions. Perhaps Anna's parents saw the news, and the story of the near rioting outside the store caused them to worry for their daughter's safety.

Jo pursed her lips. In any other circumstance, Jo might not insert herself into the workers' personal lives. But this was no normal circumstance. And so she pressed Anna for details.

Anna set down her drink. She grabbed a rubber band from around her thin wrist and fixed her hair into a low ponytail. Looking at her just then, her serious face weary, Jo had a flash of what Anna might be like as the doctor her parents wanted her to become. She'd be hardworking and methodical—all the things she was in the store—and whether her heart was in it or not, Anna would likely give it her professional all.

"Well, for one thing," Anna said, "they've always considered my job at the bookstore a big distraction. I mean, they're glad I'm making money. And I suppose they'd be more horrified if I slung drinks in a bar. I mean, at least here I'm surrounded by literature. What academic-minded parents can argue with books, right?" Her easy laugh was laced with sadness.

"Right." Jo felt her heart crack a little as she tried to return the smile.

"My parents have worked very hard to get where they are in life. My dad has three degrees, for God's sake. And my mom worked in a lab until she got pregnant with me—she likes to bring this up whenever we argue—and she put her career aspirations on hold to raise her two girls. Because of this, there's a lot of pressure. They want my sister, Lucy, and me to be successful professionals. Preferably in the science and medical fields. The fact that I've taken an unplanned and unapproved path toward social activism, of all things, has sent them over the edge. Like, big-time."

Jo leaned back and considered this. This thoughtful young lady sharing her personal struggle with her family brought up a fresh wave of compassion. Anna had been holding on to a lot of stress. She was juggling what sounded like an impossible balance of her parents' wishes and her own happiness for too long. And all the while, Anna was doing her best to be the perfect daughter and the perfect employee. No doubt she'd also put the same effort into being a premed student as well. It was enough to make anyone fold.

Jo recalled the stress she'd been under as a young adult, trying to form a plan and make her life work. In a way, parts of Anna's current struggle mirrored her younger self. But Anna had family. Jo wanted to encourage her to lean on them, even if that meant allowing vulnerability.

"What about your younger sister? Is she held to the same gold standard that you are?"

"Lucy?" Anna put her chin in her hand as she thought about this. "Yes and no. I mean, she's the baby, so she gets away with more. There's a certain leniency allowed for her that isn't for me. That's for sure. She got to go to parties and homecoming with a boy in high school. That never happened with me."

"Because you weren't allowed?"

"Yes, and probably because it just wasn't encouraged. My parents wanted me to focus on my academics, not my social life. Plus, I was probably too scared anyway. With Lucy, it's different.

She has this fearlessness about her. She's not afraid to take a risk, to fail. If I'm honest, I guess I've always been kind of jealous in that regard. It's stupid, I know. But that's just how I feel. Does that make any sense?"

"It makes perfect sense." Jo slid a hand across the table and patted Anna's arm. "But I've got news for you."

"What?"

"You, my friend, are taking the ultimate risk right now. You're smack in the middle of a nationwide news story because you're standing up and protecting something that's important to you—to the entire literary community—and city officials and protesters be damned. You're in this thing. You represent the Bruebaker Movement!" Jo raised her beer bottle in the air.

Anna grinned and snatched up her drink. The two women clinked bottles and exchanged a laugh. "Wow, I guess you're right. That is pretty risky of me."

"Damn straight it is." Jo was beginning to feel the effects of multiple beers. Her head was growing fuzzy, and her insides were warm. But mostly, she was buzzing because of her admiration for Anna. Whatever happened in the days to come—whether Anna eventually decided to stay or go—Jo would be forever grateful. She was lucky to work with such an incredible human being. And more than that, Jo was fortunate enough to call her a friend.

"Jo?"

"Hmm?"

"I just wanted to say I think it's pretty cool what you're doing for Sierra and Rain. A lot of people talk about wanting to make a difference, but they never really get around to it. I know Adam feels the same way. You actually listened to his idea about saving the store, and you supported it, even if it meant taking a big risk and breaking the rules. I really like that about you. We all do."

Jo felt a lump rising in her throat. She knew the employees liked their jobs, but she hadn't stopped to consider whether they liked her. Well, maybe she had on a professional level, but not like this. "Wow, thank you, Anna. That's very nice."

"You're welcome."

The two sipped their drinks. Jo realized she wouldn't trade her time in the lockdown for anything. She was glad to know the others felt the same way.

Thirty

The next morning, Jo woke in a haze. She and Anna had knocked off more beers than she was used to drinking, and Jo was beginning to regret her lack of restraint. The clock on her phone read 6:15 a.m., and only the smallest sliver of light bled through the window shades. Rubbing at her eyes, she scanned the dim room. Most everyone was asleep except for Sierra and Rain. The sight of two vacant sleeping mats in the corner of the room raised a flag of concern. It was still awfully early for anyone to be awake.

Were they already busy working?

Sitting upright, she felt around for her sweater. Mornings were always chilly inside the vast rooms. Jo liked to warm up her muscles as best she could before getting to work. Her joints were getting stiffer by the day. Lifting books and boxes was taking its toll on her body. And so was the unforgiving floor. If she was honest, she wasn't sure how much longer her body could handle the accommodations.

As she pulled her cardigan around her shoulders, her nose wrinkled. A sour odor wafted up from the fabric under the arms. After nearly three weeks, despite her clumsy hand-washing in the bathroom sink, Jo's clothes were holding their smell. She hoped the others hadn't noticed, but whom was she kidding? They all smelled.

Making her way downstairs, she checked the break room and then her office. Only empty darkness stared back at her. Sierra and Rain were nowhere in sight.

Darn it! She wasn't a fool; she hadn't expected the pair to stay in the building forever. She hardly knew anything about them, really. Maybe they were just nomads at heart, content to stay on the move. Or maybe they viewed a bookstore full of strangers, all sleeping, eating, and working together like some kind of literary commune, too bizarre. Perhaps Sierra and Rain weren't as comfortable in their temporary shelter as Jo thought.

And yet, Sierra had become quite nervous when she learned Casey had been lurking outside the building. Jo was so sure the mother and daughter wanted to stay hidden from sight.

But now she wasn't sure of anything.

Flipping on all of the lights in her office, Jo scanned her desk for a note. She stuck her head into the bathroom, searching for their belongings, and frowned.

Well, that's puzzling.

Sierra's backpack was gone, and so was Rain's jacket. But a sweatshirt and one of Rain's doll-sized T-shirts were folded over a stool. Had they left in such a hurry that the clothes were simply forgotten? Or were they planning to return? Deciding to confirm her suspicion, Jo wound her way through the rest of the building. Maybe they'd just been up early and were keeping themselves occupied by exploring.

After she had examined each of the book rooms, Jo slumped. The two girls weren't anywhere in sight. She had to face the idea that they might not be coming back. Disheartened, she made her way to the break room to start her usual routine of making coffee and scrounging up breakfast. There was nothing left to do but go back to work.

Plus, there were other concerns pulling at her. In a few short hours she was scheduled to finish her chat with Regina. No doubt there'd be some kind of negative feedback from the mayor's office. Jo needed to prepare herself should she get bad news. And then there was the frustrating fact that Suzanne wasn't responding to her messages. It had been days since her last update, and Jo had no idea how Mr. Bruebaker was doing. She'd already tossed and turned half the night, fighting off bad dreams about his well-being. If nothing else, Jo just needed to know he was all right.

"Sleep okay?" Truman entered the kitchen and plucked his regular coffee mug from the pile of washed dishes. Jo noticed that even with his graying blond hair standing on end and a face full of day-old stubble, he still managed to be his charming, rugged self. She envied this about men. They could get away with bed head and sleep lines, whereas women her age could not.

Using a palm to smooth her frizzed hair, she tried to hide her embarrassment. Perhaps she should have at least brushed her teeth or splashed some water on her face. "Hi. Good morning to you. No, I can't say I've slept well in a while. You?"

"Nah, me neither. That Grayson is a rough sleeper. Who knew a kid so young and slender could make such a terrible racket when he sleeps? Talk about snoring!"

Jo chuckled. Though she'd kept her mat on the fringe of the carpeting, away from the others, in an effort to get some quiet, she had heard the noises coming from Grayson's side of the room.

"The other two around here somewhere as well?" Truman asked, his head swiveling around the room. "They must've heard the snoring too."

"No." Jo's smile dropped. "I'm afraid they left."

"Sierra and Rain left? For good?"

"I don't know. It doesn't make much sense. Yesterday we

talked about the need to stay hidden from sight, and then this
morning, poof! They're gone. Most of their stuff is gone too, save
for a few articles of clothing in my office. I can't figure it out. But
then again, I can't say I knew them all that well either. It's hard to
say."

She sat down, her head bent low over her coffee. The reality
of the day was beginning to weigh heavy on her. Truman came to
sit beside her, his cup pushing onto the table. Jo placed her head
in her hands and watched the hot steam rising from the brim.

"Hang on a second," Truman said. "What do you mean about
'staying hidden from sight'? That doesn't sound good."

Jo sighed. She hadn't told the others about seeing Casey or
the fact she suspected he might be a danger to Sierra and her
daughter. She thought she was doing the right thing by protecting Sierra's privacy. But looking at Truman's confused expression
now, Jo realized this might have been the wrong decision.

"I didn't say anything at the time, but I saw Sierra's boyfriend
out on the street yesterday."

"Okay . . ."

"And while Sierra hasn't actually confirmed it, I'm pretty
sure he's the one responsible for her bruises. I've seen him once
before, and there's something very hardened about him. He has
an edge. Anyway, Sierra made it sound like no one knew where
she was. And then this guy's face is suddenly staring into the
windows. I didn't get a good feeling. So I told Sierra to stay out of
sight."

"And now she's gone."

"Yes."

Truman forced air from his nose and worked his jaw. Jo
couldn't tell if he was concerned for Sierra's safety or if he was
upset she had kept this kind of information from him. If someone

dangerous was hanging around the building, it impacted all of them. Once again, Jo had made a decision alone instead of involving the group.

"I didn't say anything because I didn't want to cause unnecessary stress," she continued, hoping to make him see her side. "Plus, I don't even know if this Casey guy was hanging around here because of Sierra. He could've just seen the crowds and the commotion and been curious. For all I know, the entire thing could've been one big coincidence."

"Yes, but you should have come and confided in me. I can understand you didn't want to upset the rest of the staff. Yesterday was dramatic enough as it was. I'm pretty sure it unnerved Adam to see so many angry faces in the crowd. The poor kid has been beating himself up about it. I think he expected nothing but rounds of 'Kumbaya' from the locals. He assumed the only pushback would be from city officials."

"I know. I saw the look on his face."

"But, Jo," he continued, "I could've handled the situation. I feel just as responsible for this place as you." Truman waved his arm. "If there's some kind of threat out there—other than the ones we already know about—you need to tell me. We're a team. I've got your back. But only if you let me."

Jo blinked. She didn't know what to say. Heat filled her cheeks as a mixture of shock and embarrassment swept over her. *Truman had her back.*

Here was a man who was kind and supportive and willing to take on the growing burden right alongside her. And yet Jo hadn't given him the opportunity to do this. Why? Had she been operating on her own for so long that she'd forgotten what it was like to rely on someone other than herself? She silently sipped her coffee and willed her face to stop burning.

After Michael left, Jo had pretty much given up on the idea of getting close to someone again. If she really thought about it, she supposed over the years she'd placed more importance on the store than actual people.

Now, sitting there with Truman, Jo understood how much she'd held him at arm's length. It was one thing for him to comfort her during a weepy breakdown; they were confined to the same building day after day. But, Jo realized, it was an entirely other thing to *rely* on someone else. Looking back, Truman's efforts to share the burden of responsibility with her had been rebuffed.

The shame in her flared.

Maybe she was more stuck in her ways than she understood.

"You're absolutely right. I should've come to you. I guess I was caught between trying to protect Sierra's privacy and, well, my own stubborn pride of thinking I could handle everything all by myself. I've just gotten used to only relying on myself for so long. Please don't take me not trusting you as anything personal. It's my own hang-up. Truly. And, for the record, I'm grateful for your support. Really, I am. I hope you know that."

As soon as the words left her mouth, Jo felt like she could breathe again. It was good to get it off her chest, to let him know she was sorry and hoped to do better. This was becoming a running theme for her, and yet she kept tripping on her own feet anyway.

"I do know it. I'm not upset, just a little stung maybe."

This was the first time Truman admitted his feelings had gotten in the way. Jo was a little taken aback at the admission. And she was also endeared. This man continued to surprise her.

"Here's to doing better." Jo swung her coffee mug in the air.

Truman did the same.

Thirty-One

*D*espite the good feeling that accompanied Jo after her heart-to-heart with Truman, nothing prepared her for the onslaught of bad news that followed. After a dismal call with Regina over Sam Turnbull's rising unhappiness with Bruebaker's, an unsuccessful scouring of the alleyway for Sierra and Rain, and an announcement from Anna that the food supply was officially dwindling into nothing, Jo found herself confronted with the reality of their situation.

Reaching for her phone, she held her breath and punched out a text to Suzanne, asking once again if she might be able to speak to her father. Surprisingly, three dots appeared in response:

Suzanne: Maybe a bit later.

Jo: Okay. Thank you.

Jo closed her eyes. It wasn't much, but it was something. She'd get through the morning and then circle back around with Suzanne later in the day. Nothing would bring her more relief than to hear her boss's voice, finally. However brief the connection might be, Jo would gladly take it.

At noon, over a meal of runny peanut butter and stale rice cakes, Jo gathered the group for a briefing. Bleary from another restless night of thin sleeping mats and growing concerns, Anna, Jade, Grayson, and Adam wandered into the kitchen with dull expressions. The lack of creature comforts was getting to everyone—and so was the lack of laundry facilities. Jo thought if an outsider could see them now, they'd think them a ragtag bunch of workers that resembled nothing of the bright and engaging employees normally found inside the bookstore.

She doubted they could keep this up much longer.

"Well, do you want the good news or bad news first?" She decided it was best to be frank. They'd gone through too much together for her to sugarcoat the facts.

"The good news," Grayson piped up. In spite of her weariness, Jo couldn't help but grin at the way he sidled up to his plate and slathered on peanut butter with gusto. Clearly, the diminishing conditions weren't enough to kill Grayson's appetite.

"Okay, so the good news is we still haven't been shut down. The mayor's office did say us vacating the building is unavoidable, but not today. They want to focus on their messaging first. It's all a political show apparently."

"What a joke. So what's the bad news then?" Adam folded his arms, an invisible shield dropping down. Jo had noticed a shift in him lately. It was as if a small light was slowly being extinguished. She suspected the turn of events on the street had everything to do with it.

"The bad news is that the contention outside is growing. You've all seen how many people showed up yesterday. And I expect more this afternoon. I've been told the police presence could ramp up because of it. This isn't something any of us wanted. Crowds are multiplying. If things get ugly, we could be held responsible."

The group emitted a collective grumble.

"Seriously? We can't control what goes on out there."

"Yeah, I mean half of those people protesting out there own businesses in the area. Why aren't they being held accountable too?"

Jo shrugged. "I don't know. Maybe they will be. But we've been warned. I think the mayor's office is hoping we'll give up the ghost and go home voluntarily before he has to force us out. That way, he doesn't look like the bad guy."

"Too late," Adam grumbled.

Jade's hand went up in the back of the room.

"Yes, Jade?"

"Um, I was just wondering—where are Sierra and Rain?"

Jo's gaze flicked over to Truman, who'd just entered the room with extra bottles of cleaning spray. Setting the box down, he cast Jo a look that said she might as well tell the truth.

"I'm afraid they've left."

"Really?" Anna raised a brow. "They seemed like they were relieved to be here, the last time I talked to them. Rain was really liking her stay in the Beatrix Potter room."

Jo sighed. "I know. I think Sierra was too. But for some reason, when I woke up this morning, they were gone."

"Where'd they go?"

A heaviness returned and settled on Jo's chest. She'd done her best to compartmentalize her worry over the girls for the time being. After all, Regina had taken up a lot of her energy that morning. But now as she faced the group's questions, Jo felt the despair leaking back out from its hiding place. What could she do? She obviously couldn't contact the authorities. Sierra might get into trouble for not properly housing her small child. Jo could get into trouble too. As far as any outsiders knew,

Jo was keeping her promise not to let anyone inside the building.

Still, Jo couldn't help but feel the disappearance of Sierra and Rain was somehow a failure on her part. Perhaps she should've kept the news about spotting Casey to herself. Maybe that guy, no matter how bad, was Sierra's only sense of family. Jo understood all too well the dull ache that took over when she no longer had her own parents. It was like living with a hole in her heart. If it wasn't for Mr. Bruebaker and the bookstore, Jo didn't know what other ways she might have sought to soothe her emptiness.

Sierra, it seemed, was attempting to fill that void with Casey.

Suddenly Adam stood. He frowned and cocked an ear. "Do you guys hear that?"

A faint knocking was coming from the front room.

Sierra! Jo thought, jogging past the registers. Before she could even discover whose face was on the other side of the glass windows, a warm trickle of relief poured through her.

When she got to the front entrance, however, all of Jo's good feelings drained away. "Who's that?"

A compact young woman, with a pretty face and long dark hair hoisted high on her head, was peering inside. She seemed to be around the same age as Jade and Grayson, just barely out of high school. Perhaps she was a friend of theirs coming to deliver food or fresh clothes. Still, it was unusual for visitors to come to the store alone, given the recent uptick in activity. Even Adam's roommates always made sure to come in pairs when delivering meals from the pub.

As Jo got closer, she knew she'd never seen this person before, and yet there was something strikingly familiar about her all the same. The others seemed equally confused as they looked from one to another, asking if anyone knew her.

It wasn't until Anna walked up that Jo understood.

"That's Lucy," she said. "She's my little sister."

Ah.

"What's she doing here?" Adam folded his arms in his usual stance, suspicion creeping over his face.

"I don't know." Just as Jo had done with Regina, Anna pulled out her phone and dialed. The two of them moved closer to the window and stared at one another.

"Lu, what are you doing here?"

Jo squinted her eyes and tried to read the girl's lips. She thought she could make out a muffled "I came to see you."

"Do Mom and Dad know you're here?"

Lucy shook her head.

Anna turned to the group, her hand over the phone. "Um, guys? Can you give us a minute?"

"Oh!" Jo stepped back, suddenly embarrassed. "Sorry, of course. We'll just go back to work." Then, turning to the rest of them, she shooed the air. "You heard Anna—let's give her and her sister some space. Everyone back to work."

They all inched away with a bit of reluctance. Only Adam lingered the longest, studying Anna's sister with a slight expression of distrust. His arms remained locked tight across his chest even as he turned and walked away. Jo wondered why he was acting so protective all of a sudden. Was he merely concerned about letting people into the store, or was it perhaps more than that? Maybe he was protective over Anna.

Jo wondered how much about her personal life he actually knew.

"Come on, Adam. I could use your help in the fiction section. Jade and I have old inventory that needs to go back down to the basement. Without Sierra, we're down a man." She patted him on his back, noticing his tense muscles.

"Yeah." He finally broke his annoyed gaze and met Jo with a nod. "That's fine. I can help you. Let me just tell Grayson."

Thank goodness I can rely on these guys. Jo watched his back as he caught up to Grayson's loping strides, and the two began chatting in voices too low for her to make out. They peeled off from the group and climbed the stairs, and it dawned on Jo how much she'd learned to trust the members of her staff. Adam and Grayson were so much more than a wannabe anarchist and a directionless millennial with an affinity for vintage T-shirts. This was made clear early on. But her understanding of this ran deeper now. These were young men of substance and intelligence and, most of all, heart.

The guilt of misjudging them hung like a dark cloud.

Adam clearly had a natural ability for leadership and vision, and Grayson offered selflessness and a yearning to try new things. It was remarkable that she'd not noticed any of this before the movement began. This crazy experiment of theirs was turning into so much more than Jo could have ever imagined.

She made a mental note to tell Adam and Grayson how much she valued them. It wasn't something she did enough of. They deserved to hear it.

This thought carried her up to the second floor and back to where she and Jade continued working their way through the most recent orders. At least this activity kept her spinning mind busy. While the fates of Sierra and Rain were a gnawing concern, Jo could at least do her best to focus on what little she could control.

And for the moment, that was still a lot.

Thirty-Two

The second Anna came upstairs, Jo watched Adam slide over with a face full of curiosity.

"So what'd she want?" he asked. His gaze traveled over her shoulder, as if he half expected Anna to have let her sister inside.

Anna's expression darkened, her arms hanging limply at her sides. Jo waited for her to answer. Whatever Lucy said to her had knocked Anna sideways. Jo could sense it.

"She wants me to come home."

Adam snorted.

"Because she's worried about you?" Jo asked.

"Yes. I mean no. I don't know." Anna sagged against a display of thrillers and pushed a few paperbacks to the side. Jo wanted to remind her not to mess up the shelves. But she held her tongue when Anna hugged her middle and continued.

"Lucy is the baby of the family, and she's used to a kind of freedom I was never allowed. With me gone now, my parents have nothing to focus on but her. And apparently, she doesn't like it. It's funny," Anna said, her voice drifting off.

"What is?"

"I've always been kind of jealous of her. Lucy gets to do whatever she wants, and she never gets into trouble. If she stays out late or drops a class, my parents tend to look the other way. My dad chalks it all up to Lucy being an 'artist,'" she said, hooking her fingers in the air. "Which, I mean, she's not. But for me, it's always been different. I'm held to a higher standard. It's totally stupid. And now that I'm doing something my parents consider radical, Lucy is suddenly jealous. That's why she wants me to come home. It's like she doesn't want me to be happy or something."

"Man, that's uncool." Adam's tone softened. "My brother and I fight sometimes, but he's pretty chill in the grand scheme of things. I can't imagine him not wanting me to be happy."

Anna's shoulders seemed to sink even further. "Yeah, well. Lucy's pretty self-centered."

"I'm sorry, Anna," Jo stepped forward, wanting to console her. "You don't deserve that. You deserve happiness. But I have to ask, are you happy remaining here? Because if you're not, please know it's okay if you want to go. I'd completely understand if you're worried about friction with your parents."

"Yeah, totally," Adam chimed in. "I mean, we want you here, but if you need to go, that's totally okay."

Jo nodded. She could tell it took a lot of self-control for Adam to swallow his passion for the movement and instead put Anna's well-being first. He clearly wanted her there just as much as all of them did. Anna was a vital member of their team. But her home life was feeling the stress. It wasn't fair to ignore that.

"Thanks. That means a lot. I want to be here, but honestly I need to process everything for a minute. Jo, is it okay if I go for a walk?"

"Yes, of course." She hesitated. "But I recommend you steer clear of the streets out front. Take the side door leading into the alley. Be careful, and please keep your phone with you in case you can't get back in. Do you want Adam to go with you? Maybe you shouldn't be alone."

Jo was not keen on any of her staff wandering around outside at the moment. Not only was there still a potential problem in the form of Casey possibly reappearing, but also the protests were drawing opposing factions. Thankfully everything so far had remained fairly peaceful. The last thing she wanted, however, was for Anna to get caught up in a scuffle. Yet she understood the need to get fresh air and clear one's head. Being locked up in the building day after day was making them all feel cagey.

To her relief, Anna agreed.

"Sure, why not? Adam?"

Adam straightened; his need to feel of service was clearly renewed. "Yeah, sure. I'll meet you downstairs in five."

When Jo heard the voices of Adam and Anna returning nearly an hour later, she relaxed. The scene in front of the store had once again escalated, and she'd begun to worry Adam might not be able to control his urge to confront some of the protesters. She'd even gone as far as to ask Truman if he might keep an eye out until the two of them returned. Jo couldn't do it herself. Every time she went downstairs to view the swelling crowd, her heart palpitated at an uncomfortable rate. The whole thing made her terribly uneasy.

Jo's relief quickly morphed into surprise when she saw that Adam and Anna weren't alone. There, standing beside them, were Sierra and Rain.

"Oh, you're back," Jo exclaimed. She snatched off her eyeglasses and went over to greet them. "What happened? Is everything all right?"

"We ran into them as we were heading back to the building," Adam said. His hand went to the back of his neck, his voice a bit hesitant. "I, um, assumed you'd want them to come back inside.

You know, for everyone's safety." His eyes flicked to Sierra's neck. Jo followed his gaze in horror to discover a nasty bruise the size of someone's hand. She sucked in her breath.

Sierra contracted, her fingers tightening around the drawstring of her dirty sweatshirt. Jo watched her jaw set.

"Yes, of course." She nodded a silent thanks to Adam. He'd done the right thing by ushering Sierra and Rain inside. Jo knelt down to Rain's level. She smelled of unwashed hair and something sticky. The hooded eyes had returned. Something inside Jo boiled.

"Why don't we go into the kitchen? It feels like the right time for an afternoon snack. Would you like that, Rain?" She wondered if Adam and Anna had to convince them to return or if they'd already been on their way back. She planned to pull Adam aside and get the details later. But for now, she wanted to make sure both girls were all right.

"Okay," Rain said, reaching for her mother's hand. Jo's heart broke. Even her voice was weary.

Adam and Anna took the hint and muttered something about needing to go find Grayson. The two of them disappeared while Jo and the others made their way to the break room.

After two cups of tea and a mug of watery hot chocolate had been placed onto the table, Jo began. "So are you going to tell me what's really going on?"

Sierra pulled the cup closer and blew into her tea half-heartedly. *She's buying time*, Jo thought. Time to change tactics.

"Rain, honey. Where did you go today?"

"Don't answer that, Rain," Sierra snapped.

Jo flinched. She hadn't heard her lose her temper with Rain before. Was she seeing the real Sierra? It was difficult to tell. They'd only spent a small amount of time together up until then. In the past two days, Sierra had been a bit on the quiet side, her mouth serious and her expression guarded. And as far as Jo could tell, there hadn't been any signs of drug or alcohol use or any kind of mental health red flags. If anything, Sierra had been fairly helpful and easygoing. She'd offered to clean the store, and she hadn't any qualms about the sleeping arrangements. She was mindful to look after her little girl. All in all, Jo would say she'd been nothing but amenable.

This was different.

The Sierra that sat across from her now was tired and agitated. She'd disappeared for the better half of the day only to return with a hangdog-looking daughter and her own body showing signs of physical abuse. Sitting there, waiting for an answer, Jo felt herself wavering between concern and anger. She was too old and too busy to be lied to. If Sierra didn't want to be honest or be helped, then Jo wasn't going to push her. Plenty of other pressing needs were waiting in the wings for Jo to address: Mr. Bruebaker's health, the fate of the store and its employees, the mounting unrest she and her staff had unintentionally attracted. Any combination of these things was enough to keep Jo up at night. Adding Sierra and Rain to the mix was only a fraction of her concerns.

Keeping her tone even, Jo tried again. "Here's the deal, Sierra," she said. "You have a choice to make. You can either choose to trust me so that I can properly help you, or you can keep on going the way you are and move back out onto the street. But there's no middle ground. I've got too much going on around here to try and guess at what it is you need. And I don't stand for half-truths. Either way is risky. I get that. There are probably repercussions if you tell me the truth of your circumstances, and there are most assuredly repercussions if you don't. I'll leave it up to you. But I urge you to look into your little girl's face and ask yourself if she deserves this kind of life. Because from where I stand, she doesn't. Neither of you do."

When she was done, Jo knocked on the table once and exited the room. It was up to Sierra to figure it out. Jo had other people who needed her too. She told herself whatever was meant to be would work out. In the meantime, she wanted to make some calls and check on the other person who was breaking her heart.

She headed into her office to check on Mr. Bruebaker.

"Suzanne?" she asked, praying she'd chosen the right time. "I'm calling to find out how your dad is doing. Any update?"

"Oh yes. Hello, Joanna."

Is it really so hard to call me Jo? She rolled her eyes. It was always as if Suzanne never intended for them to become friends, like every conversation might be their last.

"Dad's okay, considering. He's resting. A physical therapist is scheduled to do a visit later. This whole thing has made specialty doctor visits necessary. This woman comes recommended from the hospital, so we'll see. Dad still seems to have considerable weakness on one side. It's slowed his cognition way down. We'd obviously like to remedy this."

"I'd really like to say hello. I don't want him to think I haven't been checking in on him." *I'm feeling overwhelmed, and every day you keep him from me, I slip farther and farther under water. I'm adrift over here and don't know how to do any of this without my boss!*

Suzanne's response was automatic. "I can tell him you called."

"Can't I tell him myself?" She tried to keep her voice from cracking.

"I'm sorry—we're really trying to limit his visits and calls. Any undue stress could be a potential setback to his health. He's not in a strong enough position to take on all of the, you know, *drama* of the bookstore right now. But," she added with an uptick in her voice that rang of falseness, "I'm sure he'll be happy to hear that you checked in."

Jo felt her chin tremble. She'd hedged her bets and had been wrong. Suzanne had no intention of ever letting Jo speak with her father. How naive she'd been to think otherwise.

What else could she say?

"Suzanne." She straightened in her chair, fortifying her last shred of dignity. "He's still the owner of this business. Don't you think he has a right to know what's going on? At the end of the day, he's still my boss."

"No, Joanna," Suzanne replied.

"It's Jo," she said.

A huff could be heard. "Fine, Jo. Actually, Regina Anderson is your boss. She's the one in charge. And if I'm not mistaken, despite the fact you're still pulling in sales, she's the one cleaning up your mess of an incoming lawsuit and hot water with the mayor's office. So if you have any future concerns, you can take them up with her directly. But I'll tell Dad you send your best. Bye."

Thirty-Three

*B*y the time dinner rolled around, Jo was a puddle. After her defeating call with Suzanne, followed up by a terse exchange with Regina that got her absolutely nowhere, Jo locked her office door and allowed herself to cry softly into her sleeve. Her entire day held the feeling of swimming upstream against an angry current. First it was the tenuous situation with Sierra, then Suzanne, and finally Regina. Weren't they living in the age of women sticking together? She'd certainly seen enough self-help books flood into the store, with titles like *The Moment of Lift* and *Daring Greatly*, touting female empowerment and the brave act of vulnerability in an effort to be one's best self. And yet it was women with whom she'd been battling all day.

It was all too depressing.

When she was done feeling sorry for herself, Jo trudged upstairs in search of the tea she'd abandoned. Instead, she found a fidgety Sierra.

"What's up?" Jo asked wearily. She could tell the girl had something on her mind by the way she was pacing the floor. "Where's Rain?"

"She's up in the children's room with Jade. They're reading a book together."

Jo brightened. That was a first. Previously, the only things that seemed to interest Rain were everything except the books. *Good for Jade.*

"I'm going to reheat my tea. Want to come?"

"Sure."

Sierra followed behind, her sneakers scuffing on the cement floors. Jo guessed she must be tired. They'd both had a difficult day. The bruise on Sierra's neck showed as much. And while Sierra's injury was visible on the outside, Jo felt she was bruised on the inside. Both of them, she suspected, were feeling tender.

She waited for Sierra to speak first.

"I wanted to explain," Sierra finally said, lowering into a chair while Jo worked the microwave.

"Go ahead."

"Well, when you told me you saw Casey out there, looking through the windows and being a creeper—"

"I didn't say he was doing anything suspicious. I merely wanted you to know he was out there." Jo could feel the sour guilt of starting another drama coming on. Had her warning to Sierra been the reason this girl had gone out and gotten into trouble?

"I know. Casey's good at finding me, at finding us. I don't know how he does it, but he always tracks us down. Anyway, I needed a minute away from him, and he knew that. But there he was anyway, lurking around. I got worried. You and the others have been so nice to Rain and me. You didn't have to, but you let us hang out here without hassle. The last thing I wanted was for Casey to cause trouble. So that's why I left."

Jo stood with her back to the counter. She studied Sierra, considering her admission. "So you went back to Casey because it was easier? Otherwise he'd just 'cause trouble,' as you call it, and find you anyway?"

Sierra chewed her lip. "Not exactly. I went back to tell him to keep away from us and the bookstore and to give me time to think. I thought if I could explain, if I could make him understand that you all have nothing to do with me running off, then he'd stay away."

"But, Sierra . . ." Jo frowned. "Weren't you afraid he'd hurt you again? It's obvious he did. I'm not a fool. I can see your neck. Why did you put yourself in harm's way?"

"Because it was better me than you." Sierra's voice dipped, and her eyes went to her shoes. In that instant, Jo felt her insides split open to reveal a rawness she never knew existed.

"Oh, honey," she said, coming over to sit beside Sierra. It was too much. Sierra hadn't snapped at her daughter because she was mean; she'd done it because she was in pain. She'd acted selflessly, putting her body in danger to protect everyone else. A surge of compassion rose up and engulfed Jo. Without thinking, she leaned over and wrapped Sierra into a tight hug.

Sierra's limbs froze, clearly not used to this kind of intimacy from strangers. After a minute, Jo felt her muscles ease and her rigid torso go slack. With one arm, she reached around and returned the embrace.

This was how Truman found them, huddled in the bright kitchen, sniffling and holding one another. He caught Jo's eye to make sure she was okay. Jo nodded. She was.

That night as everyone was making his or her way to bed, Jo discovered Rain tugging the end of her mat with frustration.

"Hi there," she said, coming over to where the little girl stood. Jo noticed the holes in her cartoon-printed socks and wondered if they were her only pair.

"Hi," Rain said, pushing wisps of hair from her flushed face.

"Need some help?"

Rain nodded. She stepped back and pointed at the floor. Jo told her she understood and took over the task. Securing the mat in her hands, she began dragging it across the carpeting. She had to pick her feet up to avoid the collection of clothes and books that lay scattered around, evidence of so many people sharing the small space as they slept.

"Where to?" She assumed Rain wanted more privacy, to get away from the loud snores and strange faces that felt too close in the night. To her surprise, however, Rain gestured near the window.

"Can I sleep by Jade?"

"Of course you can." Jo smiled, trying to conceal her shock. Just as the little girl instructed, she moved the mat so that it was practically touching Jade's sleeping area. She looked on as Rain crouched down, fixing her pillow just so, fluffing it once and then moving to adjust Jade's with care. When she was finished, their pillows were nestled side by side, their blankets pulled taut to make it look like one giant bed.

"Wow, that looks comfy." Jo winked at her.

"Uh-huh." Rain seemed pleased with her work as she fussed with the corners and made sure the mats lined up just so. "Jade's gonna read to me tonight. She told me."

"I see." Jo's heart swelled. Beautiful, sweet Jade had magically pulled off what no one else could. She'd managed to get a child—who previously expressed zero interest in any of the hundreds of available books—excited at the prospect of a new story. Jo would hug her if she was around, but Jade had wandered off to brush her teeth in the upstairs bathroom.

"What do you think she'll read? Have you two picked out a book yet?"

Rain held up a finger and marched over to a low bookshelf. Her small face scrunched as she searched for what she was looking for. She took her time, running a tiny hand over the spines of so many books. Finally, she plucked a square-shaped hardback from its place. Holding it up, she grinned.

Jo grinned back. *Of course.*

Rain toddled back and placed a copy of *Goodnight Moon* on the blanket.

"Jade says it's a nighttime story." There was a tone of wonder in her voice.

Jo could barely contain the rush of warmth bursting from her chest. This was the perfect selection. *Goodnight Moon*'s message was simple yet powerful. The words helped children feel like they were not alone in the room and established a sense of safety as they fell asleep.

"Yes, Jade's right. It is a nighttime story. I'm so glad you two get to read it tonight. I think you'll love it."

Rain beamed and sat down, running her hand over the book's cover. It was so nice to see her feel comfortable in what was an otherwise foreign setting. She really was a remarkable child to adapt so well to what was probably a never-ending merry-go-round of change.

"Should I pull your mom's mat over too?"

Rain shook her head. "No. I'm gonna be over here by Jade tonight."

"And not your mom?"

"No."

Jo hesitated. She didn't want Sierra to think she'd conspired to remove her daughter without her permission. Yet it was obvious Rain felt a natural gravitation toward Jade. Perhaps it was only temporary and Rain liked the novelty of receiving special attention from a teacher-like figure. *Or,* Jo thought, *perhaps it's more than that.*

Was it possible Rain was beginning to doubt her mother's decisions? Was she losing faith in Sierra's ability to protect her? Jo shuddered. What exactly had Rain witnessed when they'd left the store to go find Casey?

"Rain, honey." Jo lowered down and peered into her big blue eyes. "Are you hurt anywhere? Has anyone touched you?"

Rain blinked. Her face was open, calm. "No. Mama's got an owie but not me."

"Yes." Jo considered this. "But is it ever you that gets an owie instead?"

Rain shook her head and held Jo's gaze. Satisfied, Jo stood again. "Okay, well, that's good. Not about your mom, but about you. I'm going to go find Jade. Are you okay here by yourself for just a minute?"

Rain nodded and turned to busy herself fluffing her bed again.

Thank God, Jo said to herself as she walked away.

As she went to let Jade know her story-time services were required, Jo made a silent promise to herself. She was going to protect that little girl. No matter what.

Thirty-Four

$\mathcal{J}$o awoke to a loud sound. Disoriented, she pushed onto her elbows and waited for her eyes to adjust. As the room came into focus, she saw that most everyone was still in bed. The clamor continued, and like a field of prairie dogs, heads began popping up one after another, to pause and listen.

Bang!

"What on earth is going on?" Jo was the first to her feet, still hazy with slumber. The previous day had drained her more than she'd realized. Her body felt leaden. By the way pink light filtered into the room, she guessed the hour to still be early, probably around sunrise. After spending so many nights there, she gained the ability to tell the time from the way light moved through the building.

The clanging sound paused and then started up again, sending her hands over her ears and her heart into her throat. She checked where Jade and Rain slept. Thankfully they were still on their mats. Sierra stood and crossed the room, tugging her hoodie over her head. Jo noticed a strange look in her eye.

"What is it, Sierra?"

"I'm not sure yet." She moved past Jo and toward the stairs. Her fists clenched at her sides as she quickened her pace.

"Wait!" Jo didn't want her to go alone. Thankfully, Adam and

Grayson seemed to read her mind. The two of them leaped from their beds, thrusting on shoes and forcing their tired eyes awake.

"We'll go." They ran ahead with Sierra.

"Where's Truman?" Jo spun around but didn't see him. She frowned. Was it possible he was repairing something? If so, why was he being so loud?

It wasn't until she heard a shout echo through the building that she understood the sounds didn't mean Truman was working. They meant something was wrong.

"Jade." She whirled around and pointed. "You stay here with Rain. Keep her safe, okay?"

Jade's face went white. She reached over and wrapped a protective arm around Rain's sleepy frame. "Yes, of course."

Jo ran off.

The shouts grew louder as she flew down the stairwell and onto the main level. It took a few seconds for Jo to decipher what she was seeing. There, inside of the still-boarded-up entrance, were Grayson, Adam, Anna, and Sierra, tense and staring. Next to them was Truman, his hair wild and clothes rumpled as if he'd been ripped from sleep. Jo's gaze traveled to his side, where he gripped what appeared to be a long hammer. He waved it once in front of the window, and Jo realized he was hollering to someone on the other side.

When she looked out, Jo froze. Casey was back. And he was angry.

Truman glared at Casey. "Get out of here!"

The banging stopped as Casey yelled, but Jo was too far away to understand what he was saying. From her vantage point, she noticed the crimson color of his face and the bulging in his neck. He raised a middle finger to Truman and then aimed his focus at where Sierra stood, just a foot from the glass.

"What's he saying?" Jo scurried over to Truman, ignoring her desire to run away.

Truman had fire in his eyes. This was something new. Jo had never seen him so enraged. He waved the hammer around as he spoke. "I woke up to this lunatic trying to pry the doors open. He's been at it for ten minutes, yelling obscenities and threatening to bust the place."

Jo tensed. Whatever Sierra did or didn't do the day before had clearly agitated Casey beyond the brink of sanity. It was as if she'd poked the hornet's nest and this was the result. Because there, on the other side of the store windows, was a wild-eyed man demanding his girlfriend be released or there'd be hell to pay. This guy wasn't fooling around. He meant business.

"Sierra, I think you should get away from the window." Anna tugged on her sleeve.

"Do you know that guy?" Adam turned, his face a mixture of fright and confusion.

"Yeah," she answered. "That's my boyfriend. He's pissed because I'm here. Maybe I should go out there and talk to him."

"No!" Truman and Jo shouted at the same time.

"That's a bad idea," Truman continued. "I don't like the look in his eyes. He's out of control. Is it possible he's on something?"

Sierra's mouth twisted. Jo watched her struggle to answer.

"Sierra, you need to tell us the truth here. What are we dealing with?"

"Yes, it's possible he's taken something. I mean, he also just has a bad temper. But he, like, also does speed. His cousin deals it."

Adam groaned. He and Grayson traded looks of dread, mirroring exactly how Jo felt.

"Is that why he's acting so crazy right now?" Truman had to

raise his voice to be heard over Casey's shouting, which penetrated the thick glass window.

Sierra sagged. "Yeah, pretty much. Sometimes he's just more alert, but a lot of the time, he gets kinda paranoid. And that usually turns into anger."

"Man." Adam's hand went to the back of his neck. "What do we do? We can't have him breaking into the building."

"Maybe we should call the cops," Grayson suggested. He'd shuffled over to stand beside Anna and Sierra, eager to escape Casey's line of vision.

Jo bit her lip and tried to think of what to say. Casey was getting more agitated by the minute.

"I see you in there!" he yelled, thrusting a finger in Sierra's direction. His loud voice was muffled, but they could make out what he was saying anyway. "Don't you think I can't! Come out here, Sierra!"

"Go away, Casey!" she yelled back, her voice audibly shaky. "Go sleep it off!"

"Sierrrrra!" he hollered, his chest heaving.

"Go away!" She was screaming now, her slender frame pitching forward. "I don't want you here."

Without warning, Casey hauled back and launched something hard and round. The group collectively recoiled as a rock bounced off the glass and tumbled onto the sidewalk.

"Dude." Grayson's eyes bulged. "If he does it again, he might crack the glass."

"That's not okay," Truman fumed. "This is getting out of control."

"Oh my gosh." Jo felt sick. She wanted nothing more than for this guy to disappear.

Immobilized, they all watched as Casey's temper continued

to ramp up, the blue veins in his neck darkening by the millisec-ond. Insults were hurled at the building as he waved his fists and paced the sidewalk. Sierra's answer wasn't what he wanted to hear.

Jo debated whether or not to call the police. Casey was putting them in an impossible position. On one hand, calling the police would eliminate the immediate crisis. They really needed Casey to go away. But alerting the authorities would also bring attention to the fact they'd gone against the mayor's orders and opened their doors to more people. Jo and the others already had enough unwanted attention with the protesters. The last thing they needed was added chaos. Yet if they didn't find a way to stop Casey, he might actually succeed in his mission to break inside. And that would undo all the hard work Jo and the others already accomplished.

Whatever they decided, Jo realized, they would lose.

"I'll go out there and deal with him," Truman said, his voice steely. He held up his hammer. Jo sucked in her breath. A con-fusing mixture of fear and awe swirled through her as he moved toward the door. "I've had about enough of him banging on my building."

"Wait," Jo yelled. Her voice came out too loud. Everyone turned to look at her, as if she'd said more than she intended to. She may have. But the thought of Truman getting out there, possi-bly fighting this drugged-up guy, sent her into hyperventilation. "Let's think this through for a minute."

"What is there to think about?" Adam asked. "Truman's right—he's going to trash the building. If you don't want one of us to handle it, then let's call the police and get this guy yanked out of here."

"Okay, that's fine," Jo said. "But then what? What do we do when those same cops start asking questions and wonder why he's here in the first place? They're going to wonder why Sierra and Rain are here. And then what do we say when the protesters and the media show up—because you know they will—and we've suddenly caused yet another unwanted scandal for Bruebaker's? How are we going to address all of that? Are you prepared for our movement to be completely dismantled?"

Suddenly, Sierra was crying. Her hands went to her face. "I'm so sorry. This is all my fault. I shouldn't have come here. This wouldn't be happening if I'd have just stayed away."

Jo closed the gap between them and pulled Sierra farther off to the side where Casey definitely couldn't see her. "No, honey. Don't say that. If you weren't in here where it's safe, you'd be out there in danger. None of us want that for you and Rain. Would we, you guys?" She glanced over at her team with a pleading expression. They caught on and muttered shaky reassurances.

"Yeah, we don't blame this on you. He's insane. It's good you're safe."

"Totally. Don't feel bad, Sierra."

"Jo's right—we don't want you in any danger. But in the meantime, we need to know how to deescalate this situation," Truman said. He was still gripping his hammer. "In your experience, what's the best way to calm him down?"

She sniffed. "The only thing that's gonna calm him down is to have me and Rain go out there. As mad as he is, he also doesn't like to think we can ever break up. It's twisted, I know. But that's just how Casey thinks. He feels better knowing we're around."

"Well, that's not going to happen." Jo locked her arms. There was no way she was letting those two girls out of the building. God only knew what might happen if she did. She only hoped Jade was keeping Rain distracted upstairs. The child had been through enough.

Casey thudded on the windows again, and Jo jumped. He

would not be ignored. Jo worried the glass really would break if he kept it up. This was a complete disaster.

"Can't we negotiate or something? You know, talk to him on the phone like you did with Regina?" Grayson asked.

"He's high." Truman shook his head. "Look at him. There's no way he's in the frame of mind to be rational."

"Sierra," Jo asked, willing her heart to move out of her throat, "how long does this type of thing typically last? When will he come down from whatever he's on?"

Sierra shrugged. "It depends. Sometimes it's all day, sometimes it's less than that. Judging by the early hour, he's been at it all night. When he crashes, he's pretty moody. That's when Rain and I try and stay away. He can get kinda dark."

Darker than this? Jo couldn't imagine poor Sierra and Rain having to endure such a roller coaster of ups and downs with this lunatic. How could they bear it? But then again, Sierra made it clear her choices were limited. Staying with Casey was likely her only option for support—until now.

"Maybe if we disappear back upstairs to where he can no longer see us, he'll give up and go away," Sierra said.

"Or maybe we just tell him the cops are on their way, but we don't actually call them. Would that scare him off?"

Sierra shook her head. "I don't think so. He knows I don't want the cops around any more than he does."

"What does that mean?" Jo stiffened. Had Sierra not told her the whole truth after all? Was there a warrant for her arrest or something worse? "Why don't you want the police around?"

Sierra's chin trembled. She dragged the sleeve of her sweatshirt across her damp face. "Because they'll just call child services. If they see Rain's situation is unstable or whatever, they'll take her away from me."

Of course. Why hadn't Jo thought of that? She'd been so naive. Sierra's life was tenuous enough as it was. Adding an additional layer of scrutiny would surely be trouble in her eyes. Rain was the only good thing she had in her life. If Rain was taken away from her, then what? Jo could only imagine.

"Okay, okay." Truman lowered his hammer, his anger subsiding. "Let's not get ahead of ourselves here. No one wants to involve child services. Right now our immediate concern is Casey. Let's just figure out how to remove him. Jo? Any other ideas? Otherwise, the boys and I should go out there in force. There's three of us and one of him. To me, that's still our best option."

Jo looked from one face to another. Adam and Grayson nodded stoically, apparently in agreement with Truman. She caught Grayson's leg tremble. Adam visibly swallowed. And yet their expressions remained sober. Their bravery was amazing.

I've never known people to show up in this way before, Jo thought.

Despite the heroic gesture, she couldn't bring herself to agree with their idea. Just like Sierra, if she were to risk losing the few important people in her life, her surrogate family, then what would her life be like? Jo would never be able to forgive herself.

"No," she finally said.

She thought of Mr. Bruebaker lying in a bed, too helpless and weak to defend his dream. She thought of the iconic brick building and the many years it served as a landmark to the city, tall and proud. And she thought of the supporters and activists who'd surely show up in a matter of hours, only to be confused and saddened by the sight of eminent destruction. Complications aside, Jo needed to finish what she'd first set out to do.

She needed to protect the store. But she needed to protect these people—her people—even more. Because now that she really thought about it, Bruebaker's was never really about the books, or the building. It was about the people. It was about Truman, Anna, Adam, Grayson, and so many others with whom Jo had formed a community. It was about the relationships and loyalty and sense of belonging that she'd always wanted but feared she'd never have. And here it was, all around her. And so, Jo decided, she'd call the police. Even if it meant revealing they'd let more people inside and thus dismantling the movement.

"We're going to call the police," she finally said. "Sierra is going to take Rain into my office and shut the door. The rest of us are going to wait here until help arrives. We'll take this thing one step at a time. With any luck, we can stave off any unnecessary questions and just claim Casey is a threatening person on drugs. Maybe that's all the police will care about. I'm not willing to risk something happening to you guys by sending you to confront him. End of discussion."

If Sierra was concerned over the prospect of her boyfriend being arrested, she didn't say a word. Instead, Jo watched the frightened girl nod and run upstairs to collect Rain. Seeking shelter in Jo's office was something the two of them were used to by now.

"You're the boss," Truman responded. He met her gaze and held it. The other three uttered similar answers, though worry lines were etched deep into their faces.

Jo retrieved her phone and dialed 911. With her heart still in her throat and Casey still at the window, Jo reported an attempted break-in at Bruebaker's Books.

"Please come quickly," she said.

And please let it be okay.

Thirty-Five

Within minutes, with what seemed to be a final burst of adrenaline, Casey responded to Sierra's silence with blind fury. After shouting her name over and over—not realizing Sierra and Rain had fled to the basement—with zero response, he'd had enough.

Jo and the others watched his face morph into something violent and ugly, his jaw hinging wide as he cried out. Like a flash, he darted across the street and yanked on an iron patio chair loosely tethered to a neighboring bistro. The chair freed, causing him to stumble before righting himself again. Jo and the others held their breath as he turned back toward the store, determined and angry. It was like watching a car wreck in slow motion, as Casey ran headlong into Bruebaker's front window with a sickening crack.

"No!" Jo gasped.

"Careful!" Truman shouted to the group.

Everyone sprang back in horror; Jo instinctually shielded a cowering Jade with her body. Truman braced his arms out in front as if to cushion the impact should the window shatter. The others remained frozen with shock as they waited for what came next.

The force of the chair delivered a blow that left a giant fissure along the long pane of thick glass. From it, a dozen miniature cracks splintered in all directions, like the fierce strike of powerful lightning. Both Casey and the frightened group on the other side were struck dumb by the impact, unsure of what to do next.

Jo's knees nearly gave way when she heard the police rounding the corner. She didn't think her heart could take much more— nor could their poor building.

What followed was a blur.

Casey had still been at it when a squad car arrived, its shrill siren announcing its presence at the curb. Their arrival took Casey by surprise, his paranoia clearly heightened but his reaction time too slow. It only took the officers seconds to see what had happened. There was no escaping that Casey tried to break in.

Officers arrested him with swift action. While Jo was wholly relieved, she also wished she could wake up and realize it had all been nothing but a nightmare.

As Jo stood outside in the alley sometime later and waited for the policewoman to fill out her report, she understood it was the beginning of the end. Shading her eyes, she glanced up at the sky and wondered how she'd managed to let everything she fought so hard to protect be ripped away in a single day. The glare of the midmorning sky blinked back at her, the spring rains carrying with them a familiar layer of gloom. Jo looked away and pulled her cardigan tighter. Her feet shifted on the damp asphalt. It was as if the weather were mirroring her heart.

But now here she was, answering questions and texting Regina. The police wanted to speak to everyone, given the unusual circumstances. Unfortunately, that included Sierra and Rain.

"Can't we do this at a later time, when everyone's less

shaky?" Jo pleaded with the policewoman. Perhaps if Sierra could be left alone for the time being, to gather her thoughts and recover from the stress of the day, then together they might be able to come up with a plan. The last thing any of them wanted was for Rain to be taken away. And while the police weren't hinting at this yet, Jo knew it was still a possibility.

"No, I'm sorry. We need to ask our questions now. Unless you all want to come down to the station with us?"

Jo shook her head. They most certainly did not. The idea of leaving the building carried too much weight. For one, they might not be allowed back inside to pick up where they left off. Regina had had enough. And it was likely so had the mayor. Chances were he was no longer waiting for Jo and her staff to vacate the building voluntarily, not after everything that had happened.

And, if Jo was honest with herself, she wasn't even sure what it was that she wanted anymore.

The resilience of her team was beginning to fray at the edges. Anna was caught between the persistent wishes of her family and her desire to remain loyal to her job, Adam's faith in activism and his ability for positive change had been shaken, Truman's patience was running low now that the building had been threatened, and the others were exhausted. Providing a sanctuary for runaways and creating a fortress against opposing forces were not what any of them had signed up for. Despite their best efforts, all six of them had gone off course from their original purpose. And, after three weeks, it seemed doubtful they could right their course.

Too much had happened.

Jo's phone pinged. She glanced down to read the text. Regina was on her way.

Great. Jo could practically feel the control slipping away from her.

"My boss should be here shortly. Should we go inside to wait?"

The officer agreed and said she'd be there in a minute, after radioing her partner. At the moment, Casey was being held in the back of the squad car until a second vehicle arrived to take him away. From what Jo gathered, Casey's hand was bloodied and required medical attention. His high was fading. The police would likely keep him locked up until his arraignment. He was being arrested for attempted breaking and entering, public intoxication, and endangerment. Jo prayed he wouldn't make bail and would remain in jail for some time.

At least that was the silver lining in the whole mess. As for the fate of everything else, Jo had no idea.

"So what do we do now?" Truman was the first to greet her as she stepped inside. Jo wondered how long he'd been waiting there.

"Well, first I need to check on Sierra and Rain. I'm assuming they're still down in my office."

"They are."

"Okay." She exhaled. At least they hadn't been tempted to run off. "And then we need to sit down with that female officer so she can ask some more questions. I tried not to involve you guys, but I wasn't successful. Apparently you're all witnesses. And then . . ." She pinched the bridge of her nose. A thrumming behind her eyes had developed. "We have to brace for the arrival of Hurricane Regina."

"Oh boy."

"Yeah, I know. She's on her way, and she's fuming. I don't want to scare the others, but I'm guessing she's going to make us all go. At the very least, she's going to get rid of me. That's something she's wanted to do for a long time. I've basically just handed her my head on a silver platter."

"Wow, Jo. What a mess."

"I know."

"What do you want me to do?" Truman asked. "I already nailed extra boards in front of the cracked window. It's not pretty, but I got the job done."

She offered a sad smile. "Thanks for that. I'm sure it's fine. Maybe you can go round up the others and then listen for the police to knock? I suppose everyone can meet in the break room." Even as she said it, Jo couldn't believe it had come to this.

Tapping on the door to her office, Jo poked her head inside. Sierra and Rain sat on the floor, just where they said they'd be, surrounded by blankets and books. Rain's short legs were tucked underneath her as she rested her head on her mother's shoulder. If Jo didn't know better, she'd think it was a picture-perfect scene of a family enjoying a bookstore.

"You two doing okay?" She came inside and lowered into the roller chair.

"Yeah, I guess so. Just a little shaken up, that's all."

"I can understand that." Jo wasn't feeling so hot herself. Now that her adrenaline was subsiding, she detected a nauseating unease moving in. These poor girls had been through hell and back. And just when they'd found some small semblance of security, within the walls of the store, their world was about to be turned upside down once again. Sierra wasn't going to be able to hide the fact she and her daughter were homeless and unstable. She wasn't going to be able to prove she could provide food and shelter for her four-year-old. And her connection to a now criminal would mar her chances for anonymity.

Sierra wasn't perfect. Jo knew this. But that didn't mean she wasn't worthy of a second chance. Somehow the police needed to see this. The question was, how?

"So what did the cops say? We heard the sirens. Did they arrest Casey?"

"Yes, he's being taken to jail on a number of counts. Hopefully you won't be seeing him in the near future." Jo hoped this would offer a small measure of comfort. She suspected, however, that Sierra might have mixed feelings. Casey was her boyfriend, after all. But he was also dangerous. And now he was gone.

"And what about me and Rain? Did the cops ask about us?"

Jo pursed her lips. This was the part she so desperately wanted to avoid. "I'm afraid the police do want to question you. I'm so sorry, Sierra. I really tried to leave you two out of the report, but there really wasn't any way around it. Besides, Casey was still calling for you even after the police took him into custody."

Her face fell. She hunched over and rested her chin on Rain's head. "I figured."

"Listen, I'm going to be right by your side when we go upstairs. I know this isn't easy. I recommend you just tell the truth. Like I said before, we'll take this thing one step at a time."

Including Regina firing me and all of us getting kicked out of the building once and for all.

"Okay, thanks." Sierra rose and took Rain by the hand. "Let's go upstairs and talk to some people, honey." Rain only nodded and clutched her blanket. Just before they exited the office, Rain tugged on her mother's hand.

"Wait." She let go and walked over to their little nest on the floor. Crouching down, she picked up the copy of *Goodnight Moon*. Satisfied, she hugged it and came back.

"Ready?" Jo asked.

"Ready."

As they ascended the stairs for the final time together, Jo remembered the promise she'd made to herself. She was going to protect that little girl. Somehow she'd make things okay for Sierra and Rain. Even if everything else had failed, she could at least plan on this. Because without planning, what else was there?

Thirty-Six

"I've already made assurances to Mayor Fink," Regina informed the questioning officer a short while later. "He knows we intend to lock up the store and move everyone out of the building today. We'll make a public statement, letting our supporters and the other, er, protesters know that the Bruebaker team has ended this whole affair. The mayor believes this should quell some of the noise out on the streets, and with any luck, this whole thing will blow over. You have my word that you won't need to come back here. There won't be any more disturbances at Bruebaker's Books."

The female officer nodded and scribbled another note on her pad.

Jo couldn't look at Regina as she spoke; instead, she let her gaze drift over her shoulder to where Adam deepened his sneer. Just like the others, he was disgusted at how easily Regina could dismiss all the good that had been done in the past weeks. There was no mention of the peaceful shelter in place that occurred earlier, nor the dozens of boxes brimming with newly purchased inventory by loyal online customers, nor the valiant effort by the staff to preserve Mr. Bruebaker's beautiful store.

Regina dismissed all of this. The only thing she cared about was getting Jo and her crew out of there as fast as humanly possible.

And while she knew it was for the best—they really couldn't go on living in that building much longer anyway—it still stung. Jo always assumed that when they left, it would be on their own terms, not Regina Anderson's.

Unable to contain her rising agitation, she spoke up. "Does Mr. Bruebaker know all of this?"

Regina's expression shifted. "We can discuss the details of Arnold later, Jo. Right now let's focus on the problem in front of us."

"Phhht," Adam huffed and walked away. He clearly couldn't listen to any more. Judging by the incredulous looks from the rest of her team, neither could anyone else.

Over in the far corner of the room, the male police officer was still taking down Sierra's statement. Jo couldn't hear what she was saying. She hoped that it was just truthful enough to be helpful but not enough to get the mother and daughter into more trouble. Her gaze landed on Sierra's tight grip around Rain's hand. By the whitening of her knuckles, Jo could tell she was scared.

Tuning out whatever Regina said next, Jo found herself drifting across the room. The two officers had intentionally separated the groups for questioning, but Jo no longer cared. Instead, she wanted to find out what would happen to Sierra and Rain.

"Is everything all right over here?" she asked, coming to stand next to the girls. She searched Sierra's tight expression and then arranged her face into a smile for the officer.

"Yes, we're just wrapping up," the policeman said. He was frowning and looking over his notes, as if something didn't add up. Or maybe it was just that Jo's interruption was poorly timed. "Miss Kelner here has given me what I need. The good news is her boyfriend won't be bothering her any longer."

"Is there bad news?" Jo held her breath.

"Well . . ." He tapped his pen. "It sounds like living conditions for these two are currently insecure. A child's welfare is at risk because of that. So—"

Jo's throat constricted. She knew where he was going with this before the words left his mouth. He was going to put these girls into the system, where the fate of their future together couldn't be guaranteed. She couldn't let Sierra and Rain be broken up. Not now. Not after witnessing Sierra's cut lip and bruised skin from her effort to face Casey's anger. Not after seeing Rain's tiny little fingers clasped around her copy of *Goodnight Moon* and the tender way in which she sidled up to Jade during their reading sessions. Not after the brave words Sierra uttered in trying to protect Jo and the store.

Jo had grown to care for these two girls in a way that surprised her. The thought of watching them slip away, and possibly slip from one another, sent an aching pang straight through her heart.

Her mind raced as she thought it through. Her townhouse was small and certainly not set up for guests. She was soon to be without a salary and had no idea how she was even going to support herself, let alone two more people. And yet, as soon as the policeman spoke of Rain's welfare, she knew exactly what she had to do. She was going to move Sierra and Rain in with her.

"They're staying with me," Jo blurted out to the officer.

"They are?" The officer raised a brow.

"We are?" Sierra appeared equally stunned.

Jo nodded. "It's a temporary solution, but I think that's best for now, don't you?" Without waiting for an answer, she bent down and peered into Rain's expectant face. Two blue eyes shone back at her. "Would you like to bring your mama and your new books to my house? I can set up the spare room for you to sleep and have your things. It's not far from here. Just a five-minute drive in my car. Does that sound like something you'd like to try?"

Rain squeezed her book tight against her chest and looked up at Sierra. "Can we, Mama?" The hopefulness in her high little voice made Jo's heart ache.

Sierra seemed to exhale, her shoulders easing back down from around her ears. Jo noticed her eyes grow damp. "Yeah, we'd like that."

Jo clapped her hands together. "Good, it's settled then. Officer? We all good here?"

The officer cleared his throat. "Yes, fine. Since the minor is still in the custody of her mother and they are going to be under your care, Ms. Waterstone, I believe that's sufficient. All I need is your phone number and home address."

"Your partner already took all of my information down."

"Okay." He tapped his pen a final time. "You all are free to go then. Thank you."

"Thanks." Jo turned to Sierra and Rain. "Let's gather up your things, shall we? I'm pretty sure we're all about to be sent home."

Home. It felt so strange to say it out loud. For the past nineteen days, the bookstore had been home. And now Jo was not only leaving but taking two new people with her. Never in a million years did she envision such a scenario. She'd resigned herself to the idea of living alone forever. It wasn't that Jo wanted to be alone, but she'd stopped believing there were many options. Now, with Sierra and Rain, Truman, and the rest of the team, Jo understood what she'd been missing out on all along.

She now had people in her life beyond her work. And that felt wonderful.

The three of them fell into step and strode past Regina. Out of the corner of her eye, Jo caught Regina's jaw hanging open at the sight of the two newcomers. Her instructions not to let anyone else into the building had not only been defied but also caused far more trouble than anyone had bargained for. Jo lifted her chin into the air and kept going.

In the hour that followed, Jo found herself wavering between the bittersweet goodbyes and cautious optimism. Just as she'd suspected, Regina had given the team a tight timeline to pack up the remaining items and get out. Jo figured her boss would rather have them vacate the building immediately, but the reality of finding someone else to properly identify and relocate piles of sorted and sold inventory was slim. And, despite Regina's displeasure with Jo, the team was still given certain responsibilities.

Anna was tasked with sending out Regina's approved messaging via the bookstore's newsletter and social media platforms. Jo looked on with agitation as Regina sat in the break room, her legs crossed and her foot tapping impatiently, dictating a "corporate" response for Anna to type up.

"It's imperative for people to know we've held ourselves to a high standard in an effort to keep this iconic piece of Portland's culture alive. We are so thankful for the outpouring of support from the reading community and beyond. It's with a heavy heart, however, that we must shutter the business in the face of an ever-changing retail climate and the sudden decline of our founder, Arnold Bruebaker."

Jo pulled a face and turned away, her blood boiling. What did

Regina even know about what they'd done to preserve the store? It was like a slap in the face to hear her ramble on in such a holier-than-thou manner, acting as if she were the one to toil away the past four weeks on her hands and knees, sorting and organizing, with the rest of them.

How dare she? Jo thought.

Anna kept her head down, her fingers frantically typing as if she too wanted to get the awkward exchange over with. Anna was still an employee, and she likely wanted to keep any chances of a good severance package. Her obedience, however uncomfortable, was understandable. Jo admired her for doing her job.

Plus, Jo knew that letting herself get worked up over Regina wasn't worth her time. In her heart, she knew who'd done the real work, who'd sacrificed their personal lives to put in the real time. That's all that mattered. Because of Jo's team, the bookstore was going out of business only after a valiant effort. Perhaps everything would be divided up and sold off to other stores—in the grand scheme of things, they'd hardly made a dent in the nearly one million volumes filling three levels and nine rooms. But the spirit of the store and its memory remained. Jo and her staff knew this—so did the good people of Portland.

Perhaps somewhere down the line, someone would reopen the place and start small.

"Jo," Regina said, her voice suddenly surprisingly unsteady, "you've been a dedicated employee, and Arnold's family appreciates your loyalty. But you allowed your emotions to get in the way. I'm afraid you lost your better sense of judgment in many regards, and now we're ending in near disaster. I don't have to tell you that the mayor is beyond irritated he has to deal with the melee of protesters out on the streets, and you know all of the other unfortunate events that were also born from this experiment."

Jo tried to keep her composure. Someone like Regina would never understand what it was like to love something so much you'd sacrifice everything and risk your own well-being just to try and preserve it. It almost made Jo feel sorry for her—almost.

"Does Mr. Bruebaker know?"

Regina paused.

"Regina?" Jo didn't know why, but her heart shot to her throat. There was something Regina wasn't sharing. The twitch of her mouth told Jo that much. "Does he know?"

Regina exhaled like she was tired of holding something in. For the briefest of moments, her face softened. "He doesn't know."

"Okay . . ." Jo frowned. Something wasn't adding up.

"Arnold's health took another turn for the worse sometime in the night. He's back at the hospital now."

"What?" Jo shouted. Everyone in the room turned as her knees buckled. She gripped the table for support. "What do you mean, he's taken a turn? How could you not lead with that, Regina? Oh my God, is he going to be okay?"

"I don't know yet. It's doubtful."

The room spun. Jo wasn't sure if she would crumple to the floor or bust through the barricaded doors and run to the hospital. How could Regina hide something so monumental from her? Surely Jo should be sitting at Mr. Bruebaker's bedside and not still inside that store, where she was apparently no longer welcome. Just the very idea of Mr. Bruebaker impaired and in pain sent a choking sob up from her chest. Why hadn't she been told?

Truman was suddenly at her side, a steady hand going to the small of her back. Anna was there too, touching Jo's shoulder in solidarity.

"Perhaps you can tell us what you do know," Truman said. He kept his hand on Jo as he pressed Regina for details.

"Well, I got a voice mail from his daughter, Suzanne, about an hour ago. All she said was that her father's breathing seemed labored and he was fairly nonresponsive when the night nurse at the nursing rehab center checked on him. He'd been agitated before bedtime, and then he seemed to decline." Her gaze landed on Jo like a silent act of blame. Jo narrowed her eyes and tightened her grip on the table.

"Anyway," Regina continued, "the next thing Suzanne knew, her father was being packed into an ambulance and rushed back to the ER. She said it was likely his heart, but she couldn't confirm with doctors until more tests were done. He's alive. I mean, obviously. I would've told you right away if that weren't the case."

"Would you?" Jo scoffed in her direction. She wanted to reach out and slap the righteous expression right off her face.

Regina reddened. "Well, of course, Jo. I'm not that unfeeling."

A low cackle escaped. Jo pushed the hair from her face. She felt deranged. Was this even happening, or was it all a sick dream? She no longer knew.

Truman's furrowed brow deepened. He kept his hand on Jo's back, firm and reassuring. "What else can you tell us, Regina?"

"Not much. Suzanne just said the doctors told her this might happen. Stroke patients often experience multiple episodes. She was warned her father wasn't out of the woods. I guess people who suffer one stroke are then even more susceptible to a second or third event."

"Yes, I've heard that before too," Truman responded.

Jo couldn't take it anymore. Why were they all still standing around, speculating on Mr. Bruebaker's condition when he was lying on a hospital gurney? And why was Regina so hell-bent on closing the store and relieving Jo of her duties before announcing this terrible news? Thoughts swam around in Jo's head as she tried to make sense of it all. Did Regina—and Mr. Bruebaker's daughters for that matter—want to gain control of the business and make autonomous decisions while Mr. Bruebaker was incapacitated? Was she cutting Jo out of the picture because she didn't approve of the movement, or was she getting rid of her because Jo was the very source of their boss's stress-induced condition?

Either way, Regina saw Jo as the cancer that needed to be cut from the equation. Suzanne and Jane's father was overwhelmed with worry and stress—and Jo was the cause. Eliminating her might eliminate further risk.

Was she the reason Mr. Bruebaker was sick?

"I need to go," she murmured. Her eyes were beginning to brim, and she very much wanted to get out from under Regina's accusatory stare. But her legs wouldn't cooperate. Jo turned to go but felt as if her limbs might turn to jelly. Blinking away tears, she sent a pleading look to Truman for help.

Thankfully he understood. He nodded and placed a strong arm around Jo's shoulders, leading her from the room. Anna was at her side in an instant, hooking an elbow through Jo's.

"Yes, that's probably best." Regina stood awkwardly alone, watching them go.

The three of them made their way through the building and into the quiet of Jo's office. Truman closed the door and pulled out her chair for her. Anna put her back to the wall and slowly sank to the floor.

"I'll go tell the others that we're done here. I think they're all just about ready to go as well," Truman offered with a worried expression. He lowered to peer into Jo's face, and his hand slipped from his side and wrapped around hers. Jo could feel the warmth of his palm covering her own. With a gentle motion, his thumb swept over the tops of her fingers, briefly caressing her skin.

Jo swallowed hard, a flood of emotions coming over her.

"Jade's upstairs putting things away with Sierra and Rain in the Beatrix Potter room," Anna said, averting her eyes. "And the guys are moving the last of the boxes from the nonfiction area."

"Okay." He nodded. And just like that, he was upright again, pulling his hand back to his side. "You'll stay here with Jo?"

"Yes."

Jo said nothing. She retrieved a package of tissues from her desk drawer and blew her nose. She knew what they were doing. Truman and Anna were worried she might crack, that she couldn't be left alone. Jo didn't try to correct them. At present, she was barely holding herself together, afraid if she stood, she might shatter into a hundred pieces. The loss of the store, her boss, and the life she knew sent a wave of grief rolling through her in a way that was too overwhelming for words. All she could do was sit and wait for it to subside. When it did, she would go to Mr. Bruebaker.

If it was the last thing she did, Jo would let him know that despite everything, his wonderful legacy would live on—even if only in spirit.

Thirty-Seven

*N*avigating out of downtown and to the hospital proved more of a production than Jo imagined. After handing over her car keys with instructions for Jade to take Sierra and Rain to her townhome, she followed Truman out of the building.

She would look back later and remember that morning as a blur: the incident with Casey, the police, Regina's cold dismissal, and the heartbreaking news of her mentor. And also the unmistakable tenderness from Truman. Like a cruel twist of fate, everything occurred in the span of a single day. And yet Jo could also see how all along there'd been a slow build leading up to it for nearly a month.

Sitting in the passenger seat of Truman's truck felt foreign and yet wholly comforting at the same time. The two of them bumped along, Truman reshuffling used coffee cups and a stack of books as he waited at a stoplight on the near-abandoned city streets.

"Thanks for going with me," Jo said. She was sure her face was puffy from crying, and she couldn't recall if she'd even brushed her teeth that morning. Truman was seeing her at her lowest point. That was for sure. But none of this really mattered. What mattered most to Jo was getting to see Mr. Bruebaker as soon as possible.

"I wouldn't have it any other way." He smiled, sending her a sideways glance. Jo looked out the windows as he drove, marveling at her city. She'd been cooped up for a month, but it felt like so much longer to her. How strange to have taken her old life for granted. Now everything she once relied on hung in the balance. It would take a long time to process what happened and what she might've done differently if given the chance.

As they pulled into the hospital parking lot, Jo's eyes pricked. A bright red EMERGENCY sign reminded her why they were there. This was Mr. Bruebaker's second trip to the hospital in less than two weeks. And, according to Regina, this time around was much more serious.

"You know," Truman said as he eased the truck into a vacant spot, "there's a chance we may not be able to see him."

"I know." Jo had considered this too. Between the severity of his stroke, his overly protective daughters, and the precautions of the emergency room, it would be a miracle if they let her inside. Still, she had to try. She'd never be able to forgive herself if she didn't. "I just want him to know I'm here. To put him at ease. And also . . ." She hesitated before meeting Truman's gaze. "And also to let him know I've learned a very valuable lesson. People matter. People like you, and the others from the store, matter more than a building with four walls. I know this now. That lesson has been a gift."

"I understand." Truman's eyes were damp as he reached out and gave her hand a small squeeze. It wasn't a large gesture, but it meant everything.

As the automatic doors slid open, the two of them entered the expansive hospital lobby. The overpowering smell of latex gloves, cheap flower arrangements, and something sharply antiseptic greeted them. Jo's nose wrinkled. She very much missed the reassuring smell of books.

She also missed the comfort of her familiar surroundings. As she scanned a large directory, she felt her pulse quicken. She had no idea where they were going.

"Maybe I should try Suzanne's phone one more time."

"Okay, but hospitals are notorious for poor cell reception."

Frowning, she saw that Truman was right. If she wanted to call Suzanne and get directions to the right room, she was going to have to go back outside.

"Let's start with the emergency waiting room. We don't know if he's been admitted yet. They might still be working on him in there."

Working on him. It sounded so clinical, so grim. Jo nodded and tried to hold her composure as they picked their way through a series of corridors. At last, they arrived in the correct spot. Jo scanned the room—a sea of downcast faces—searching for either Suzanne or Jane.

"They're not here." She looked up at Truman, hoping he'd have a better plan. "Now what?"

"Hang tight," he said. Jo leaned against a wall as he made his way to the front desk. He was too far away for her to hear what he was saying, but after a series of head nods, she believed he had luck.

"Okay," he said, coming over to where she stood. "The intake nurse isn't allowed to give me personal information. She did, however, tell me that if he was admitted, he was probably taken to the acute care rooms on the sixth floor. We should go there next."

They jogged back to the bank of elevators they'd passed earlier and rode five levels up. Miraculously, a nurse at the desk located Arnold Bruebaker's name and told them that, yes, he was indeed admitted that morning and was down the hall to the left.

"But"—she held up a hand—"because you're not family, you'll have to remain outside the room. There's a window. You can stand in the hallway and wave. New precautions. And I'll need to go make sure there aren't any other visitors. We can only allow one at a time."

By the time Jo was led down the hall to stare into a plexiglass window, she was a mess. The idea of what she might see frightened her. She was told he wasn't awake, but she could visit him nonetheless. Suzanne and Jane were thankfully elsewhere, and Truman promised to head them off should he see them coming off the elevators. All Jo wanted was a moment alone with the man who'd been a dear friend and mentor for most of her adult life. If she could just reassure him somehow, let him know his store might make it and that she'd be there to support him in whatever he needed, then she'd be satisfied.

When she arrived at the window, however, Jo's vision swam. She spotted Mr. Bruebaker on the other side, asleep on a narrow hospital bed, the sheets pulled taut and an oxygen tube fastened to his lifeless face. Wisps of his fine gray hair cascaded backward. His once-bright eyes were now closed and quiet. It was another version of the man she knew so well, a version she didn't recognize.

Her mind went blank. She forgot everything she wanted to convey. The only thing that flooded Jo's brain was an apology.

I'm sorry I couldn't do more. Her palm pressed up against the glass as she willed her silent message to be heard.

Looking at him like that, so frail and alone, Jo wondered how he could possibly recover. Closing her eyes, she blinked back the tears. She tried to drown out the low din of beeping machines, chatting nurses, and nearby patients coughing. Concentrating, she tried to imagine a happier time, when her mentor and friend had been at his very best.

As her mind slowly quieted, she recalled him the way he'd want her to: that broad smile, the warm brown eyes, the way he lingered in the rooms of the bookstore for hours shaking hands and inquiring after titles customers liked to read. He was the kind of man who had no walls, no boundaries. Jo often overheard customers remark how approachable he was upon meeting, as they wandered through the aisles admiring newly snapped selfies with him on their phones. Jo was proud of him in a way a daughter might be of a father. She wondered now, as she opened her eyes and stared through the glass, had he been proud of her?

A nurse walked by just then, offering a polite smile in Jo's direction. Jo hoped maybe she'd be able to tell her some information.

"Excuse me?"

The nurse stopped. "Yes?"

"Can you tell me anything about this patient, Arnold Bruebaker? Has he woken up very much since he was admitted?"

"Well, I just came on shift, so I don't know too much. But I think he's only been in this room a couple of hours. He was in the ER before that. The doctor does his rounds in the morning. Do you want me to page him now?"

Jo shook her head. She thought of Suzanne and Regina and all the reasons why getting involved with Mr. Bruebaker's care might get her into further trouble. This wasn't the right time to insert herself. "No, that's okay. Thank you though."

Just as the nurse started to walk away, Jo remembered something.

"Wait," she called. "Could you possibly give him something for me? Maybe leave it by his bed in case he wakes up?"

The nurse smiled. "Sure."

Dipping into her tote bag, Jo fumbled around. She'd almost forgotten.

In the minutes before leaving the store, amid all of the confusion and goodbyes, Jo had enough clarity to do one last thing. Stealing away to the third floor, she arrived at the door of the rare-books room. She hesitated before producing a small key from her pocket to unlock the door. Stepping inside, she was met with a fine haze of must and leather. Flicking on a table lamp, she crossed the room to the far wall. Spying the weathered, rust-colored hardback, she snatched it from its resting place and tucked it under her arm. As she strode from the room, she took one last glimpse of the treasured space.

Jo was acutely aware she might never be alone in that room again. It was important to take a mental snapshot just as it was: a remarkable stillness that held the written word of so many precious voices. She hoped whoever came after her would take great care of each and every volume in that room.

All except for the single copy in her hands.

"This is very special," she said, handing it over to the nurse. "It's important to him."

"I'll put it in his room." She put her hand out as Jo carefully placed the book in her grasp. "Wow. This looks really old."

Jo smiled. "It's a first edition of Walt Whitman poems."

"Wow, cool."

Jo had no idea if the nurse even knew who Walt Whitman was or if she was familiar with Mr. Bruebaker's favorite poetry collection, *Leaves of Grass*. But she knew what it would mean for him to wake up and see it there. He'd know it was from Jo, and he'd understand its meaning. This book didn't belong in the store, left alone to collect dust. It belonged with him.

Jo thanked the woman and walked away. As she did, she recited a verse in her head. It was one Mr. Bruebaker often shared with Jo, reciting it as if it were a mantra. She'd come to know this quote not as Whitman's, but as that of her boss. He never ceased to inspire Jo. And for this she was forever grateful.

> *Not I, nor anyone else can travel that road for you.*
> *You must travel it by yourself.*
> *It is not far. It is within reach.*
> *Perhaps you have been on it since you were born, and did not*
> *know.*
> *Perhaps it is everywhere—on water and land.*

Making her way back to Truman, Jo wiped the last of her tears from her face. It was time to go home.

Thirty-Eight

That evening, as Truman dropped her at the curb and waited until she went inside, Jo crossed the threshold of her townhome for the first time in weeks. She hadn't realized how much she missed the sight of her living room, with its dark wood floors and buttery cream sofa set against a pine bookcase. When Jo first moved in, she'd consciously made an effort to decorate the front room in pacifying, neutral tones to ensure a place of sanctuary. Oftentimes, she'd come in the door from work, kick off her shoes, and collapse into the folds of the couch cushions. With a carton of takeout from her local Thai restaurant and an anticipated hardback from her to-be-read stack, Jo was content to spend her time off curled in that very room.

That night, however, was different. There, resting on her sofa with a chunky knit blanket draped between them, were Sierra and Rain. Half-eaten pasta dinners sat on the coffee table in front of them.

"Hello there," she said, placing down her tote bag. Her face felt swollen from crying, but she tried to brush away the dark feelings. It was important that the girls feel welcome in her home. "Everyone doing okay?"

"Yes," Sierra said. She scooted forward on the sofa, her voice soft. "I hope it's okay we ate. Jade helped us find a box of spaghetti and get it cooking. We saved some for you in the kitchen."

"Thank you." Jo was so tired. Her appetite was all but gone. But she appreciated the gesture anyway. No one ever cooked for her. "Please don't get up. I'm just going to go wash up, and I'll be back. It's been a long day. You two just relax."

"Thanks." Sierra leaned back again, her arm going over Rain's prone frame. "Your place is really nice. It's like an Instagram photo."

Jo smiled. "That's very nice, thank you. I like living here."

She moved down the hallway. Poking her head into rooms, she saw that everything was as she left it. Moisturizers and brushes still lined the bathroom counter, mail was piled on a desk in her office, unfolded laundry waited on the daybed (she'd have to clean this up for the girls), and her bedroom was cool and tidy. Making her way to her bed, she fell back onto the duvet and groaned. Soy candles, the light hint of dryer sheets, and a slight woodsy smell that clung to the wood floors reminded her she was finally home. Lying there, Jo suddenly had a new appreciation for her beautiful things.

Three weeks of sleeping on a thin floor mat had been much harder on her than she realized. Her muscles ached and her head was sore, but she was relaxed knowing she was home.

After taking a long, luxuriously hot shower with extra soap and then pulling on a favorite sweater, Jo wandered out to find the others. Under the soft glow of a table lamp, Sierra and Rain lay asleep on the sofa. She paused to take in the sight of their matching bare feet propped on the coffee table, their heads bent toward one another and their eyes closed. She pressed her lips together and wondered if she should wake them. They were so peaceful there. And Jo noted how at home they seemed, surprisingly. This made her happy. She was glad her place could be a refuge. She'd been alone for too long, and it was nice to share it with someone else.

Jo hadn't any idea how long Sierra and Rain would stay. Her intention was to shelter them but also to find out whether there could be extended family or friends she might help Sierra contact. Surely there had to be someone who missed the girls. But right then, her goal was simply to provide a good night's sleep.

"Sierra," she whispered, gently shaking her shoulder. "Let's move you into the daybed."

Sierra blinked and yawned.

"Rain can stay here on the sofa for tonight. I brought her an extra pillow." Jo watched as Sierra nodded and rearranged her daughter into a better position. The two of them tiptoed out of the room and down the hall.

"I moved my stuff out of here. It's actually a good little bed. The sheets are clean, and the bathroom, as you know, is across the hallway. Maybe leave your door open in case Rain wakes up and worries?"

"Ummm, hmmm. Thanks, Jo." Sierra was half-asleep as she climbed into bed. She didn't bother to remove any of her clothes, and Jo didn't blame her. She had a feeling all three of them would sleep like the dead.

"Good night," she said, switching off the light.

"Night."

Jo crept away with gratitude in her heart. So much had gone painfully wrong that day—Mr. Bruebaker, Regina, the store—but she was home, and two of the people she worried about were safe. This, she understood perhaps more than ever, was a gift.

Come morning, when the world was once again awake and people would most likely need answers, she'd deal with reality.

Right then, however, she'd crawl under her comforter and be soothed by the knowledge that there was peace.

If only for one night—where they would go from there was still a question.

The following morning, Jo woke to the clanging of pots and pans. The light chatter of laughter floated in from the other side of the closed bedroom door. Squinting, she checked her phone. She'd slept well past 10:00 a.m.

Propping up onto her elbows, she looked around her room. Daylight streamed in from a crack in the curtains, giving every-thing a cheery feel. Jo smiled. It had been forever since she'd been so lazy.

More kitchen sounds could be heard, followed by what was definitely more than one voice. Who was in her kitchen?

Snatching up a terry cloth robe, Jo padded down the hallway. The aroma of bacon and something distinctly maple filled the house. Her stomach gurgled. It had been a while since she'd eaten.

"Oh, hey, Jo." Jade popped around the corner. Her face was clean and scrubbed, a topknot of hair piled on her head. "I hope you don't mind that I came over. I brought groceries for you guys."

"Hi." Jo pushed her hair back and attempted to straighten her robe. She could only imagine what she looked like after such a hard night's sleep. But then again, Jade had seen her at her worst, so what did it matter? "That's so nice of you."

Once inside the kitchen, she noticed Sierra standing at the counter, cracking eggs into a glass bowl. Rain balanced on her knees; a wooden stool was dragged over so she could reach.

Jo smiled at the two girls. "Hi there."

"Hi!" Rain piped up. She waved a metal whisk in the air to show she was helping with breakfast. "We're cooking!"

"I see that." Jo winked. "Did you both sleep okay?"

"Yeah, it was awesome. Thanks." Sierra's expression was wistful.

"I'm so glad." Jo took a steaming mug of coffee that Jade made for her and cocked a hip against the counter. She couldn't help but smile as she watched the three of them bustle about, making enough food for an army. "Anyone else coming over?"

Jade blushed. "Oh, well, Grayson said he was going to stop by. If that's not okay, I can totally text him not to come. He crashed on Adam's couch last night. I told him I went to the store, and he got excited about eating something other than toaster waffles."

They all laughed. If Jo never saw another frozen waffle in her life, it would be too soon. She knew the others were just as thrilled as she was about breaking from their isolation menu.

"That's fine. I'm happy to have him come over. What about Adam and Anna? Have you spoken to them?"

Jade shook her head. "No. After you and Truman left the store, Regina took the key and locked everything up. Anna went home to her parents' house, and I went home to mine. The boys headed off in Adam's car. I guess you could say we were all kind of sad to go. But our movement played out to its end, it seemed, so . . . yeah, that's about it."

Jo blew on her coffee and tried to envision the store empty. She imagined Regina didn't waste any time in closing the place down. Jo wondered what the response had been to Anna's postings on social media. A shudder ran through her. People were most likely upset. Adam's initial article sparked a movement that people could get behind. And now it had been taken away. Despite her curiosity, Jo decided against looking online. It was too soon, too raw. For now, she would focus on her small circle of friends.

She wondered if she should call Truman. He'd gone home and was likely all alone. A big breakfast might be exactly what he needed.

"I'll be right back," she told the others as she went in search of her phone.

When she glimpsed the screen, however, she saw a text had come in from Suzanne.

> Looks like we missed you at the hospital. Dad's not doing
> well. Call me for an update.

Jo's throat constricted. This was bad. She just knew it. Numbly, she dialed Suzanne's number. Each ring felt like an eternity. At last, Suzanne picked up.

"Jo?" Suzanne's voice was hushed. There was noise in the background, but Jo couldn't define it. She had to assume Mr. Bruebaker's daughters were still at the hospital.

"Yes, it's me. I just got your text. What's wrong?"

"I'm just in the waiting area; let me walk outside."

Jo waited, her feet pacing the floor.

"Okay, I'm in the parking lot. It's the only place I can get good reception. I thought you'd want to know he's in surgery. The doctors first thought they would treat any clotting in his brain with medication. But he wasn't responding the way they hoped, and things seemed to deteriorate overnight. And I can't say anyone has given Jane or me a whole lot of hope."

"Oh no." Jo sank onto her bed. She wanted to say more, to ask questions, but she was afraid if she opened her mouth again, a giant sob might come rolling out. It was all she could do to hold herself together.

Suzanne seemed to sense this, because her voice softened. "When I saw that book beside his bed and the nurse told me you stopped by, I knew you'd want to know. Business aside, my sister and I know how close you are to Dad. It's been a series of terrible events this past spring, and you and I most likely hold a difference of opinion about a lot of it. Especially when it comes to keeping my eighty-six-year-old father so tightly involved in the daily running of the bookstore. But on a personal level, I know you care for Dad and he cares for you. Whatever happens, Jo, you should know that."

A million thoughts swirled. Part of her wanted to jump in her car and storm into the hospital waiting room and be there the minute Mr. Bruebaker's surgery was over. But another, more practical, part of her knew that she wasn't family and it wasn't her place. She'd been let go from a job and a life that she loved. And although Suzanne was updating her on his well-being, Jo was also being held at arm's length for a reason. Mr. Bruebaker's daughters didn't think Jo was the best thing for their father or his business. She'd gotten too involved and hadn't let the aging owner retire in peace. Perhaps the two women even blamed Jo for their father's sudden decline. Keeping her at a distance would prevent further damage.

Jo sagged. She couldn't say she blamed them. Who was to say they weren't right? A sour mix of guilt and grief began to roil around in her gut. How had everything gotten so bad?

"I'm sorry." *I never meant for this to happen. I only wanted to carry out your father's dream. I didn't know when to stop. And now it's too late.* There was so much to say, so much to explain, but when Jo opened her mouth, nothing came.

"I'm sorry too," Suzanne said. "I've been under a lot of stress. It's no excuse for my harsh behavior. I know that. You've been nothing but faithful to Dad, and that's commendable. He may not be able to express himself right now, but I think I can speak for him when I say he's always been proud of you."

Jo swallowed hard. The grief rose up like a wave and threatened to pull her down until she could no longer breathe. There were no words.

"Thank you," she murmured. "I have to go. Please tell him I love him."

"You take care, Jo."

Jo hung up the phone.

Wow, she thought. *So Mr. B really did love me and was proud of me.* Perhaps his biggest legacy wasn't the bookstore after all, but rather the trust he put in Jo. She was a better person than she used to be. Because of that, Jo understood that everything would be okay. She would eventually find a new job and continue to surround herself with the people she cared for.

Brimming with gratitude, she wandered out to find the others.

Thirty-Nine

Jo sat on her front steps and tilted her face toward the sun. Spring had finally arrived, bringing a burst of balminess as it chased away the rain. Having lived in the Pacific Northwest for two decades, she knew the dry weather wouldn't last. After all, the rains were what kept the landscape so delightfully green. For the moment, Jo would relish the inviting temperature and appreciate the pine-scented air. Her soul required it. Too many hours were spent indoors. It was time for a change.

Every so often, a neighbor would emerge and wave from afar. After being secluded for so long, Jo found it strange to suddenly be among other people again.

Sitting there, Jo attempted to define her new life.

In the handful of days that followed her departure from Bruebaker's Books, she struggled to ground herself. Mr. Bruebaker remained in intensive care after his surgery, and the outlook was bleak. Visitors weren't allowed, but Suzanne kept her updated with brief texts. The bookstore was still shuttered, and Jo was cut off from access to any future plans. And while Sierra and Rain were still with her, the others had begun to splinter off in different directions. Jade, of course, was good about checking in. Jo looked forward to her phone calls. But the other staff members were less communicative. Jo suspected everyone was busy decompressing.

Leaving the store for good had been a lot to unpack—for all of them.

There wasn't yet a clear path forward.

Because of this, Jo found her emotions fixed to a giant pendulum, swinging from low to high, depending on her focus. For so long, her work life and happiness had been tied together in a perfect knot. Everything in her world was connected, and she'd liked it that way. Now everything was different. With the termination of her job and the closing of the store, the secure knot was suddenly yanked free, and the result had left her untethered.

There were positives, however, she had to admit. Little Rain was thriving in her new environment. Over the past few days, she and her mother adopted a routine of cooking meals (macaroni and cheese was a favorite), going for neighborhood walks, and curling up to enjoy the early-reader books Jade gifted them. Witnessing her daughter's delight, Sierra appeared brighter now, the color returning to her face. Jo noticed how her shoulders no longer rode up around her ears, and the bulky hoody had finally been shed. There was a lightness about Sierra that hadn't been there before. It was like watching the metamorphosis of a butterfly.

This change in Sierra had much to do with the fact that Casey was out of the picture. The mother and daughter now possessed the security of stable housing and an absence of violence. Thankfully, the three of them were getting along surprisingly well in Jo's cozy townhome. Jo knew their arrangement wouldn't last forever. She and Sierra had already begun to broach the idea of contacting family members back in Idaho, along with trying to find a job and possibly even day care. Sierra was still rather guarded when it came to her past, but there was a yearning in her tone that made Jo believe she missed her family.

It was something to consider, Jo told Sierra the previous

night over dinner. Even if she didn't reunite with her parents, at the very least Sierra could let them know she was all right. The rest would come naturally.

As for Truman, Jo wrestled with a tangle of both longing and regret. She never did get around to inviting him over for breakfast, despite the fact he'd left a couple of messages asking how she was. In fact, they hadn't spoken since the trip home from the hospital. The only real communication was a couple of texts relaying the news of Mr. Bruebaker's surgery. That was nearly a week ago. The guilt of ignoring him ate away at Jo's edges.

She often thought of the way her hand felt wrapped inside of his. If she closed her eyes, she could almost imagine the warmth of his touch. She missed his companionship. She missed his soothing voice, the way he always had the right thing to say, and she especially missed the way his intoxicating scent of sawdust and aftershave caused her to go weak in the knees.

And still, Jo couldn't bring herself to face him.

Reaching out meant opening the aching wound of leaving the store and her old life behind. Every time she thought about it, her eyes welled up and her stomach clenched. It was as if her brain couldn't hold anything more—the loss of her job, the condition of her boss, the caring of her houseguests, and the uncertainty of her future. Trying to make space for Truman in all of that was overwhelming. For that reason, she'd yet to return his calls.

Where do I go from here? Jo rearranged herself on the steps and watched as a young couple walked by with bags of groceries tucked under their arms. She dipped her chin as they passed, saying hello. It was nice to be an observer on her street. Living downtown was never dull. Even though her townhome was on the edge of the city, on one of the last few quiet streets within walking distance of the local shops, things were changing. Two new hotels were being erected on the nearby city blocks. The small park on the corner, really only a patch of green space for dogs, was being ripped out to make room for new construction. And the longer Jo stayed, the more she noticed a much younger demographic moving in. She'd been so busy that these developments, while noticed, were always pushed to the back of her mind. But now, as she continued to observe life from her front stoop, these things stood out to her in a way they hadn't before. Just like the bookstore, life as Jo knew it was changing. It was inevitable.

The question was, would she change too?

The front door clicked open just then, interrupting her thoughts. Jo turned to see Sierra hovering at the threshold.

"Hi—everything all right?"

"It's your phone," Sierra said, extending her arm. "I thought you'd want it. The ringing hasn't stopped. It's Suzanne."

Wordlessly, Jo reached out and took the device. She didn't bother getting up. Instinct told her she needed to be sitting down for this call. Suzanne would have texted if it was a good update. She wasn't in the habit of calling to chat. This was different, and Jo knew why. She could sense it.

With slow movements, she hit redial. Everything else melted away as she closed her eyes and waited for an answer.

"Joanna?" Suzanne's voice was hoarse.

"Yes."

"He's gone," she said.

"Oh no." A heavy stone sank in Jo's gut. *Mr. B.*

"We lost him this morning. He just sort of slipped away. I thought you should know."

Jo nodded, allowing the tears to come. "I understand. I'm sorry for your loss. He was a good man." *And I'll miss him more than anything in this world.*

"Thank you. We're just glad he's no longer suffering. It wasn't any way to live. He'd had enough, and I think he decided to let go. He's at peace."

Jo bowed her head, unable to respond.

"There will be a service. My sister, Jane, will reach out with details. He'd want you there, Jo. We want you there. You were a good friend to him. We'll make sure you get all the information. Okay?"

"Yes, okay. Thank you."

"Goodbye, Joanna."

"Goodbye."

Jo let the phone fall away as she buried her face and continued to cry. She was never going to be able to sit with Mr. Bruebaker again, never going to be able to share stories about the bookstore or ask for advice on how to proceed. The once-constant voice in her life had been muted. And while Jo had been silently preparing for his loss, the pain of it hurt like hell. Mr. Bruebaker was gone.

Jo didn't know how long she'd been sitting there or what her houseguests may have thought, but she discovered Rain's soft, tiny hand settling onto hers and squeezing tight. She hadn't noticed them come out, but there were Sierra and Rain, lowering down onto the stoop to flank Jo on either side. Neither of them said anything. They just scooted in close and kept her company as she quietly sniffed and grieved her beloved boss.

Forty

$\mathcal{T}$he memorial service was a blur. What was supposed to be a private affair for friends and family quickly morphed into a very public event. Even though the mayor discouraged the public from any large gatherings, considering the unruly protests, neither the police nor the city officials stood in the way of the event. It was an important day for many. Nothing was going to stop them. People were moved to participate.

Jo couldn't say she blamed the hundreds of mourners who came out. Bruebaker's Books was a central fixture in the community. The store was, as the media often pointed out, a cultural touchstone. The success of the business was due to its founder, Arnold Bruebaker. Everyone wanted to pay their respects. They each wanted to return the love they felt every time they had walked through the front doors. Mr. Bruebaker had been a staple. Without him, there was loss.

Jo had been seated up front near Suzanne and Jane, on the wooden pew of the old downtown church, in what was a packed house. Later on, she'd read the news and see images showing the lines of people snaking from the entrance, mourners holding up signs and crying. Customers laid flowers along the perimeter of the building, paying their respects to a man they considered a local icon.

It was all quite touching, looking back. But on that day, Jo found herself conveniently numb. She'd glimpsed a few familiar faces in the sea of bodies and offered a small wave. Regina was there, of course, overdressed in all her designer glory. She'd traded a nod of recognition with Jo on her way out. That was as much as either of them cared to engage. Jo pushed onto her toes, wondering where Anna, Adam, Jade, and Grayson were sitting. But every time she tried to find them, someone else popped their head up to shake her hand or offer condolences. As a result, she never found her friends. There were too many people in the way.

As for Truman, Jo wasn't sure if he'd even come. He'd left her more messages, but Jo hadn't had a moment to respond. She kept telling herself that she would, but time kept escaping her. Of course, there were things to say, but the lump in Jo's throat always prevented her from following through. The day of the service proved no different.

Perhaps, she told herself, *connecting with Truman isn't meant to be.*

Why else would it be so hard?

Later on, when she'd gone back to her house, Sierra and Rain were waiting. They'd opted to stay behind. Sierra wasn't a fan of big crowds, and she worried the event might be confusing for Rain. Jo understood. It was best to be alone that day anyway. She didn't have the capacity to worry about anyone else. Despite this, it was nice to walk into her kitchen and be greeted with two happy faces. They'd been busy with a tube of cookie dough and the oven. Everything smelled of sugar and joy.

Jo was comforted by their presence. She realized she needed them just as much as they needed her. However temporary their stay, she was grateful.

When her doorbell rang a little while later, she was surprised to find her friends on the other side. They were all together: Jade, Anna, Grayson, and Adam. And they'd come to see her.

"Oh my gosh, how lovely!" Jo quickly stepped aside and ushered them in.

"We didn't see you at the after-party," Adam said.

"It wasn't a party, Adam." Anna rolled her eyes. "It was a reception."

"Same thing." He shrugged and grinned at Jo. "There were way too many people inside that place. I guess none of us are used to being around people after a month of solitude. So we bailed."

"We thought you might've felt the same way and come back home, so here we are. I hope that's okay." Anna lifted up a glass dish brimming with what looked like a casserole. "And we brought food!"

"Well, that Suzanne chick kind of shoved it at us. She claimed there was too much stuff on the buffet table and we'd be doing her a favor. She was pretty freaked out by all those people. I don't think she realized how popular Mr. Bruebaker really was."

"I can imagine." Jo chuckled. She could picture Suzanne scurrying about her father's house, straightening furniture and attempting to direct a flood of unexpected visitors. She bet Mr. B was somewhere looking down in amusement. He would have loved the chaos. "Let's go into the kitchen."

The four of them followed Jo through the house, with Anna and Adam murmuring how nice everything was and asking how come they'd never visited before. If she hadn't been so emotionally drained, Jo would've thought it amusing her staff found her home so intriguing. What had they expected to find? She wondered.

"Hi, Sierra. Hey, Rain."

"Wow, smells good in here! You guys making cookies?"

"Chocolate chip!" Rain said.

Everyone exchanged hellos and smiles. The impromptu reunion provided a happy distraction for each of them. Jo looked around the room and realized how much she'd missed seeing their faces. They were all there—all except for one.

"Anyone see Truman today?" Jo ventured. Maybe he'd been with the others and was on his way over. A tiny bubble of hope rose at the thought.

"No." Anna shook her head. "We assumed he'd be with you."

"Yeah, I thought we'd see him today for sure. But who knows? There were so many people in that church. It was crazy," Adam said.

"Yeah," Grayson said between bites of a cookie. Rain looked on as he ate, waiting to see if he approved of her baking skills. "It was nuts. Did you guys see the photos online of the bookstore? There's like a hundred cards and flowers piling up at the front doors."

"Yeah, I saw that too. It's really sad, but it's also pretty beautiful. I mean, everyone loved old man Bruebaker. He was like a celebrity. People are grieving him," Anna said.

"I even read there's a petition going around to rename the street outside the store after him."

"Wow, really? That would be amazing."

"Gosh," Jo said. "I haven't had a chance to read the news, but that all sounds wonderful. I bet he would've liked that."

"We should all go down to the store and see all the stuff people have left in tribute to Mr. B," Adam suggested. "It might be a cool way to say goodbye to the place."

Everyone looked around the room.

"So what do you say?" Adam raised a brow. "Should we all hop in our cars and head downtown? See how locals are paying their respects at the store?"

Jo hesitated. Part of her really wanted to go with the others and see the flowers people set out in homage to her boss. It warmed her heart just knowing this was happening. The spirit of Mr. Bruebaker deserved to be celebrated.

But she just couldn't bring herself to go. Not yet—she wasn't ready. She still felt too tender. Glimpsing over at Sierra, she could tell the girls weren't ready to go back either. It had taken some time for Sierra to shake off Casey's traumatic visit. Going back to the scene of the crime to view the large window crack and boarded-up doors would likely trigger her angst all over again. Jo didn't want that for her. She didn't really want it for herself either.

It was best to remember Bruebaker's how it was before all the misfortune.

"I think I'm going to pass," she said. "You all go ahead. I'm going to stay here with Sierra and Rain and eat some of these cookies." She winked in Rain's direction. Rain stood over the baking sheet and beamed, looking more grown-up than when they'd first met. *So much is changing*, Jo thought. It was difficult not to let it all break her heart. But sooner or later, she was going to have to let go.

She may as well start today.

"Aw, Jo. Are you sure? It won't be the same without you."

"I'm sure," she said. "You guys go, and take a photo for me, okay? I'll go another time." *And if you see Truman, tell him I miss him*, she thought.

"When will we see you?" Jade asked Jo, reaching out to fix a strand of Rain's blonde hair. "Are you guys going to be around?"

"How about all of you come back here next week? Sierra, Rain, and I will make you dinner. Say, Wednesday night?"

"You know I'm in!" Grayson announced. He grinned as he popped a second cookie into his mouth.

The group laughed. They promised to be there. Jo told them she couldn't wait.

With hugs and assurances, she sent Anna, Adam, Grayson, and Jade on their way. They would be back soon, and Jo would be happy to have them.

Leaning in the doorway, Jo hugged her middle. Having people in her life—people who really cared and showed up no matter what—was the best gift of all. Watching them go, Jo felt unbelievably lucky.

They were like family, each of them bonded by circumstance. And Jo wouldn't have it any other way. Closing the door, she made up her mind. It was time to call Truman.

Forty-One

Later that evening, Jo sat on her front step and waited for Truman to arrive. After she'd called and asked if he might come over, and he said he would, she immediately went to listen for the hum of his truck approaching. To her relief, it took no time at all to drive right over.

Oh my. Just the sight of him ambling across the road, in his jeans and flannel shirt, jolted her with a magnetic pull. Before she knew what she was doing, her feet carried her onto the sidewalk in his direction.

"Truman," she breathed. Why had she stayed away? She could no longer remember. "I'm so grateful you came."

"Jo." He closed the gap between them and folded her into a hug. "I've been calling for days. Of course I'd come. I've just been waiting for an invitation."

"Oh." She stepped back and pushed the hair from her face. "I'm sorry. Please don't take it personally. I've just been feeling kind of . . . I don't even know. Lost, I guess? With Mr. B's death and me trying to get centered back at home, and everything else, I just kind of . . ." She drifted off, not sure if she could articulate the way she'd been feeling. All she knew was that she didn't want to spend any more time away from him.

"I know," he said, his voice soft and low as his warm palm

stroked the side of her face. "I know, Jo. It's okay. You don't have to explain. I just missed you, that's all."

"I missed you too." It came out like a sigh as she reached up and pressed her hand against his. How foolish she'd been to retreat. "I'm so sorry. Can you forgive me?"

He peered down at her, the creases around his eyes deepening. "Jo, you have nothing to be sorry for. We're all grieving in our own ways. But I'm here now, if you want me to be."

Jo watched as he swallowed, waiting for her to respond.

"I do."

"Okay."

"Truman?" she asked, inching closer. She tilted her face up to meet his.

"Yes?"

"I think you'd better kiss me now."

"I think so too."

He drew her in and pressed his lips against hers, softly at first, then with a gradual intensity that made her head swim. Jo clung to his middle, feeling as if she couldn't get close enough, and kissed him back. It was as if she were in a dream. All the magic of her books couldn't compete with the way Truman made her feel in that moment. And Jo never wanted it to end.

"Have you heard anything more since the new owners have taken over Bruebaker's and moved it into a smaller building?" Anna asked over the phone a month later. "They didn't waste any time in reopening."

"Yes," Jo said, glancing out the window. "I agree. But no, I haven't talked to anyone. I heard Regina had been discussing the sale of the business in secret conversations earlier than any of us realized. Only Suzanne and Jane knew." It was true: the original location sat empty for now, but a smaller space had been opened under the same name by a couple out of Salem.

"Have you been to the new location?"

"No," Jo said. After Mr. B died, she didn't have any real desire to follow the new store's progress. It just wasn't the same.

"I have," Anna continued. "It's pretty nice, actually. It's modern, but it's got a cozy feel all the same. I guess the new owners knew it would be too hard to replicate the feel of the old place, so they clearly went in a different direction. There are a lot of books, though. I heard their goal is to one day grow the inventory back up to a million volumes. Like the original store."

Jo tried to picture the scene Anna was painting. It was hard to fathom anyone else achieving what Mr. B had done for so many years. Still, Jo didn't begrudge someone else for trying. Who didn't love a bookstore? "I haven't had a chance to visit. As you know"—she paused—"I've been a little preoccupied."

"Right." Anna's tone turned playful. "So you and Truman are pretty serious, huh?"

Heat rose in Jo's cheeks.

Anna kept going before she could answer. "Good for you guys! I mean, no offense, Jo, but we all kinda knew you two would eventually wind up together. I mean, you guys were pretty close, even before."

Jo laughed. "Really? Was it that obvious?"

"Uh, yeah." Jo could practically hear Anna smiling through the phone. She was glad her friend was happy for her.

"Yes. Truman and I are having a lot of fun together. We go to the movies and cook in at home a lot. I guess you could say we're trading our busy life for something a little simpler. We're both ready for a new chapter."

"That sounds really nice," Anna said. "And what about the others—have you heard from anyone lately?"

"Well, everyone's called a few times," she answered. "But they have their own busy schedules. It took a while, but I think everyone is landing on their feet after leaving Bruebaker's. You're obviously busy with medical school up at OHSU. And I understand Adam started working for a nonprofit in the city. You probably know Grayson announced he wants to be a chef, so he got a job as a line cook at a hotel downtown. And Jade is getting her teaching degree."

"Yeah," Anna said. "I guess we all found a path after all."

"Yes, we really did."

"What about Sierra and Rain?"

Jo's chest swelled at the mention of the girls. She missed having them around most of all. "Sierra and Rain are doing just fine. They were able to connect with an aunt back home just last week. She took them in, with no questions asked. Last I heard, both mother and daughter were doing well. Sierra has two job interviews scheduled, and Rain is possibly starting day care. I usually get a phone call from them every few days or so. I hope they'll be in my life for a long time."

"Wow, that's really nice," Anna said.

"It is, isn't it?"

"Maybe we can meet up for lunch sometime soon?" Anna asked.

"I'd love nothing more." Jo's heart swelled with gratitude. She wouldn't trade the new relationships in her life for anything.

Jo said she'd be in touch and said goodbye. Looking at the time on her phone, she went into her bedroom to get ready for the night. Truman was coming over soon to take her out to dinner— her choice. Making her way to her pine dresser, she paused and glimpsed at a hardback book she'd purchased for herself. Her fingers ran along the cover of Walt Whitman poems.

Raising her eyes skyward, she smiled. She bet Mr. Bruebaker was somewhere smiling too.

Acknowledgments

In the spring of 2020, at the height of the pandemic, the famous Powell's Books in Portland, Oregon, closed. This surprising event devastated those who loved it. I was one of them. Thankfully, the legendary bookstore has since reopened, but it caused me to imagine a world in which a fictional bookstore in trouble is saved by its employees. And while my story is loosely inspired by Powell's, this book is a love letter to independent bookstores everywhere.

So, my very first thank-you is to all of the indie booksellers who have supported and championed my books. A special acknowledgment goes to some of my favorites in the Pacific Northwest: Roundabout Books, Dudley's Bookshop Café, Paper Boat Booksellers, and Powell's Books.

To my early readers, Gretchen, Tiffany, and Kerry, thank you! Lidija Hilje, thank you for being an awesome book coach and developmental editor. Jennie Nash, thank you for our heart-to-heart in Santa Barbara about the author life and what happens when you "know too much." To Brooke Warner, Lauren Wise, and the rest of the team at SparkPress, thank you for welcoming me back into the fold. I missed the wonderful boutique experience of your press and am thrilled to have returned to my roots.

Suzy Leopold, thank you for your enthusiasm and help spreading the word. To the writing community on Instagram (#Bookstagrammers!), you are so valuable and appreciated. Thank you for supporting each of my books. A big shout-out also goes to the Women's Fiction Writers Association. To say you are a community of supportive and inspiring writers would be an understatement.

A sincere thank-you also goes to my book-coaching clients. Thank you for being excited about my work as you thoughtfully navigated your own writing journeys.

Finally, thank you to my friends and family for your never-ending support. Greg, Lauren, Natalie, and Ben, you are my heart. I love you.

About the Author

NICOLE MEIER is an author and certified book coach living with her family in the Pacific Northwest. Her novels include *The House of Bradbury*, *The Girl Made of Clay*, and *The Second Chance Supper Club*. You can visit her at nicolemeier.com or on Instagram @nicolemeierwrites.

SELECTED TITLES FROM SPARKPRESS

SparkPress is an independent boutique publisher delivering high-quality, entertaining, and engaging content that enhances readers' lives, with a special focus on female-driven work. www.gosparkpress.com

Murmuration: A Novel, Sid Balman Jr, $16.95, 978-1-68463-091-2. One of the first Muslim women to graduate from West Point, a Jewish US Army captain, and a Somali migrant nicknamed Charlie Christmas risk everything for a refugee boy on a three-decade odyssey that takes them from Africa and Europe to Texas and Minnesota—and redefines what it means to be American in the twenty-first century.

Riding High in April: A Novel, Jackie Townsend, $16.95, 978-1-68463-095-0. *Riding High in April* takes us across the world as one man risks it all for a final chance to make it big in the tech world. At stake are his reputation, his dwindling bank account, and his fifteen-year relationship with a woman grappling with who she is and what really matters to her.

Charming Falls Apart: A Novel, Angela Terry, $16.95, 978-1-68463-049-3. After losing her job and fiancé the day before her thirty-fifth birthday, people-pleaser and rule-follower Allison James decides she needs someone to give her some new life rules—*and fast*. But when she embarks on a self-help mission, she realizes that her old life wasn't as perfect as she thought—and that she needs to start writing her own rules.

That's Not a Thing: A Novel, Jacqueline Friedland. $16.95, 978-1-68463-030-1. When a recently engaged Manhattanite learns that her first great love has been diagnosed with ALS, she is faced with the impossible decision of whether a few final months with her ex might be worth risking her entire future. A fast-paced emotional journey that explores whether it's possible to be equally in love with two men at once.

And Now There's You: A Novel, Susan S. Etkin. $16.95, 978-1-68463-000-4. Though five years have passed since beautiful design consultant Leila Brandt's husband passed away, she's still grieving his loss. When she meets a terribly sexy and talented—if arrogant—architect, however, sparks fly, and neither of them can deny the chemistry between them.

Elly in Bloom: A Novel, Colleen Oakes. $15, 978-1-940716-09-1. Elly Jordan has carved out a sweet life for herself as a boutique florist in St. Louis. Not bad for a woman who left her life two years earlier when she found her husband entwined with a redheaded artist. Just when she feels she is finally moving on from her past, she discovers a wedding contract, one that could change her financial future, is more than she bargained for.